LARGE PRINT EDITION

TUESDAY JANE

D1329561

PAUL MIKAELS

McBride/Malloy series prelude

BOOK ONE

Arizona - October 1991

⚔

PROLOGUE

Josie stepped from the eighteen-wheeler just as a hot, suffocating wind erupted. She brushed the hair from her face and watched with amusement as several plastic bags and various paper products twisted across the asphalt and floated into the blue beyond.

"Dust devil!" George yelled, still holding his trucker cap.

It was early October, but the sun was scorching. Luckily Phoenix was only a momentary stop. George could drive as far north as Cordes Junction, halfway to Flagstaff on I-17. He mentioned there was a travel center

4

along the highway, and hitching from there would be no problem. They had driven together from a truck stop on I-10 near the outskirts of Los Angeles. She had slipped into the Iron Skillet, and George was the first trucker she approached. Four hundred miles wasn't a bad first run.

Her friend Sara Wilcox planted the idea in her head. Sara once described how she hitchhiked across the country from one truck stop to the next. Sixteen years old and not a nickel in her pocket. Her one rule was to only ask gray-haired men for rides. The older truckers were safe. Besides, they could use a little companionship on the lonely road and must've felt good knowing they were keeping a young girl out of harm's way. Josie was using the Sara Wilcox method of travel, and so far, it was working splendidly.

As George finished with the diesel pump, she headed to the restroom. Inside, in front of a sink, a woman was splashing her face. Next to her, another woman was brushing her teeth. They both watched Josie pass the mirror. She nodded and smiled and entered the first unoccupied stall.

She had gone by a pay phone on her way to the lady's room. She'd let Danielle know she was on her way home. The last time they talked, Josie told her she was kicking around the idea of returning. She hoped to stay at Danielle's place when she got to Indiana, so now that she was on the road and making progress, she should at least ask.

Josie washed her hands at the sink next to the woman who had been brushing her teeth. The woman beamed a broad smile and remarked, "You're a beautiful girl!"

"Thank you!" Josie replied. Although she often received such compliments, they never failed to make her feel special.

The round dial clock above the Southwestern Bell pay phone showed two o'clock. Was it two or three hours later in Indiana? If it was only four p.m. in Shawneetauka, Danielle could still be working at the restaurant, not at home. She'd better call later or the next day. Josie wouldn't call the restaurant. Someone else could answer the phone, and she'd have to explain. Nope, she'd wait to call.

As she went through the travel store, George appeared.

"You want a Coke or something?"

"Sure!" Josie said and went with him to the soda fountain.

"I'll get nachos too. Are you hungry?"

"A little."

"Get whatever you want. I'm buying!"

She grabbed a Snickers bar from the snack aisle. A young man was noisily stocking the opposite shelf, punching boxes open while whistling a tune, and eyeing her conspicuously. She slid her finger along her light blonde hair and flashed her bright blue eyes. He fumbled with his cardboard box and dropped several bags of Ruffles onto the tile. He laughed nervously, his face turning a dark shade of crimson. Josie giggled and walked away, meeting George at the cash register.

"This all you're gettin'?"

"All I need!"

"You're a downright inexpensive companion," he said. "You can share my nachos."

Holding an icy cola in one hand and a candy bar in the other, she pushed open the exit door with her backside. George followed, carrying his cheesy nachos with drink pressed to his chest, balancing them precariously.

Once they settled into the Peterbilt and hit the highway, George said: "About you thumbing it to Indiana . . . I'm starting to feel anxious for ya. We've got a northbound bus that stops in Cordes. Coulda already come and gone today. But I could put you on it tomorrow. And I'll pay the fare, so no excuses!"

"Thanks. But that's too much."

"My little place is just a short way to town. You can stay overnight in our spare room. Then be off tomorrow. The bus goes through two or three o'clock, I think."

"I don't know . . ."

"Well, think it over. You shouldn't look a gift horse in the mouth!"

"I've got peculiar ways. Hitchhiking is an adventure!"

"An adventure? You've got me worrying over it."

"It's nice of you to be worrying for me, George. That means you're a good person."

"I reckon I'm better than most. That's what worries me."

↔

He parked his Peterbilt in the overflow lot of the truck stop in Cordes. His light-blue Chevy pickup truck was ready to go so he could swap. He joked that his driveway was too short and narrow for the big rig. Besides, his wife didn't drive anymore, so she didn't need the Chevy at their place. "Well?" George asked her without actually asking again. Josie shook her head. She thanked him graciously, grabbed her duffle, then headed to the Cordes travel center. He was disappointed, but he gave it a shot. He left in the Chevy. His home wasn't even a minute's drive from the truck stop.

He found Marge in the kitchen, working a crossword puzzle. She was tuned to the country

& western radio station and didn't hear him come in. She liked the classics; Hank Williams sang "I'm So Lonesome I Could Cry." A fresh pot of chili simmered down on the stovetop. George could smell the chili cooking before he even got inside the house. He threw his trucker hat on the table, sat across from Marge, kicked his legs out, and leaned back in the chair with his hands locked behind his head.

She lifted herself from the table and went to the fridge to get him a beer. She popped the cap with the churchkey and handed George the bottle. "Why the long face? You just tired?" she questioned, still standing next to him.

"I'm dawg tired, as usual. But I'm worried about a girl."

"What girl?" She tugged at the cottony fabric of her floral-patterned muumuu gown. It was sticking to her skin.

He told her about Josie.

"And you just let her go? Just like *that*?"

"I offered . . ."

"Must not have been good enough, George! Think she's still there? We'd better go ask her again—*insist*." Marge practically yanked him off the chair. She turned the stove's burner off and let the chili rest in the pot. She snatched the beer bottle from his hand and stuck it in the fridge. They went out the door.

"She reminds me of our Tammy," he said quietly from behind the wheel of the Chevy.

"Don't say that," Marge replied, now understanding his long face.

"This girl is a bit older, but damn if I don't see Tammy every time I look at her!"

Marge kept quiet and looked out the passenger window. Their girl ran away sixteen years ago that month. She was just fifteen. She bolted through the door because they wouldn't let her go dancing with a boy much too old for her. Tammy ran out the door, never to be seen again.

The police were no help. Marge followed up with their office frequently. She checked for leads or reports. But it was all for naught. She usually left with an ache in her heart that wouldn't quit. Gradually she checked in less and less. Then, finally, she stopped bothering at all. They couldn't do much. Tammy could have gone anywhere. But not a day passed in all those sixteen years that Marge hadn't thought about her little girl.

The first few days after Tammy left, Marge was angry. She couldn't understand how Tammy could be so selfish—not calling or letting them know her whereabouts. But by the end of that week, she was despondent. She prayed Tammy was safe and would return no worse for wear. By the second week, Marge was crushed. Some mornings it was hard to even climb from bed. She slept until noon when George was working, driving his truck. She could have slept all day. An unbearable weight pressed over her—a crushing burden of grief and sadness.

It went on like that for years.

When they pulled into the truck stop, George smiled. Josie was standing near the door with her bag. "Here she is!"

Marge slowly extracted herself from the pickup. She was a portly-shaped middle-aged woman who rarely moved with much speed.

"Hiya George!" Josie said with a big smile as they approached.

"This is my wife, Marge," he said to her.

"Sweetie, we're not gonna take no for an answer!" Marge said straight out. "You'll stay with us tonight, and we'll get you on that bus tomorrow afternoon!"

Josie just grinned and lifted her bag.

George put her duffle in the truck bed. Josie sat in the middle of the bench seat, looking past the wooden beads and crucifix hanging from the rearview. Marge glanced at her with a smile.

When they got into the house, Marge fussed about getting new linens on the guest bed. The ones on the bed were clean but maybe dusty; no one had slept in there for a while. The last time was over a year previous when George had gout and needed to stretch his leg out so his throbbing-red big toe could hang over the side. She swapped out the linens.

Later Josie helped her make cornbread to go with the chili for dinner. They baked it golden brown. The radio played, and George sat at the table and drank his beer. Marge hadn't felt that happy and content in years. Josie's presence warmed her soul.

The next day George called Greyhound. The bus would go through at three o'clock. It was eighty-nine dollars to Middlebury, Indiana, the closest stop to Shawneetauka. So he pulled a hundred out of his wallet and handed it to Josie. She was hesitant about accepting it.

Even though it was Sunday, George had to take the Peterbilt over to his buddy's place in Prescott to perform the truck's scheduled maintenance. He wouldn't be able to put Josie on the bus and see her off. So he wished her luck and godspeed and headed out the door.

For most of the morning, Josie and Marge played board games, and then they watched television until the early afternoon. They made a big bowl of chili mac and cheese for lunch using leftovers. Marge cut up a watermelon too. Finally, at half-past two, Josie grabbed her bag and headed down the road to the bus stop at the McDonald's parking lot. It was a short walk to town. Marge stood on the porch and watched her go. She had tears in her eyes.

It wasn't until the following day that she went into the guest room to pull off the bed sheets. Josie used the shower and left the white towel hanging from the back of the chair. So Marge pulled down the sheets and grabbed the towel to wash.

Josie had left a note on the nightstand. It was short and sweet, thanking Marge and George for their kindness. Marge grinned when she read the message, but her grin quickly faded. She found George's hundred dollars partly tucked beneath the writing pad. She let out a long, heavy sigh in a weary way. If Josie hadn't taken their money, she probably wasn't on that bus. George came down the hall and stopped at the doorway. Marge was sitting on the bare mattress, upset. She looked over, shook her head, and held the cash for him to see.

CHAPTER ONE

Recently back from the Middle East and Operation Desert Storm, Dolan McBride hit the road from Fort Riley when his discharge came through. So he said adiós to his pals of the 1st Infantry Division—The Bloody First—and headed west from Kansas.

It had been four years since he'd been to Arizona. The last time it was him and Bree. They headed out together just before graduation. But this trip, he was riding solo. The Jeep's passenger seat was empty aside from crumpled-up snack bags and a Rand McNally road atlas.

The San Francisco Peaks were in view, and the ponderosa pines were getting taller along the highway. He was hoping to bypass Flagstaff and head straight to his aunt's estate in Sedona, surrounded by the beautiful red rocks, but the Jeep's low fuel gauge urged otherwise. So he pulled into a Mobil station for one last fill-up.

While the fuel was flowing, a Northern Arizona University bus chugged on by. Then he remembered: it was the same gas station they had stopped at previously, and Bree asked to see the college. She was still undecided about schools.

Bree was a competitive swimmer and had heard about NAU's impressive program, so after bouncing around the administrative offices and making inquiries, they met with the swim coach.

"It helps that we train at an altitude of seven thousand feet," the coach said. "Strengthens the blood!"

"We're from the Midwest, so the highest I've ever trained is about here," Bree replied, holding her hand outstretched to show a height above the ground at about three feet. "Yay, high."

"Do you swim?" the female coach asked Dolan, whose physique resembled the sport's most outstanding swimmers. He was tall and lean, with strong shoulders and back tapering to a narrow waist and long arms that could wrap around the world.

"Only when I fall from the fishing boat! But seriously, no."

"I'm afraid our women's team is squared away, but we're starting a men's team and could use help."

Bree's face fell flat. She thanked the coach, left her office, and they walked to the far north side of campus until coming to a historic red-block building with twin spires called Old Main. They sat on the stone ledge next to the entrance stairs.

"This place isn't for me," Bree said. "I'm not feeling it."

She had already been accepted to Michigan State University but wouldn't be swimming there. She had been considering smaller schools for a better chance to make one of their teams.

Bree pulled out the Fuji disposable camera she had purchased from the Mobil gas station. She pressed her face next to his and snapped a picture with the camera facing them, smiling naturally, apparently forgetting the minor setback she had suffered. Dolan grabbed the camera, held it portrait-style, and stood back so he could get a good shot of her sitting next to the steps of the old building. Bree stretched her long legs in the sun; her strawberry-blonde hair blew lightly in the breeze. She looked damn good.

Later, when they had the film developed, she saw that photo and lost all interest in competitive swimming. Instead, she'd become a model.

Bree was often capricious, but this wasn't just a whim. Agency talent scouts had interviewed her when she was fifteen, but her parents were unsure about the people and their motivations. So the idea had been bouncing in her head for some time.

She attended MSU that fall and also pursued a modeling career while living in East Lansing. That one excellent photo, produced from a cheap disposable camera, taken on the steps of the historic building at NAU, altered the trajectory of her young life.

Dolan snapped out of his daydream when the gas tank was full. He jumped back into his garnet-red Jeep, departed Flagstaff, and headed south on State Route 89A through the canyon toward Sedona.

The trip through Oak Creek Canyon was awe-inspiring. The cool, crisp air blew through the open windows. The road twisted and turned. The scenery was perfect: the rocky outcrops along the red canyon walls, the big pines, the orange and red changing leaves of the overgrown brush along the creek, the rock slides, and the sheer wildness of the place. It sure beat Kansas.

He pulled over and parked where the road straightened, and the terrain flattened. A nice clearing was cut between the road and Oak Creek. The creek wasn't far across the grassy flats. The water was clear and flowed briskly over the gray and reddish rocks. No trout floated through the crystal clear water, but the undercuts and deep pools possibly held many. He had packed his fly rod in the Jeep and planned to use it.

Dolan thought about Allman as he looked across the creek.

His school-buddy Bobby Allman had a trick to pull trout from the cut banks, tangled bushes, fallen logs, and other water-related obstacles.

He sawed a fishing rod down to a short length and used it to jig the impossible spots that held all the big footballs—the fat, rounded brook trout. They'd camp near the creek and cook up the brookies he pulled out—throw them in the fire, wrapped in foil, smothered in butter, and sizzling.

They were about thirteen the first time they had a fish feast. Allman's dad got laid off from the phone company that summer, and they spent most of it up near Grayling in a rundown cottage on twenty acres in the woods. A boy's dream—motorbikes, rifles, and fishing rods.

Like Dolan, Allman joined the Army out of high school; but with him, it didn't last. Something snapped in his head, and he never recovered. No one knew why. He was a tough kid, so it made no sense. A month after he went

AWOL, he was found dead in a hotel room, his wrists cut.

Goddamn, Allman.

A gnarled, old tree along Oak Creek was full of apples. Dolan stretched himself and pulled a branch to grab one. He took a bite; it was sweet and crisp. He reached again with his long arms to get a few more nice ones for his aunt. She always liked apples.

↔

The famous red sandstone formation known as Cathedral Rock was visible through the oversized sliding glass doors that led to the balcony of her home office. She had grown accustomed to the view. Now she only occasionally felt the same wonderment when looking over from her desk at the image of the dual red buttes and smaller central spires as she did when she and her husband first picked this acreage to build on some years ago. Back then, she stood on the red earth and felt the power and energy of the vortex; she was sure of it, even if her rugged cowboy husband teased her for thinking so. She was excited about her incredible new world: the world of crystals, meditation, and healing. She sank to her knees and wept when she saw that Cathedral Rock view. Actual tears. Her husband smiled, nodded, and tossed the FOR SALE sign to the dirt. They started to build soon after. Occasionally, she remembered those days long past and got a sense of that rare feeling that swept over her like a whirlwind. But presently, she did not reminisce. Instead, she carefully examined her work schedule and prepared for the day.

Lauren "Doc" Halleran practiced natural medicine in the Sedona area. She'd primarily perform house calls for wealthier clients, provide natural remedies and whole-body wellness, and instruct yoga and meditation techniques. She also volunteered a few hours weekly at the county health department, assisting expectant and new mothers.

Her nephew Dolan was arriving later that afternoon. She had scheduled a light day so she'd be home early enough to see him in. She grabbed her bag and went to the patio door.

"Come on, Charlie," she said, looking around the room as she slid one of the glass doors open. "I'm hittin' the road, kitty."

A large cream-colored cat darted from the hallway and beelined through the door without even glancing at its owner. The fluffy long hair disappeared off the balcony, went down the steps into the courtyard, and lay on a spot of sun that shone brightly on the pavers.

"You lazy cat!" Doc shouted and slid the door shut.

Doc wanted to remind Red that Dolan was coming in that day. Her father-in-law lived in an adobe guest cottage on the property. Harold "Red" Halleran, Sr—an energetic, mischievous old cowboy—moved in a few years earlier when his eyesight faded, and he gave up driving. It was morning, so he was still home. He often wasn't. Friends frequently dragged him out for lunch or a drink.

"I'm already cooking up plans," Red said. "I hope he stays with us for a while so I can show him a thing or two!"

"He may stay a few weeks, maybe a whole month . . . so that should give you time to get into trouble!" Doc replied.

"A month? That's great! But I reckon I'll just plan something for the next few days to get things rolling. You know as well as anybody, Doc, I won't even buy green bananas at my age!"

She laughed at his oft-heard joke, then headed out for the workday.

↔

It was afternoon when Dolan came in the front door. Red leaped from his chair with the agility of a man half his age. "Here he is, Doc!"

Doc was busily cooking Mexican for three. She dropped her apron on the granite countertop and came around the kitchen's island. Dolan hugged his aunt, and she asked how the trip went. Red came over, shook his hand, and tapped him on the shoulder. "You must've gained twenty pounds since you were last here. Packing in the feed, eh?"

"I'm up to 198 but no heavyweight. I'm still lean," he said. "That cooking sure smells nice. Sure beats MREs!"

"What's that, you say?"

"Meals, Ready-to-Eat. New and improved Army field ration. A so-called meal in a bag!"

"Doesn't sound too appetizing. Like my hardtack and beef jerky when I'd get caught out on the range."

"Hey, I remember your beef jerky. It wasn't bad. You just needed great teeth!"

"Well, I made steak fajitas and enchiladas for you boys!" Doc said. "And everything's ready, so let's eat."

They sat at the long, rectangular Spanish Colonial-style dining table with oversized leather-backed chairs. Doc poured the red wine and made a toast to Dolan, the war hero. He shook his head, not feeling worthy of such a distinction. He turned to the large canvas painting of Doc's husband hanging above the fireplace and lifted his glass. "I'll toast to Uncle Harry, though," Dolan said. "Now there's a *real* hero!"

They all followed suit, and an awkward quietness fell over the table. It usually happened any time Harry was mentioned.

"Wow, this is great grub!" Red said, breaking the silence. "I wish we had a pretty cook like you tending to the chuck wagon back in the day."

"Well, thank you, Pops!" Doc replied, smiling. She was a gorgeous forty-four-year-old.

"So, Dolan, do you have any plans right off? Because I know Pops already has something lined up for the two of you."

"How about we head to Vegas for a couple of days?" Red said to Dolan.

"Sure . . . I'm game!" he answered. "Been a while since I've played poker."

"I'm gonna have you drive my Lincoln because I don't think I'd make it in your Jeep. I don't drive her anymore due to my eyes. Although, I still like to get her on the road to keep her in shape!"

"But it's you and I all day tomorrow!" Doc said. "We'll go on a hike near Schnebly Hill

Road, then stop by Tlaquepaque. You loved that place."

He did enjoy it there. The last time they went, he relaxed under the sycamore trees along the creek while his aunt and Bree went through the art shops of the Mexican-style village.

"Sounds great!"

Doc poured a little more wine around.

"Have you thought about what you'll do after taking time off? Maybe use your GI bill for school."

"Maybe. I've thought about it."

"I wish I hadn't sold the ranch," Red said. "I could've had you punching cows . . . You could've been my foreman!"

"Growing up in Michigan, I'm not sure I'd make much of a cowboy. But I'd be willing to try."

"I remember when you were a tiny tot, all you ever wanted to be was a cowboy!" Red replied.

"True. I never wanted to leave your ranch when I was a kid!"

"You still boxing?" Red asked.

"I trained in the ring while on base, but it's not something I'd want to do for a living. That's for sure!"

"I expect not!" Red said. "I knew a few prizefighters in the old days. Most of them poor bastards ended up punch drunk and silly when they put on age."

"What did you once say about washed-up prizefighting boxers and crippled bull riders?" Dolan asked, smiling.

"Oh sure . . . I've got this plan to build a fancy retirement home for worn-out whores, prizefighters, and bull riders. Imagine the great stories you'd hear in that place! That'd be one helluva return on investment. If I could scrape up the cash, I'd sink my last dime!"

"You may win big in Vegas. Never know!"

Doc's cat jumped onto the empty seat beside Dolan and eyed his plate. He had a flat face and big round blue eyes. He didn't blink much and had a strange, almost human-like appearance.

"Go ahead and help yourself, Chuck!" Red said.

Dolan fed Charlie a strip of carne asada, and he swallowed it whole.

"That cat will eat an entire fajita if you make him one!" Doc said. "He'd tell you to hold the onions, though."

↔

On Sunday morning, Dolan and his aunt went up the craggy and rugged Schnebly Hill Road. He pulled the Jeep over when she pointed to a flat spot near a lookout. The Munds Wagon Trail crossed Schnebly Hill Road several times, and they could hike in whichever direction they chose. However, Dolan was adventurous and usually wandered into the wild where no trails existed. So after traversing up the old wagon trail for a short clip, they went off bushwhacking through the wilderness. Then, to avoid wading through a patch of catclaw, they slipped into an *arroyo* that originated from Merry-Go-Round Rock. The dry wash started as an easy hike over fine gravel, but boulder hopping was necessary after gaining elevation. Eventually, vegetation swallowed up the arroyo. So they pulled themselves through patches of red-branched manzanita bushes, sharp-leaved scrub oak, and more horrid catclaw until they finally escaped the brush, approaching the wide-open smooth red rock at the base of Merry-Go-Round.

"Why do I follow you off the trails?" she asked, shaking her head while pulling at a catclaw branch stuck to her boot.

As they started again, they spooked a few mule deer. The deer bolted and clicked loudly across the red sandstone. "Whoa, that got my heart pumping!" Doc laughed.

"Theirs too!"

They continued along the smooth rock until they came to a rectangular white boulder that must've fallen from a higher level. They rested on the boulder's edge and looked across the vast scenery—the mint-green Arizona cypress mixed with darker green juniper and small pine trees; pinkish-white mountains and dark red buttes lined the pass on each side.

"Not a bad view, eh?" she said.

"I've seen worse."

"You know," his aunt started, "your uncle and I rode horses up through these trails."

"Seems like a nice place for it."

"Until he'd get a bug up his rear . . . and then he'd want to race me the rest of the way back!"

"That sounds like him."

"When we talked yesterday about what you were thinking about doing after your time off, you didn't mention law enforcement."

"You were asking about using the GI Bill. Not about being a cop," he said with a smile. "But truthfully, I'm not sure. I wasn't going to think about it for the next few weeks. I'll think about all of it afterward! All at once! When I have to!"

"Sounds like a plan. Just chill out for a while."

"Yeah, and you were going to teach me to meditate . . . the Doc Halleran way! So I can clear my head and screw it back on straight."

"Well, this is as good a place as any to start. How about our first session?" Doc said.

"Great! But wait a minute—I can't afford those high prices you charge your clients," he said, pretending to be worried. She laughed and nodded.

"Okay then, if you like, we will take a few slow breaths, then I'll begin the Halleran method of yoga and meditation," she said, speaking in her soothing, calm, and quiet voice. Dolan smiled as his aunt released her inner yogi, and she began with instructions.

She explained how her meditation techniques centered around breath and breathing. The inward breath is life, and the outward breath is death. The pause between the two—the gap that only lasts a fraction of a moment—is nothingness. And nothingness is the nirvana that all people strive for. So we must concentrate on the gap. On the nothingness. On the calm.

Breathe in slowly. Now mind the gap—the nothingness—fall into the gap. Breathe out slowly.

↔

Red and Dolan left for Vegas early Sunday evening, a day sooner than expected; Doc would be busy that night anyway, and Red was getting antsy. So they packed up their bags and headed out. After filling the tank of Red's big Lincoln, they went up through Oak Creek Canyon.

They were traveling west, rolling down I-40, still a couple of hours from Vegas, when Red blurted: "Turn off here!" They passed Ash Fork and were coming up on the Crookton Road exit.

"Looks like the middle of nowhere!" Dolan said. "What's here?"

"It's Old Route 66! Ain't much of this historic pavement left. So you need to run your tires on it some!"

"Just for the hell of it?"

"Sure, for the hell of it. And it's heading the same way we are—straight into Seligman."

He veered right and pulled onto a lonely-looking highway that cut through wide-open grazing land. Several reddish-brown and white cows were feeding on the dried grass near the road.

"Just need a dust devil and a couple of tumbling tumbleweeds, and the picture would be complete!" Dolan joked.

"Those are Hereford cows. See those young black steers and heifers with white faces? Those are the Black Baldies. They mix the Hereford cows with the Black Angus bulls and get those."

"Why not Hereford bulls or Angus cows?" Dolan questioned as they rolled down Route 66.

"Money mostly, I imagine. When you order a steak at a restaurant, you want the Angus, right? Well, they're still Angus! Also, baldies are born a little smaller, so it's easier for the mother. And let me tell you, those Hereford cows are tough gals. They can live off cactus and scrub brush when times get hardscrabble. They're good all-around mothers too!"

The sun was low in the sky, reddish along the horizon, and they were heading west, straight at it. Dolan flipped the visor down and squinted his eyes. Red tilted his cowboy hat lower.

"What's in Seligman anyway? You have to take a leak?"

"Sure, I gotta take a leak. But I'm gonna get a whiskey and a beer at the Blue Ox Saloon! But don't worry; I'll buy you a beer! But only one because you're driving."

"Thanks. I'll try not to drink it too fast!"

"Or maybe you'd prefer one of those tutti-frutti girly drinks! I saw you doin' yoga with Doc this morning. Just sayin'—"

Dolan shook his head, grinning.

The Blue Ox was in the middle of town. It was a plain block building with a gravel parking lot—a tough-looking place. Motorcycles lined the front, and two pickup trucks were parked along the side. Two cowboys were also walking in, and Red nodded to them.

"Tourists," Red said, motioning toward the row of shiny Harley-Davidsons. The cowboys chuckled.

"Ain't that the truth," one of them agreed.

Inside were two billiard tables, three round oak tables with chairs, and an L-shaped bar with an old-fashioned brass-pipe foot rail. The motorcycle crew took up most of the barstools. A jukebox in the corner blasted Lynyrd Skynyrd. Red pointed to the bathroom and slid in. The two cowboys picked up pool cues and started a game at the farthest table. The bartender walked over two beers and told Dolan he'd be with him in a minute. The motorcycle crew was happy and loud. They spoke some English but mainly another language he didn't recognize. When Red came around, Dolan walked toward the bar and the two empty stools.

"A whiskey, bartender!" Red said, in a rough voice, as you'd hear in an old western movie. He tapped his hand on the bar for effect. "And two Budweisers."

The bartender set up their drinks, and he turned and looked over at the motorcycle crew getting ready to head out.

"We will go back to Sweden now," a tall, thin guy said to the bartender. "We have seen the Grand Canyon, and now we can die in peace!"

"Hell of a long way on a motorcycle!" the bartender yelled.

"No, we ride from Las Vegas, where we rent them! Fly back to Sweden!"

They all laughed, and the bartender thanked them for the business.

The music stopped, and the place cleared out. The cowboys were still playing pool. It was quiet enough for Red to tell stories, which was his favorite pastime.

"The first time I stopped at this bar was in 1959. My buddy over at the Bar-T Ranch, south of town, needed a few horses broke, so I came up and stayed at the ranch. After just a week, two horses I worked on—a chestnut filly and a buckskin gelding—were as gentle as circus ponies! You could set your grandma on the saddle on either one of them. After one week! The other was a damn pretty white colt. All white. My buddy James Tilly—the owner of the Bar-T—wanted that horse for his young wife to ride. But goddamn it, I couldn't make any progress with that horse! That son of a bitch started snortin', squealin', kickin' and bitin'. And boy, did he buck! He bucked like that Steamboat you hear about from the old days up in Wyoming! So I came back the next week and gave it another shot. I tried out my tie-down trick. I'd hog-tie the son of a bitch and leave him lying in the dirt for a while. I'd do a little whispering in his ear to make a good show for the cowpokes hangin' about. Then I'd let him up again. Well, guess what? None of my tricks worked. He was an all-around ornery bastard. So since I couldn't do a damn thing with him, Tilly sent him off to a rodeo bucking ranch for training! Son of a gun if he didn't become a decent bucking horse. That bastard bucked in a few professional rodeos! He was my only failure when it came to breaking-in horses! Good ol' Whitey!"

"I guess your buddy had to find a different horse for his little wife!" the bartender said while pouring Red another shot.

"Shit, no! That pretty little woman ran off with one of the ranch hands a month later, and Jim never saw her again! That knocked him for a loop. He was never the same after that."

"That's rough."

"Speaking of a pretty little woman," Dolan said in a whisper, almost to himself, as a blonde female of about eighteen and an older gentleman walked into the bar.

The bartender slid over from his position across Red and carefully eyed the girl as she approached him. She wore tight, almost painted-on faded blue jeans and a thinnish red and white striped sweater.

"Would you happen to have any aspirin here? The store down the street is already closed. I have a killer headache," she said, smiling to keep a good face but suffering.

"Sorry, none that I know of. We may have Alka-Seltzer, though."

"I have a bottle of aspirin out in the car," Dolan said, popping up from his seat.

The man she was with stood at the far end of the bar. He looked over to her and nodded his head toward the door, signaling her to go out for the aspirin. Then he asked the bartender for a shot of Jack Daniels. "Make it a double," he added.

Dolan and the girl walked out to the Lincoln. He dug through his overnight bag and eventually found the aspirin. She'd been watching him with a bit of concern while he had trouble finding the bottle, but she smiled with relief when it appeared in his hand.

"We've got a bunch of water bottles in the trunk. I'll get you one."

"Thanks. I guess all the traveling is getting to me. This headache is something!"

He handed her two aspirin and a water bottle that he had opened. She swallowed them down.

"Thanks again! I'm amazed by all the good people I've met on the road. People seem to want to lend me a hand. I'm lucky like that, I guess!"

"The kindness of strangers?"

"Yes. Good people."

"You seem to be a nice person. That helps," he said. "You're also pretty darn cute. That helps even more!"

"That's kind of you to say. My father told me my face would get me into trouble someday," she said, smiling. "And also my pride!"

"So, where are you heading?"

"I plan on getting back to Indiana soon. Visit my friends and family. But we have to stop by a few carnivals and fairs here and there to drop off supplies. That's his plan, anyway. Do you live here?" she asked while looking up and down the empty pavement through Seligman. The town was dead.

"I've lived here for approximately ten minutes. Then I'm moving on to Las Vegas to do some living there—for a few days anyway!"

"Are you a player? Maybe you'll get lucky!"

"Poker!" he said with a smirk and a head tilt. "If that's what you meant!"

"Oh, yes . . ." she giggled. "Gambling!"

Her man companion walked out of the bar and toward them.

"Thank you, son," he said to Dolan as he paused for a second to get the girl. "We appreciate your help. But we've got to run, darlin'."

He nudged her elbow to move her along and tipped his black cowboy hat in a nod toward Dolan.

"Oh wait . . . here!" he said and tossed her the small bottle of Excedrin. "You may need more later."

She caught the bottle, then reached back and squeezed Dolan's hand.

"You're my savior!"

They went away into the dark, and he turned and closed the trunk of the Lincoln. He liked that girl and wished he'd asked her name. She made him feel clumsy, silly, and forgetful, so he assumed that was good. He hadn't felt that way around a female in some time.

He walked into the Blue Ox, and Red was in the middle of another story. He sat at the bar and ordered a second beer, even though Red said he should only have one. The cowboys were still playing pool, and Red was telling more lies. Dolan suddenly felt excellent—cheerful and relaxed. And his beer was nice and cold. He thought about that cute blonde, and then he thought about playing poker in Vegas. *Maybe get lucky*. He laughed to himself and sipped his beer.

They finally pulled into the hotel valet entrance at about midnight due to the frequent stops along the way. Some of the layovers included the town of Kingman for Popeye's Chicken; then Hoover Dam, where a still inebriated Red insisted on urinating over the rail into the reservoir; then the Gold Strike Casino a few miles past the dam, where Red won and lost over a thousand dollars on the craps table.

After checking in, Dolan wrapped his arm around the old man's shoulders, and the pair walked from the lobby toward the elevators. Red's cowboy hat was half-crooked, and Dolan knocked it back straight. "We'll get settled in first before you wander off."

Fashionably dressed, gray-haired couples waited in the corridor. A posh show must've just let out. Dolan and Red squeezed into the first elevator that opened. An uncomfortable silence prevailed once the door closed and the elevator began to rise. Red looked over to Dolan and said in one of his funny, high-pitched voices: "Now, boy, don't be bringing any of them fancy *whores* up to the room! I need my beauty sleep!"

CHAPTER TWO

On Sunday night, around ten o'clock, Yavapai County Deputy Shane McGraw was called out to Ash Fork. He found an older motorhome blocking Jose Valenzuela's driveway in town. As Deputy McGraw circled the motorhome with his flashlight, Mr. Valenzuela gave his opinion on the matter. "I think maybe kids stole it from the RV park down by I-40. Took it for a joy ride and left it here! That's happened before around town."

"Did you see anyone leave it?" McGraw asked.

"No. We didn't see anything. I saw it parked here when I went into the kitchen to get a drink of water. I asked my wife about it, and she didn't know anything. So I was gonna go to bed, but she said I got to call you if it's blocking the driveway. She wouldn't be able to get out. She'd have to go over the lawn with her car to get out in the morning because she's got to work at the flagstone yard at seven. So I call you."

"No license plates. The thing looks like it's in rough shape. All the tires are pretty low too. So it looks like it has been parked for a while, and they decided to drive it out. It didn't get far, so maybe it did come from the RV camp next to the highway," McGraw said. He suddenly made a contorted face. "You smell that?"

"Smells bad. Like someone died," said Mr. Valenzuela.

The small window at the back of the camper van was open, and the stench was coming straight out. McGraw flashed his light inside. "Jesus!"

He opened the back door and found the corpse of an older woman in a state of decomposition. The unpleasant smell hit him hard; he gagged and coughed. Jose Valenzuela peeked in and also gagged.

"Do you recognize her?" McGraw asked, flashing his light back into the motorhome.

"No. It's an old woman."

The deputy called it in and waited for the medical examiner and a detective to come out. In the meantime, he searched around the glove box and other places to figure out who owned it. But unfortunately, he didn't find any paperwork—just clothing, supplies, and plenty of trash.

"Why leave the poor woman in my driveway?" Mr. Valenzuela queried.

"That's why I wondered if you recognized her. It's like they left her here . . . special for you!"

Detective Patty Malloy arrived at eleven o'clock and, after inspecting the scene, radioed to have the motorhome and contents towed on a flatbed to the county yard for examination. As the flatbed rolled off, she turned to the deputy.

"Was the hood warm when you got here?" she asked.

"I'm sorry I didn't check," McGraw answered sheepishly. "Pretty stupid, I guess."

"Don't worry about it. But let's figure out who drove it here. The deceased surely didn't!"

"I thought she was dumped here on purpose!" McGraw said. He turned to Mr. Valenzuela, who came outside again. "So you have no idea how long the van was here before you saw it?"

"No. When I came home at five o'clock, it wasn't there. Then like I say, when I stood at the kitchen sink around nine or so, I saw it."

"Your wife didn't see anything?"

"No. You can only see the driveway through that kitchen window at the sink." Valenzuela pointed back. "And believe me, if dishes are in that sink, my wife doesn't go anywhere near it!"

They laughed.

"Tomorrow, you and Deputy Kennedy should go door to door with her photo and a photo of the motorhome to see about a connection to this neighborhood," Detective Malloy said. "And stop at that RV park by I-40 before you head home."

"Will do. Sure is a strange one, though!" McGraw acknowledged.

◄►

Detective Patty Malloy didn't get much information from the motorhome or the deceased. So she ran a trace on the vehicle identification number. But unfortunately, after spending most of Monday on leads, it turned into a dead end.

The VIN led to Ted Vickers, the former owner in California. Ted said he sold a hundred and sixty acres of land south of Ash Fork about twenty years ago; he threw in the motorhome with the deal. The motorhome was in poor condition, and he didn't want to chance it breaking down heading to California. Ted remembered signing the title and giving it to the buyer. An Asian couple from Phoenix bought the land.

Malloy tracked down Ken Choi, still the owner of the land and living in Phoenix. Mr. Choi said that he had improvements done shortly after buying the acreage. Choi had the property fenced, and one of the workers on the job—he thinks his name was Bob—asked if he was doing anything with the motorhome. Mr.

Choi didn't want anything to do with the motorhome because a bunch of pack rats had taken over the thing, and it was a mess. So he wanted it gone and off the land. If Bob wanted to try and fix the beat-up motorhome, clean it up and get some use out of it, then good for him. So Mr. Choi handed him the title. The original owner already endorsed the document, so he didn't think anything of it. Bob must've never registered it. Choi remembered that he got their phone number off a bulletin board at an Ash Fork gas station. And that was it. He never talked to them again. Twenty years was a long time, he said.

"From twenty years ago!" Detective Malloy said to Deputy McGraw when they sat down together at the diner in Ash Fork. "That's my only lead. It's starting like a crazy cold case! I can't believe Ken Choi remembered all the details he did."

"Yep. We haven't got anything either. The neighborhood sweep was a bust."

"If you can believe it, I stopped by the Shell and checked the bulletin board! I was snooping for a twenty-year-old advert from Bob, the handyman. Truthfully I don't know what I was looking for," Malloy said, stirring more sugar into her black coffee. "Well, I'll call the coroner and pester him before he leaves for the day!"

The detective went over and used the diner's phone to call the medical examiner's office. McGraw watched the waitress bounce from table to table, filling coffee cups. He held out his half-empty cup as she went by.

"Here you go, sweetie," she said. "You sure you don't want a piece of pie or something? A big guy like you needs to eat!"

"Thanks. Coffee is fine."

"Let me know if you change your mind! I'm right here!"

The detective sat back at the table. She looked relieved.

"Any information?" McGraw asked.

"Plenty of information. Just not what I expected. The coroner said she died a few days ago."

"Smell was pretty bad, though," McGraw said in a whisper, not wanting anyone to hear. "Just a few days?"

"It was hot in that motorhome. Nice and warm would do the trick. Besides, that RV stank worse than she did."

"Probably."

"More importantly, the coroner said it was pneumonia. Advanced lung cancer too, but pneumonia did her in."

"Like when we found the hoarder with all the cats last month?"

"Exactly, except no cats this time. Just a body in a camper van creating a nuisance for Jose Valenzuela's wife!"

"Yes. Weird," McGraw mused. "But we still have a crime committed, right? I mean . . . someone dumped her!"

"And I'm sure you'll get to the bottom of it, deputy," Malloy said as she stood up and put two dollars on the table. "I have a lot of important things piled up on my desk. Well, I'll talk to you tomorrow anyway."

Patty left. Deputy McGraw stared at his coffee cup and asked the waitress: "Now, what type of pie did you say you had on the shelf? Any banana cream?"

↔

On Tuesday morning, Deputy McGraw patrolled I-40. It was a beautiful October day, and all was quiet on the western front. He parked near the old highway maintenance yard between Ash Fork and Seligman. Traffic was sporadic and light, but he'd bring out the radar gun later. Occasionally truckers still pulled off the highway onto the wide shoulder to check equipment. But all the remains of the highway yard and facility were long gone, swallowed up by growing grasses and underbrush.

The chocolate-covered cream-filled Long John went well with his morning coffee. He'd get another one tomorrow. But maybe custard. He liked custard too, but they were always gone.

McGraw popped the door open and jumped from the cruiser. He set his coffee on the hood of the Crown Victoria and lit a smoke as the warm sun hit his face; it was a lovely morning with a gentle breeze. Of course, smoking was stupid, but he figured one a day hardly even counted. His pack of Marlboro Lights lasted nearly half the month.

The quiet of the morning suddenly ended. He turned his head to the sound of coyotes yipping and barking in the thick brush. It was a frenzied commotion, and curiously, the hairs at the nape of his neck pricked up.

They must've been close. Maybe they were near the asphalt pile and yard remnants. He crept toward the noise and peeked around a juniper for a better view. Several coyotes were in the tall grass, tangling around each other. Three massive turkey vultures waited their turn from a high perch.

As he returned to the vehicle, he noticed the chain blocking access to the area had fallen. It was heavy and rusty; he'd retrieve his leather gloves from the patrol car to hang it back across. Beneath the chain, drag marks crossed the pea gravel and continued straight to the coyotes through the top layer of sun-baked soil. Now he was curious. He dropped his cigarette and swiftly grabbed the shotgun from the car's rack.

McGraw made a charge with the 12-gauge pump action pointed straight while hurling obscenities to stir the coyotes. He kicked the dry dirt until his black leather boots turned gray. The skittish animals dispersed in all directions; the vultures reluctantly followed. Relieved but out of breath, McGraw lowered the shotgun and continued slowly to the area from where they fled. The dust cloud he created drifted past.

Suddenly he froze.

"My god!"

A body lay in the tall grass. McGraw took a few deep breaths and carefully moved closer. It appeared to be a young female—shirtless—wearing only jeans. The skin of her bare back was pinkish-blue. She lay contorted and twisted. Her long blonde hair spread over the light-gray caliche soil. It was bad. But it went from bad to worse as he circled: the carrion birds and wild dogs had made a mess of her face. She was a faceless corpse.

McGraw turned away, feeling nauseous. He took a few steps and doubled over, vomiting. Then, wiping his face, he stumbled back to the Crown Vic and radioed it in.

It became a busy crime scene when the forensic team, photographer, medical examiner, three patrol deputies, and the detective arrived.

"So our victim here appears to be a young woman," Detective Patty Malloy said, speaking out loud to the medical examiner, McGraw, and anyone else standing around. "She was dragged—looks like by her belt loops—from the shoulder of eastbound I-40. One broken belt loop on her denim jeans, and another looks stretched. Her sweater and bra are lying here, but they could have slid off from being dragged. She's missing a shoe. Bruising around her neck. I know, I know, we'll wait for official word from your team, but I'm going to assume strangulation—homicide. A terrible amount of animal activity. What are you guys guessing so far for the time of death? Twenty-four hours here? Thirty-six at the most?"

"I'm going to estimate close to thirty-six hours here with rigor almost fully dissipating," the medical examiner announced.

"Sunday night?" Malloy said. "Okay, so no identification. Nothing in her pockets? Could we get photos of this sweater and her jeans together? Put them together as a set, please. We need to get canvassing around Seligman and Ash Fork to show the pictures of the clothing. Maybe someone saw this young woman and anyone she was with."

The photographer was standing near the sweater in the dirt.

"My team will get proper photos of the clothing once she's back at our office," the medical examiner said.

"Oh, for sure," Malloy replied. "I didn't expect you to yank her jeans off here!"

McGraw took notes and listened to the detective. A forensic examiner stuck his partly-smoked cigarette in an evidence bag.

"That's not evidence," McGraw said, pointing to himself. "Sorry, it's mine." He felt foolish. It was bad enough that he had to mention the vomit earlier.

"What brand are the sweater and jeans and such?" Detective Malloy asked.

"The jeans are Guess," the examiner said. "The bra is from Victoria's Secret."

"A cake eater? Is this a rich girl? Probably not local, then."

The examiner shrugged. "The sweater has a Goshen brand tag."

"Goshen? I've never heard of it. A boutique brand? That could be helpful," the detective said, then lifted the shoe from the dirt. "Shoes are white canvas Keds, size seven . . . Well, one shoe. No jewelry. No piercings. No rings. Think somebody took the jewelry from her?"

"Not seeing any marks or tan lines on fingers suggesting rings," the medical examiner noted.

The detective stepped over to Deputy McGraw. "So we have a young woman strangled and dumped approximately the same time you and I are dealing with the elderly woman in the motorhome on Sunday night."

"Connected?" McGraw said, perplexed.

"And we have nothing on that one, have we?" Malloy said. "McGraw, I want you to handle the canvassing of Seligman. Start with all the businesses. Get photos of the clothing from the team. Also, get the motorhome photos from Sunday night—perhaps connected, perhaps not—but we're still working on that. Kennedy! Where's deputy Kennedy?"

"I'm here, detective," said the tall, thin, red-haired Deputy Tim Kennedy as he walked up.

"I want you to take charge of canvassing Ash Fork businesses. We'll get all the photos and information together. McGraw is going to handle Seligman."

McGraw slid his notebook into his pocket as they zipped the young woman into the blue coroner's bag. "But you just said this girl probably isn't local. And our nasty stuff and drug runners usually originate out of Vegas and Kingman. Right?"

"We have to start somewhere, now don't we, McGraw," Patty said. "Not to mention our motorhome incident appears to be local. So we start local and work our way out. I'll be starting with missing persons. Also, I'll check with the high school to see if any female students went absent."

↔

The coroner narrowed the young woman's age to seventeen or eighteen, mainly because her wisdom teeth hadn't quite emerged. Her official weight was 112 pounds, and she was 5'4" tall. She had natural light blonde, full-length hair.

McGraw started his door-to-door at the O.K. Saloon on the west end of town. He showed the owner a photo of the red and white striped sweater combined with her jeans. The deputy gave the girl's description—height, hair color, size—and showed the motorhome photos from

Ash Fork. He explained that she could be a local, but more than likely, she was just passing through on Sunday.

"Doesn't ring a bell," the owner said and shook his head.

From there, he moved from business to business, and it was the same result over and over. Finally, he crossed the road to the small ramshackle wood building housing the Stockmen's Bank office. As he walked in, he recognized the bank teller.

"Hello there, Jennifer!"

"Shane? How are you doing? I haven't seen you since Maggie and Josh's wedding. Like three years ago," Jennifer said, smiling.

They both went to school together in Prescott Valley. Shane had a little crush on her, but he never let on, mainly because his buddy was sweet on her, and they dated pretty steadily.

"You look great!" he replied. "It's nice to see you. So it's been three years, eh?"

"They've got me working up here in the wild west! Both the normal tellers went down sick, so they sent me up from my Prescott branch. Sure is a little different than I'm used to!"

"How many days have you been up here?" Shane asked.

"I've been trekking up here since last Thursday! Are you here on bank business? I heard you were a sheriff's deputy," she said, pointing to his badge.

"Yeah, unfortunately, police business. Nasty business."

He explained the situation. He gave Jennifer the standard line he had repeated previously, then showed the photos and described the girl. But with her, he added gruesome details. He hadn't meant to. It was a form of catharsis.

"Coyotes were all around her body . . . fighting each other for position. So I chased them off . . . I shouted and kicked dirt around. But I looked down . . . her face, um, it was just . . . just gone. It was horrible."

"Oh my god," Jennifer said, clearly shaken.

"I'm sorry. I shouldn't have—"

"No, it's okay. Don't worry about me. But that poor girl," Jennifer said emotionally. "I wish I could help!"

A youngish man entered the bank carrying a money pouch. Deputy McGraw stepped to the side and let him access the teller window. He was exchanging bills for change. As he transacted with Jennifer, Deputy McGraw showed him the photos.

"Looks familiar. I can't place it exactly," the young man replied.

"Really? The motorhome?"

"No, the clothing. The red and white sweater."

"Where do you work?" McGraw asked.

"The Blue Ox Saloon."

"So you think you've seen her?"

"Aspirin . . . that's it. She was asking for aspirin. Pretty blonde girl."

"Was she alone?" McGraw asked excitedly.

"Um, no, I think she was with her dad or grandpa. He was in his fifties or sixties, I think. Kinda big guy. Over six foot. Maybe 250 pounds. Never seen either of them before. It was Sunday night, I think. He ordered a shot of Jack, then left."

Shane used the bank's phone to call Patty at Northern Division.

"Detective Malloy? We caught a break on the girl! Can you send the sketch artist to the Blue Ox Saloon in Seligman? Yes, she was with an older man. So yeah, I'm with the witness here at the bank. But we'll head over to the bar to do the interview. Okay, see you there."

CHAPTER THREE

The crystal-clear blue water of the hotel's swimming pool was a refreshing change from the smoke-filled poker room of the casino. The gambling cash Dolan set aside was all but used up, so he needed to find an alternate form of entertainment. The sun warmed him nicely as pink flamingos wandered around the tropical grounds beneath the palm trees and birds of paradise. He sipped a rum and Coke while relaxing. Being only twenty-two years old, drinking in public was still a pleasurable novelty.

Even though it was a weekday, the pool was crowded and lively, with splashing and music. Lounging adjacent was a nice-looking, thirty-something couple. The man squeezed and rubbed suntan lotion on the woman's pinkish back, and the scent of coconut and jasmine permeated. They laughed and giggled like kids, and Dolan smiled too.

Sometimes he longed for those feelings and expressions—the loving and laughing—as he had with Bree. But he was quick not to delude himself, as the bitterness and bickering usually followed the loving and laughing. It was a pattern of highs and lows, from sweet to sour, that repeated endlessly—the emotional rollercoaster. But they were young when they fell for each other, only in junior high. That made it worse. They grew into an old, bickering couple before turning seventeen. She nit-picked, and he was sullen and indifferent. They were on-again-off-again repeatedly during their school years. But they were never apart for long; they always came back. But then, after graduation, it happened. It was inevitable.

"So we're agreed? Going our separate ways to live our own lives?" Bree said as they sat together in his Jeep, parked in the driveway of her parent's home.

"You go off to State, and I go to the military."

"But we live like normal—single—people?"

"Yes."

"See other people?" Bree questioned.

"Yes," Dolan replied, but he didn't want to think about that. He didn't want to think about her with anyone else.

"So we're over?"

"I think it has to be this way. To be fair to both of us. More so to you."

"I've been thinking about this for a while too. You must know that," Bree said. "I've imagined what it would be like to *really* be on my own. To be free. Exciting but scary. Scary to be away from you and alone."

"I know. Same for me."

"I'm going to miss you, you know . . . it'll be hard to be apart. But, of course, I'm a pain to you sometimes, with all my antics, little dramas, and mood swings. When you do get mad or don't seem to understand me, there are times I hate you, despise you—I don't even know why—but I do love you, and maybe I will forever," she said, turning teary-eyed as her voice trailed off.

"I know, but . . ." he started, yet couldn't say more.

She leaned over, outstretched, and fell into his lap. They held each other, and tears flowed. Bree pulled closer and reached around his neck. She pressed her wet face against his. She kissed him hard.

"I do love you," she said, barely audible under the tears and sniffles. "I love you."

He cradled his hands around her face and attempted to speak but gave in to tears and simply kissed her again. They held and pressed against each other for a long while. Hot tears rolled between their wet faces. It was a painful yet purifying experience for each of them. They didn't want to break from their embrace because it could be the last time they would be together. They stayed that way until the tears slowed, and the sobs quietly became silent.

Eventually, they walked up to her porch. Dolan dropped her hand as she turned to open the door. She looked at him, managed a little smile through her tears, and softly said a final goodbye.

The last time Dolan saw Red, he was entertaining a bunch of regulars at the sportsbook while playing the ponies. If horses were involved, he was sure to be near. So Dolan stopped by the sportsbook to see if Red was around. He was, and his entourage had grown to include a showgirl, complete with a giant pink feather plume on her head and not much else. Red's smile was as wide as ever while someone took their photo; the feathered female lifted his cowboy hat and kissed his cheek for the shot.

"Hey, kid! Get over here and get in this Kodachrome!" Red shouted as he walked up.

Dolan and Red posed with the young woman between them.

"This is a real-life war hero," Red said to the showgirl as she stood with them. "He just got back from Saudi Arabia. Got a couple of medals for pushing Saddam's boys outta Kuwait!"

"Thanks for your service!" the girl said to Dolan, then kissed him on the cheek, and the bulb flashed.

"We're gonna have a whole suitcase full of Kodachromes!" Red shouted.

↔

The next day they were heading home. Vegas wore Red out. Dolan drove the big Lincoln down the highway, and Red dozed in the passenger seat. Sin City was in the rearview mirror, and rugged mud mountains were ahead. Beyond Hoover Dam and through the mountainous desert for miles, the landscape was Saudi Arabia all over again, and memories he wanted to forget. So he blocked out the war; instead, he thought of the cute blonde girl at the Blue Ox and wondered how far across the country she'd gone. Perhaps she was already home in Indiana.

When Red woke again near Kingman, Arizona, he complained about this or that and was in a sour mood. But with a big smile, which seemed to contradict this, he said: "I'm just plain ornery today."

His smile reminded Dolan of Uncle Harry. Pops hadn't talked much about his son. Actually, not at all. Three days' worth of stories, and none were about Uncle Harry. He suspected it was too painful for him to talk about his boy. Too painful even for an old, tough cowpoke like Red.

Doc's husband was an amazing character. He was an all-around rodeo champion at the age of nineteen. He specialized in bull riding but could rope steers and ride broncs. He joined the Army in 1967 and became one of the most decorated soldiers during the Vietnam era. An *actual* war hero. Not long after returning to Arizona, he was elected county sheriff, the youngest ever at twenty-seven. He became well known throughout the state as the charismatic lawman of Yavapai County. He usually donned a Stetson hat and carried a Colt "Peacemaker" revolver.

Uncle Harry was Dolan's childhood idol. He first met his uncle when he flew to Phoenix with his mother. He was only six years old. Waiting for them was the sheriff. He lifted

Dolan to get a good look at him. He put the kid on his shoulders and carried him and all their luggage to the car. After loading their bags in the trunk, the sheriff dropped a little cowboy hat on Dolan's head and handed him a nicely worn leather gun belt with vintage metal cap pistols. They seemed heavy and real.

"This was my pair when I was your age," his uncle said.

Little Dolan buckled the gun belt on and wouldn't take it off the entire trip. He liked being a cowboy in Arizona, especially considering Red still had his working ranch near Sedona. So it was a sad day when they flew back to Michigan and left it all behind. But little Dolan would dream of returning to the wild Arizona country—to become a cowboy like his uncle and old Red.

Unfortunately, a tragedy eventually smashed his western dreams and memories to pieces. His idol was gone, and he couldn't understand why. Dolan was ten when a homeless drifter killed his Uncle Harry. The sheriff was shot in the back while walking out of a diner in

Prescott on Christmas Eve. When asked why he did it, James Earl Donahue replied: "He seemed like a helluva nice target." It was Christmas morning when the phone rang in Michigan. His parents flew to Arizona to stay with his aunt, sending young Dolan to his grandma in Detroit. The boy never cared much for holidays after that. Never much thought about cowboys and Indians anymore, either.

Dolan joined the Army because he wanted to follow in his Uncle Harry's footsteps. Maybe he'd become a cop too. But he was still chewing on that idea. He wanted to get his head on straight before making that decision.

He pulled off I-40 at Seligman to get gas. Red handed him a twenty-dollar bill and said that should fill her up. Dolan went inside the gas station. The cashier and another worker were talking about a local killing.

"What happened?" he asked.

"Young woman was strangled and dropped next to the highway," the cashier stated. "They're trying to find out who she is and chase down the killer. Here are the sketches they left us to hang up."

The colored-pencil sketch of the female resembled a drunken scarecrow with ratty blonde hair. She wore a red and white striped sweater. If it hadn't been for that striped sweater top, he'd never have put two and two together, as bad as that scribble was. But he had a creeping feeling that this was the cute girl from Sunday night. The other drawing was an older man. He wore a black cowboy hat with feathers on the front band, glasses, and a beard. Without a doubt, it was the man who accompanied her.

Countless images and thoughts flashed through his head—her pretty smile, the way she tilted her head when she talked, how she fingered strands of blonde hair behind her ear, and her adorable giggle. *Was she dead?* He couldn't believe it. As he walked away, the cashier said: "Have a nice day!"

Strange words to hear.

They drove through town, and he tried to think of anything the girl said that could help the police. A Yavapai County Sheriff's car was outside the Blue Ox, so they pulled in.

"I may hold off the whiskey this time," Red said as he jumped from the Lincoln.

It was early afternoon, and the place was empty except for the bartender and Deputy Tim Kennedy. Kennedy was sitting at a table in the corner set up as a makeshift Seligman office. He later explained how he had been taking turns with Deputy McGraw and Deputy Smith staffing the desk, hoping for any potential witnesses to return. Today was his lucky day as the two cowboys who were also at the bar on Sunday night stopped in. It was Luke Staley and Billy Espers. They were ranch hands over at the Kaufmann outfit, east of town. They weren't much help as they said they didn't see anything or hear much. They mostly had their backs to the bar while playing pool. They left an hour after the girl and man did. They headed east back to the ranch on Route 66. Again, they didn't notice anything out of the ordinary.

"We're thinking you may need to speak with us," Red announced as he walked in. "And I'll be passing on that rotgut today . . . but I wouldn't mind coffee if you've got any!"

"I'll get a pot on," the bartender replied. "I wouldn't mind some myself."

Dolan sat across from the deputy. He asked his name to start.

"Dolan McBride," he said. He explained how he saw the sketch of the girl and man at the gas station and knew he had to contact them. He went on to tell him anything he could remember the girl or the man said or did.

"She lived in Indiana? That's good information," Kennedy replied as he filled out a witness statement form.

"Yeah, they were going to make stops at carnivals and fairs to drop off supplies. So this guy must be a truck driver that works for carnivals or a business that supplies them. Get his description and sketch out to fairs and carnivals that are going on or starting soon, right?"

"Could be a strategy," Kennedy said. "Now, did you see them go? Or drive off? See their vehicle?"

"No. They went over toward the sidestreet, and I headed back in."

"So, how long before you left? I mean, how many minutes after they left did you leave?"

"Fifteen or twenty minutes, maybe."

"That's strange because Sam Mills, the bartender here, said you left just a couple of minutes afterward," Kennedy said, sounding skeptical.

"I ordered a beer and drank it slowly! It was at least fifteen minutes."

"In what direction did you head out of here? I'm assuming you went west since you were going to Las Vegas?"

"Yes. We went through town but stayed on Old 66 instead of taking I-40 to Kingman."

"Isn't that a longer drive? Not taking I-40?"

"I guess it is. We were sightseeing."

"In the dark?" Kennedy said with skepticism, taking the joke seriously.

Red made a face. He didn't seem to like the deputy's tone. He walked over to the makeshift table office.

"Deputy, are you gonna ask my name—write it down on your sheet there—before you question me? But, of course, I didn't see anything or hear much because I was over in that seat spinnin' tales for this bartender here. But if you're gonna start getting suspicious of your star witness, you may want to know who we are first."

"And you are?"

"My name is Harold Halleran, Sr."

"As in Sheriff Harry Halleran? I thought you looked familiar!"

The deputy stood up and shook Red's hand.

"Sheriff Harry was my idol! You won't believe this, but I have his photo hanging inside my equipment locker! He came to my school over in Prescott to give a talk once, and I got to meet him. I was just a little kid, but that's when I decided I'd be a lawman. That day!"

"Well, thank you, son," Red said. "That does mean a lot to me."

"Something I wanted to mention," Dolan started, "is that the colored-pencil sketch you've got circulating of the girl is horrible! I'm not sure where you found your artist, but he's no Rembrandt! Why not just use a photo?"

"A photo is not possible," he said and tactfully explained.

"I see," Dolan said quietly.

"Sam sat down with the artist yesterday," Kennedy said, motioning toward the bartender.

"That's fine. I'm not questioning Sam's recollection. It's just—look, my aunt is a naturopathic physician, but she's also a great artist. So I'll sit down with her when we get back to Sedona and put together a drawing that may help you get a name. And another of that bastard of a man. His sketch isn't terrible, but we could do better."

"That would be great!" Kennedy said. "I'll give you the phone number to our Northern Division office in Chino Valley. Detective Patty Malloy heads our division so ask for her."

Dolan stood up from the table.

"One more thing before I forget," the deputy began and fumbled with a file. "Did you happen to see this motorhome anywhere around here?"

"Nope. Sorry. Was it involved somehow?"

"Well, it's a weird coincidence at this point. It was abandoned in Ash Fork approximately the same time our Tuesday Jane was killed. And it had the body of an elderly woman inside. She'd been dead a few days or so. No foul play is suspected, but she was left abandoned. And we don't have a name on her either. She's the Sunday Jane Doe."

"Damn, that is weird."

When Dolan and Red left, the bartender walked over to Deputy Kennedy's table with his pot of coffee and two mugs. He offered him a cup and sat down.

"Thanks, Sam! I could get used to this service."

Sam poured the hot coffee, and they both sat still, drinking slowly. It was so quiet you could hear a pin drop. Sam let out a long breath through his pursed lips.

"Tell me, though, Tim," he said to the deputy. "Do you think you could move your patrol car around back? You must know you're killing my darn business!"

CHAPTER FOUR

She sharpened her graphite pencils, pulled out her Strathmore sketch pad, and flipped past the bowl of fruit, teapot with cups, and other penciled still lifes until she came to blank pages. As Dolan carefully described the young woman's facial features, a passion and fire erupted from him. He directed her hand with precise recollection and acuity. He was on a mission.

"Her chin . . . a cleft or dimple . . . not severely deep or sharp, but it was there. Her top lip, nice and full, had that heart shape, I suppose . . . What's it called? Then above her lips . . . between her nose and upper lip . . . the sharp dent."

"The cupid's bow is the nice curve on her upper lip. And the vertical dent is called a philtrum," Doc replied.

Dolan said her eyes should be a little rounder and brighter, so Doc erased what she did and tried again. Her nose was slight and gently sloping. Eyebrows were curved and thin. Her light blonde hair was parted in the middle, negligibly offset from the center, with a little body, not flat on her head.

Doc was finishing up with a bit of shading around her cheeks.

"She's very pretty," his aunt said. "I see why you can describe her so well!"

"Yeah, but she was so nice too. Grateful for the little bit I did for her. Damn—this is sickening!" He walked into the kitchen and got a drink of water. Doc kept working.

"I guess they're calling her Tuesday Jane," he said, standing near the sink. "They already had a Jane Doe from Sunday night—an older woman. You know, I'd like to help find this son-of-a-bitch truck driver! And rip his damn head off!"

When he returned to the table, Doc said: "How does this look now?"

He examined the drawing and nodded.

"Perfect! Aunt Lauren, you are one gifted woman!"

She finished the minor changes to the male suspect's sketch, and Dolan pulled out Detective Malloy's phone number.

"Patty is in charge of the investigation?" she asked. "Give me the phone."

"You know her?"

"We're old friends. Harry hired her like fifteen years ago."

He handed the white cordless phone to his aunt, and she spoke with Detective Malloy.

"Patty, this is Doc Halleran! What the heck have you been up to? You haven't come down to see us since the Fourth of July. I should come over to take you out to lunch, but I've been pretty busy here. Yeah, a strange thing happened. My nephew Dolan and Red went through Seligman the other night and came across your girl. Yeah, your Tuesday Jane. Oh, the deputy already told you? And you didn't call me right away? Jeez. He sat with me, and we have two good sketches. Dolan thinks they are excellent—a great resemblance. Listen, my nephew and I have been talking here, and he's interested in helping your office in any way he can. Yeah, so—well, I may be speaking out of turn here—but I think he would like to head over and do intern work with you, some footwork, whatever it takes. He wants to help. Also, he's recently out of the military, and I think he's kicking around becoming a police officer. No, I'd be all for it. I know, you'd think I'd be the last person. But I'd be proud if he did. I'd like him to courier these sketches over to you because we're not going to fax them and mess up the quality! Here, I'll get Dolan on the line."

He grabbed the phone. "Hello, Detective Malloy."

"Hello, Dolan. So you want to bring the sketches over?"

"Yep, I think the quicker I get them over to you, the faster you can get them out."

"I could send a deputy over to pick them up. You don't have to come all the way over."

"No, I'll bring them myself and talk to you about how I can help."

"If you say so. We're near Chino Valley at the south end of town. Right on State Route 89. Can't miss it. Northern Division Office."

"Chino Valley–Northern Division? Okay . . . I got it." He set the phone on the counter.

"I'll make you a quick sandwich, and you can take it along," Doc said, smiling.

"Sounds good! What's the shortest way to get to Chino Valley from here?"

"Up through Jerome and over the mountain."

"Nice. Too bad I won't have time for sightseeing in town."

Red came in through the front door.

"Am I late for dinner? I was napping for the last couple of hours. Boy, I kinda wore myself out over in Vegas."

"I'm heading back out to deliver these to the detective." Dolan showed the sketches to Red.

"You're gonna be on the road more than a long-haul trucker!" Red said. "These pictures sure look good. Of course, I never did pay much attention to what this pair looked like, but you sure did! This one is a scary-looking creep, isn't he? And she sure was a cute one. What a damn shame for that poor girl."

"The detective said she could send a deputy over to get the sketches; I told her no. I figure you're right," he said, turning to his aunt. "If I show up there, maybe they'll put me to use."

He drove his Jeep over the narrow, steep, and curvy road through the town of Jerome, then up and around Mingus Mountain, where tall pines intermixed with changing oak and the yellowing aspen dotted the landscape of the Black Hills range. He thought of his aunt's stories as he passed through town.

Dolan liked Jerome—a historic mountainside mining town that nearly busted when the copper and gold mines closed up in the old days. The original miners established a camp at the current site on Cleopatra Hill. Several fires burnt much of the town early on when it was mostly wood shacks and tents. The brick buildings were built in the 1890s. Then the town and copper mines boomed, with as many as fifteen thousand people living and working there by the 1920s. But it didn't last. The depression hit, and copper prices slid. By 1953 all the mines were shut. The town fell into disrepair. Some of the structures were dangerously close to sliding off their foundations into oblivion. Many had. Starting in the 1960s, free-spirited artists and counter-culture individuals began arriving and taking up residence, forming an artist colony of sorts, joining many long-standing residents and shopkeepers who stayed on through thick and thin. The newcomers and old-timers worked together to bring the broke town back to life, mainly by selling artwork and various trinkets to tourists and building on its haunted-ghost-town backstory.

After college, Dolan's aunt came to Jerome on the back of a Harley-Davidson motorcycle, sitting behind her first boyfriend, Davey. It was 1969. She stayed and started drawing and painting. Davey only lasted a week, then rode on. She thinks he ended up in California but never saw him again.

When Dolan and Bree were out in Arizona four years earlier, they spent a day in Jerome with Doc. She guided them to all the places where she lived and worked. Like the corner hotel, then just a low-budget flophouse for artists and hippies, to the lower-level apothecary shop across the street, where she experimented with herbal remedies and essential oils—some of which she still used in her practice. But it was with nostalgia and a little sadness that she brought them around to other sites, like the park in the center of town, where she'd do caricature sketches of tourists for tip money and, incidentally, where she'd meet a young cowboy soldier recently back from Vietnam who was losing himself in a day of drinking. He was lounging in the grass with a bucket of ice and Budweisers. He told her some jokes. She laughed and thought he was too funny. Then he convinced the auburn-haired beauty to put away her drawing pencil and join him for a cold beer. They sat on the grass together the rest of that afternoon, talked, laughed, and kissed. A few months passed before they married at the Halleran ranch near Sedona. She wore flowers in her hair; he wore his Stetson hat. They left on horseback and spent their honeymoon up the West Fork of Oak Creek Canyon.

↔

The Northern Division of the Yavapai County Sheriff's office was north of Prescott near Chino Valley. The county covered a vast land area encompassing over eight thousand square miles, similar in size to some smaller states back east. When Harry Halleran was sheriff, he devised a plan to divide the county into three unique areas and patrol divisions. He put a commander in each division, and he would oversee the entire operation. Detective Patty Malloy eventually headed the Northern Division, which contained thousands of square miles from north of Prescott to Ash Fork, Seligman, and farther northwest toward the Hualapai Indian Reservation near Peach Springs, where tribal police had jurisdiction.

He met the detective at the division office.

"I'm Dolan McBride, ma'am," he said and shook her hand. Patty was short and squatty with a bob-type haircut. Her face was round with thin lips and an inverted smile.

"Let's see what Doc did for us," she said, pulling the sketches out of the large envelope from which they came. "Nice!"

She walked the drawings to the desk sergeant with instructions to get them out to all media outlets.

"The murder of a pretty female like this should get the media buzzing. That will help."

"Any progress?" he questioned.

"It's early yet. But these sketches will get the ball rolling. I can almost guarantee it."

"So, have you checked the local fairs and carnivals?"

She chuckled a little.

"So you want to be a cop? Or are you just interested in helping a bit on the case?"

"Truthfully, I'm not sure."

"Well, to be an officer here, we have a five-month training course through the academy. At a minimum. Unless you were military police?"

"Was not an MP. But I want to help in any way I can."

"Look, I know what your aunt said, but you're all jacked up because you're one of the last people to see this girl alive. Perhaps she made an impression on you. Maybe you feel a little guilty for some reason. But how could you have known, right? Anyhow, I'm going to get Chinese food down the street. It's late, and I'm hungry and tired. How about we talk there?"

Dolan nodded in agreement. "Sure."

So over a plate of egg foo young, Detective Malloy cautiously opened up regarding the case.

"Her being from Indiana, like she told you, makes sense. The brand of her sweater was Goshen, which I had never heard of, but it's a boutique firm in Goshen, Indiana. They sold it. So perhaps we confirmed that bit anyway. We'll ask the Indiana State Police to run with the sketch tomorrow. I'm sure their news services will get it covered."

"And the suspect?" Dolan questioned.

She reached over for the soy sauce.

"Yes, we're working on the fair/carnival angle and have already found three going on this week in the southwest. We faxed the original sketch to management at two of them, and they circulated the fax among their staff. In addition, the St. Sebastian Catholic Church will be running a fair in Albuquerque, New Mexico. We faxed the sketch to their parish, and they'll be on the lookout for such an individual making deliveries for the set-up."

"No big state fairs this time of year?"

"Quite a few . . . Texas, Mississippi, Georgia, South Carolina, and our own."

"Arizona State Fair is going on now?" he asked excitedly.

"Yes, Phoenix Police is already cooperating with us."

"But he would have already been and gone. It was Sunday night when he was here so—"

"There are many, many deliveries for these big state fairs. Ours goes on for the entire month of October. They regularly get new inventory . . . stuffed animals, food, other prizes, you name it." Malloy said. "And they'll be circulating his sketch tonight and tomorrow. So if any of the workers recognize him, they'll be able to give us the name of the company he works for. So we'll find him."

"Good, but I figure he'll be halfway to Indiana now," Dolan insisted. "And if he knows the heat is on, he may disappear!"

"Yes, possible. We are also working on other angles at the moment. We're not going to release these details now, but they look promising."

"So you are running a few leads down?"

"You're a persistent bugger; I'll give you that! Yes, we've already got a couple of names. We're following them up. Doing good police work. But it takes time."

"Seems like it. The good police work, I mean," he acknowledged.

"Look, I was close with Sheriff Harry. He taught me a lot. Your Aunt Lauren is great . . . Doc is my good friend. You seem to have a passion in your belly. If you want to be in law enforcement, there could be a spot for you here. Someday, if you choose to complete our academy program, as I said, I think we'd be proud to bring you into the department. But I think you are too close to this. You are emotionally involved and jacked up. This happens with law enforcement officers too, and we take them off the case when it does. No questions asked. So I'm sure you can understand my hesitancy in letting you get too involved?"

"I understand," he admitted.

The restaurant's waiter was standing near the cash register, looking at his watch, fidgeting. But he was smiling and affable.

"Also, maybe now that you see the department is working hard on this, you can rest easy. We'll get this young lady her name back and find this guy. We've got a dragnet running. We may need your help identifying truckers that get pulled in. So that'll be important."

Patty never handed any payment to the waiter at the register when they left. They walked out, and she said to Dolan: "It's a little game we play. He hands me a bill at the table, then I hand it back to him at the register, and he charges nothing. So I leave a huge tip at the table that pays the check anyway. They refuse to charge us police for meals here. Gratis!"

"Nice of them!"

"But to avoid the look of impropriety, I pay at the table anyway!"

They returned to the Northern Division parking lot. Patty told him to thank his aunt for the sketches. She'd owe her.

"I'll call my aunt. I may stick around this side of the mountain for the night. I wanna go fishing in the morning. Any cheap motels?"

"The Roadhouse Inn down the street here isn't bad. The cheap ones are north of here in Paulden, but especially up in Ash Fork. You can get a room for eighteen bucks a night up there!"

"That's my kind of price! Beats sleeping in my Jeep," he said. "It also puts me closer to the nice little lake off I-40. Cataract Lake, I think it was."

"Yeah, Cataract is near Williams. Good luck! I'll keep in touch!"

CHAPTER FIVE

He slept well at the motel in Ash Fork. Management hadn't freshly decorated the room in forever. The 1950s came to mind. The red, white, and blue *I Like Ike* sticker on the dressing mirror may have been the reason. But regardless, the sheets were clean, the towels fresh, and the steamy hot shower that morning helped wipe away the mild headache he woke up with, which was a good thing since his bottle of aspirin was gone. He left the bathroom without shaving, put on the t-shirt he'd been wearing, and slapped his old, worn-out John Deere cap on his head.

Dolan usually looked one of two ways. He typically appeared with an unshaven face, a baseball cap on his head, a regular t-shirt, or a long-sleeved flannel, culminating in an outdoorsy *Field & Stream* look. But on days when he appeared too much like a slob and decided to make an effort (or when the military required it), he'd shave close with a blade and use a little gel or pomade on his typically short brownish hair. He significantly transformed himself with this minimal effort and grooming. Bree dubbed this his *GQ* look, as she said he was pretty enough to be on the magazine's cover. Dolan, of course, was never sure if she was complimenting or disparaging him, considering she explicitly used the word pretty instead of maybe, handsome. Since Dolan was only planning on fishing that day, there was no question whether he'd shave or not. Consequently, he wasn't very pretty that morning.

He ran across the road to the diner and ordered a Denver omelet for breakfast and a coffee. Two hunters were sitting across the aisle, both wearing camouflage. They were exchanging hunting stories. The man nearest—a short, fat man with a long red beard—was telling a tale that involved a supposed trophy elk. He did so in an animated way, as his hands were moving as much as his mouth. He explained that he was on an archery hunt, crawling on his belly with a bow and arrow strapped to his back until he was close enough to "the monster elk" to take a chance at him. Little did he know another hunter from his party was also moving oppositely, stalking the same elk. The other hunter took his shot first, and the arrow only grazed the elk's enormous rump. The trophy animal bolted and leaped into the air and began charging in the direction of our red-bearded storyteller. The fearless hunter hit the dirt as hard and fast as possible, and the big elk hurdled directly over him. He pulled himself off the ground and spun around. He fumbled with his bow and arrow, but before raising it straight, the elk disappeared into the thicket, stopping briefly in a clearing well beyond range. He never saw the beast again. He said that was off Devil Dog Road, down I-40 a few miles toward Williams.

"The biggest trophy elk you'll ever see! I've been hunting that area ever since!" the red-bearded man shook his head. "But damn, if I ever do see him again . . . he ain't getting away. After that, it'll be him or me!"

When Dolan hopped in his Jeep and exited the motel parking lot, he could only turn right onto the one-way street. So he began heading west through town. Finally, he got to the end of the line in Ash Fork and merged onto I-40. Unfortunately, he was traveling westbound, not east, but he kept going regardless.

The day before, after giving his witness statement to Deputy Kennedy, he and Red traveled on I-40 eastbound and passed the crime scene at the old highway yard. He'd seen the crime tape still wrapped around the juniper trees near the shoulder of the highway. Today, since he'd accidentally gone out of his way, he would go even farther out of his way to loop back and pass the crime scene again. Only this time, he'd stop.

When he pulled off the road at the scene, he remembered the girl's pretty face as she smiled back at him for the final time, squeezing his hand. It was strange, but something zapped in his head when he met her. Even though he was only with the young woman for a minute, she affected him. It was a physical attraction, but more importantly, he had a genuine, tender feeling for her. The feeling intensified a hundredfold when he heard she was dead. Almost hauntingly so.

He stood on the freeway shoulder in front of his Jeep. The yellow crime tape, now partially dangling and torn, flittered in the light breeze of the morning. He tried to imagine what went on there. They say she was dumped and dragged.

Dolan could see what he believed to be the drag marks in the light pea gravel along the shoulder, and onto the whitish-gray dirt, through the brush and scrub. He was picturing a semi-trailer parked on the road here, the big man jumping down from the truck's steps, leaning down to grab the girl by the foot or hair, and dragging her for fifty yards into the overgrowth. But a large man at six feet plus and close to 250 pounds would have an easier time throwing her over his shoulder and walking with her. She didn't weigh much more than 110 pounds. Maybe he was worried passing drivers could see him, so he crouched as low as possible. Perhaps he was weakened from an old injury or age, and awkwardly dragging was the only way. Any reason was possible. Still, he could see a puny guy dragging her body or a woman. That made sense. But such a big man?

A vehicle pulled off the highway onto the broad shoulder. It was a sheriff's patrol car. Dolan walked closer to the front of his Jeep and stood and waited. A large doughy-looking young man emerged from the car. He had brown, combed-over hair and a fresh face, not much older than Dolan.

"Do you need assistance?" the deputy asked.

He walked over to the officer.

"I'm Dolan McBride. I'm the guy that talked to the victim on Sunday night."

"Oh, you're Sheriff Harry's nephew!" he said, reaching out to shake his hand. "I'm Deputy Shane McGraw."

"I didn't go into the area or anything." He pointed to the partially cordoned perimeter.

"That's fine. Forensics have finished with it, I'm sure," McGraw said. "Yeah, I'm the one that found her body over there. It was bad."

"How did you find her? Did you happen to see her from the interstate?"

"Nope. I pulled off here for a minute and was standing next to my cruiser, and I heard a bunch of coyotes yipping—hey, you want a cigarette?" McGraw offered. "I'm trying to quit completely, but I usually have one in the morning."

"No thanks," he replied. "You know, I was standing here wondering why such a big, strong dude would drag her all that way and not just throw her over his shoulder."

"Interesting point. I thought she was dragged by her feet. One of her shoes was missing. But we never found it. So it could've stayed in the truck," McGraw said. "But you can never tell why people do anything . . . push, pull, carry or drag or whatever! It could be laziness. If you pushed her body out onto the ground from the truck, it might not be as easy as you think to pull her up and throw her over your shoulder.

You'd have to squat down low to get your hands on the body. Rather cumbersome."

They walked closer to the perimeter.

"The detective thinks someone used the belt loops of her jeans to drag her. One loop was torn, and the other stretched."

"I don't know. That seems awkward."

"Maybe he was yanking at the jeans, trying to pull them down. Get at her. That's what I thought, anyway. Those jeans were *tight*," McGraw said, then got fidgety with his hands, looking embarrassed for saying such a thing. "But, of course, they didn't violate her like that . . . Um, I usually don't speak this freely about cases. I shouldn't!"

"I was with Detective Patty Malloy last night in Chino Valley, so I know a little already," Dolan replied. "I want to help any way I can."

"Well, those new sketches are running now, and we're getting leads rolling in. Most will be a waste of time, but one or two won't!"

"That's good. I guess I've helped with something."

"This guy here—our suspect—looks like he could be a serial killer or at least a guy with a pattern!" McGraw said.

"What? You've got other victims or something?"

"Not here, but a few along I-40 out to Oklahoma. It all happened a few years back. One of our deputies, Tim Kennedy, went through FBI files and found a guy that fits the description. He seems to work the I-40 corridor. He's a trucker. Rodney Russell Lee. He wears a black cowboy hat with feathers on the front."

"No kidding? That sounds like our guy. So he's already wanted?"

"He was awaiting trial a couple of years ago for kidnapping two sisters from Oklahoma, sixteen and fourteen years old. But, unfortunately, he got off on a technicality. And they never found the girls either."

"Son of a bitch!"

"The lawyers are as bad as the damn criminals! It was the second time they got him off!" McGraw said, then turned up his leather-banded wristwatch. "Well, I better get going. We have a briefing in Chino, so I shouldn't be late!"

"Nice meeting you."

"Same!"

The deputy pulled onto I-40 while Dolan remained a few more minutes at the crime scene. He felt slightly better knowing the bastard hadn't sexually assaulted the girl. *Small favors.*

He was on his way down eastbound I-40 again and started thinking about fishing at Cataract Lake. He thought about using his fly rod along the shoreline and the type of artificial flies he had in his vest. He never fly-fished in Arizona, only in Michigan, but most any fly would do. He had quite an assortment of them, so the trout at the lake should hit on one kind or another. "Goddamn fishing license!" he shouted out loud.

It slipped his mind; he needed a license for Arizona. So again, he pulled off the interstate at Ash Fork and went to the gas station. It was a touristy place geared for visitors on the way to the Grand Canyon, loaded with souvenirs and snacks. He found a big ol' gal working the counter, and she was happy to help him get a license.

She was filling out all of his pertinent information on the form. First, she used his driver's license for most of the particulars, then asked about the extra stamps.

"What stamps?" he inquired.

"A two-pole stamp. Gonna use two poles?"

"Nope."

"What about city lakes? Gonna fish a lake in a city?"

"Maybe. I guess."

"What about trout? You gonna fish for trout?"

"Wow, I assumed trout were fish. Weird that you need a stamp for trout. Yes, I guess I'll need one of those too!"

"The darn government gets you coming and going," a gray-haired man said. He was sweeping the floor near the counter but stopped and leaned on his broom. "I own this place, you know, but I have to sweep the floors and clean up because I can't afford more employees after paying the darn taxes!"

She tore out all the stamps he needed, then flipped the paper license over.

"Here, you got to lick these and stick 'em on these boxes on the back. It'll be twelve dollars extra for the stamp taxes."

"I'm not a big fan of licking and sticking," Dolan said.

The woman leaned across the counter and said in a whispered, southern drawl: "Honey, I could make a funny joke about *that*!"

"No, thank you, Vera!" the owner chimed in while he continued to sweep. "You've scared away customers with your bad jokes in the past!"

Dolan laughed as he licked the stamps and stuck them into place. He paid her and headed out, eager to use his brand-new Arizona fishing license.

CHAPTER SIX

His right rear tire was a little low—a slow leak—so he pulled over to use the air hose before leaving the fuel station. He filled the tire until the gauge read thirty-five psi. Maybe he'd get that leak patched someday. Or maybe not.

As he returned the hose to the hook, a scruffy-looking individual popped from behind the stainless steel housing of the air pump. He smelled like he'd been sleeping off a week-long bender in the grass. He was a skinny guy with curly hair and a nervous tic. His eyes blinked incessantly, and he jerked his head a lot. But he seemed cordial enough.

"Hello, friend," he said. "Would you happen to have some spare change for a man in need?"

Dolan shook his head and started walking away, but then he stopped, reconsidered, and returned. He handed him whatever few singles and change he had stuck in his front pocket from the prior transaction.

"Thank you so much, my friend!" the man said politely. "You know, I don't do this too often. Ask for handouts. But my momma died, and I'm not sure what to do now."

The man was about thirty-five or forty years old, but he felt for him. "Sorry to hear that."

"You see, we live south of Seligman, down around the national forest, and never get to town much. We live on the land going from camp to camp in our motorhome. My brother Buck used to live here in Ash Fork, so I come looking for him the other day and never found him. He'd know what to do about burying Momma. But his landlady said she ain't seen him in near a year."

"Like having a funeral here in town?"

"Well, sure, a preacher saying words would be nice. Look, I want to do right by her, but everything got all messed up, and I lost her."

"Lost your mom?"

"Sure. The motorhome got to running poorly, then stopped altogether, so I left Momma where she was. That's when I went looking for Buck. I walked all the way to the place he was living—about five miles north of town—and when I get there, the landlady said she ain't seen him in pretty near a year, so I walk all those miles back, and she was gone!"

"I see," Dolan said, clearly remembering Deputy Kennedy's story.

"So I went on to the mission at the end of town. They feed you and put you in a bed for the night. I knew about the mission because I stayed there once when I come to town for piecework. But they kick you out during the daytime, so I've been wandering."

"Didn't you ask the people at the mission to help find your motorhome?" he questioned reluctantly.

"Well, you see, the motorhome isn't exactly legal . . . The guy who gave it to us said he didn't know about the title and all that. He wasn't so sure if it was stolen. But we rarely brought it up to town or anything. It don't have no registration papers or insurance. Buck would know what to do. I need to find Buck."

Dolan needed to return to the gas station to call the sheriff's office to tell them about the motorhome mystery.

"Hey, I'm Dolan, by the way. What's your name?"

"Andy . . . Andy Bergeron. My brother is Buck Bergeron."

"Well, Andy, I'm pretty sure we should contact the sheriff's office and let them hear your story. They'll help you find your brother. You didn't do anything wrong that I can tell."

"You think they can find my brother?"

"Sure . . . they've got all kinds of computers and records. So they know where everyone is! And they can help get a proper burial for your mother."

"But someone took the motorhome. And Momma too!"

"The sheriff took her, Andy. They're waiting for someone to come forward to identify her. Look, how about you sit in my Jeep, and I'll call the sheriff's office. Maybe we'll go to the diner and wait for them to show up. Get you something to eat."

"I don't know. You think it'll be okay? They won't put me in jail or nothing?"

"Nah, I think they'll wanna help you."

"Well, maybe they'd find Buck too. I'd like that."

"Great," Dolan said. He ran back into the gas station to use the phone.

They sat at the diner and waited for one of the deputies to arrive. Andy ate a stack of hotcakes and a mess of sausage. In between bites, he explained that he was a trapper. That trapping goes way back in the family tradition. He explained that he and his mother moved around to find coyotes, bobcats, and foxes. He said a prominent rancher pays him for the pelts he brings in.

"Like a bounty?" Dolan asked. "Because the coyotes are a threat to the livestock?"

"Well, maybe partly so. They worry more about mountain lions. They've got a professional hunter that takes care of those. But anyway, they sell all the pelts I bring 'em for profit. They get good money for 'em, I reckon. But the men at the Bar-T don't pay me in cash money, but mostly supplies. Like a trade. We got our fuel for the motorhome right from their tank pump at the ranch, and water, of course, and they give us lots of canned goods and other provisions, like the cough syrup Momma was using. So we like it better that way. Cash isn't handy down in the forest."

"I've heard of that Bar-T Ranch."

"It's a big spread, and they're real nice fellas. I do other work too. They say we could camp anywhere on the ranch. But Momma preferred the forest because it was nicer and prettier."

Deputy Kennedy walked into the diner and stood near the register. Dolan and Andy popped up and went to meet him. The deputy put Andy in the patrol car and came back to talk with Dolan.

"Hey kid, you're making me look bad!" he said to Dolan, giving him a playful tap on his shoulder with his fist. "You wrap up our case and tie a pretty little bow on it!"

"I was only buying a damn fishing license and filling air in my tire. I didn't do anything special!"

"Well, I'm sure everybody at Northern Division is already talking about how Sheriff Harry's nephew is coming for their job!"

"I don't want their jobs. I just want to go fishing! And you know, that's what I'm going to do now."

"Well, catch a biggie," Kennedy said. "Thanks again!"

Kennedy started for the patrol car and Dolan for his Jeep. Then he remembered he wanted to ask him about the trucker. "Hey, deputy . . ."

"Yeah?" he turned.

"Don't you guys need me to look at photos of this serial killer suspect?"

Kennedy seemed surprised. Not pleasantly.

"How do you know about that?"

"Deputy McGraw mentioned it."

Kennedy shook his head and scrunched his face up. "That's on the down-low! We're waiting on info from the Oklahoma City branch of the FBI. He shouldn't—"

"I get it. I'll forget it until you hear more or need me."

"Good man," Kennedy said. "Now go get some fishing in!"

Finally, Dolan was on I-40, heading in the proper direction, east toward Williams, leaving the cedar and scrub ranchland for the high country. Ponderosa pine was growing taller as he passed Devil Dog Road. He chuckled, remembering the red-bearded hunter and his story about getting leaped over by the monster elk. There was a small canyon pond near the exit, and he almost turned off to try his luck, but he'd keep driving until Cataract Lake. The rugged westerly side of Bill Williams Mountain was in view; it was some wild country he would like to explore someday. He'd put it on the to-do list.

↔

The breeze let up, and the small lake was still. The east side of Cataract had craggy gray boulders piled up, creating a dam. A concrete spillway on the north edge of the boulders had water leaking through, forming a little stream on the other side. A tiny campground bordered the southeast portion of the lake with six or seven campsites for overnight stays. An older, bearded man had a blue tent with a gray rainfly. His tent occupied the only site in use. He had an inflatable boat with an electric motor which he dragged out of the water. He told Dolan that trout were hitting by the tall pines near the southern edge, especially in the marshy area, but he was fishing deep in the center for catfish.

Dolan put on his rubber boots, snapped the four sections of the long fly rod together, and grabbed his vest. A professional fisherman would go and examine the water and discover what insects were present or if larvae or nymphs were emerging to the surface, then attempt to match that pattern from his assortment of artificial flies. But he'd use the first fly that popped out of the box as he normally did. So he tied what appeared to be a small mayfly to the leader line and started fishing near the marsh where the man had pointed. He didn't have luck initially and worked his way to the edge of the pines. After the fourth cast, he got action at the surface—a sizable fish broke the water—but he missed setting the hook. He flicked the line a few more times and soon got action again. He felt a light pulse on the rod and kept the line tight as he reeled. It was a small brown trout. The hook slid off the fish's lip as he reached for it. It quickly swam away. Eventually, he caught three fish: two small brown trout and one reasonably large sunfish. He sat beside the shore, rested his back against a giant ponderosa pine, and looked over the lake.

A folded, partially torn, handwritten letter was in the upper left pocket of his fishing vest. It had been in that pocket for over four years. Bree wrote the letter a week after they split up. It ended up in his fishing vest because he discovered it one morning on his driver's seat the day he was heading up to the Au Sable River with Bobby Allman. They planned to get some fishing in before going off to basic training together. He found the letter on his seat, along with the picture Bree took of them, with faces pressed together, at the NAU campus. He liked that photo. He read the letter and put it into his fishing vest pocket before picking up Allman. It was an excellent place to stick something you wouldn't want your buddy to read. But maybe he should have let him read it. That's the problem with most guys—the things they should share and talk about, they never do. *Goddamn, Allman.* So he stuck the letter in his vest, but the photo eventually made it into the Jeep's glove compartment. It was still there.

Dolan assumed, way back when, that Bree wrote the letter on impulse and possibly forgot she even did. But that's how she was. She was impulsive and flighty. Her mood swings and capriciousness were hallmarks of her personality. She could be silly and fanciful one moment and then dead serious for days thereafter. He loved her silly side; he couldn't help himself. He pulled the letter out and read it once again. He grinned because it was so Bree, through and through. Or at least how he remembered her to be.

Bree had a plan. Her letter outlined it. She admitted she stole the idea from a classic Cary Grant film she had watched with her grandmother. Her plan wasn't exactly the same, but the premise was similar. She wanted to meet and possibly reunite in four years if neither were in a serious relationship. Then, they could try again as adults. Of course, in *An Affair to Remember*, Cary Grant was supposed to meet Deborah Kerr in six months at the top of the Empire State Building, but Dolan wouldn't like that since he didn't favor big cities. So she decided the cemetery park at Thompson Lake in their hometown would be more appropriate. That'd be the place. The day and time would be Halloween 1991 at noon. Their four-year stints would be up (her college and his military), and they should be ready to move on to the next stage of their life. So it was all set.

But that was the condensed version of her plan. The actual letter contained a thousand tiny, handwritten words. It explained why they were perfect for each other, the many reasons she chose that specific time and place (the backstories and little romances which Dolan knew all too well), that she still loved him and expected she still would in four years, and that she wrote all this out to make herself feel a little better. She had a miserable night thinking about him, and writing this down made her feel much better.

Dolan folded the letter and shoved it back into his pocket. It was hard to believe her day was coming in only three weeks. Strange how those four years went by in a blink. He wished he could forget about her and her plan. He wished he could but knew he couldn't.

The lake was calm, with a surface like glass. The man at the campsite was starting a fire, and gray smoke drifted straight away. It was close to lunchtime. A silvery fish emerged from the top water, flashing prismatically in the sun. It was a large fish, most likely a rainbow trout, and it made a big splash when it flopped back into the water. Circular ripples showed on the surface and gently expanded outward until they vanished into the shoreline. Once again, the lake became still.

CHAPTER SEVEN

Detective Patty Malloy was sitting behind her desk at the Northern Division, speaking with Deputy Tim Kennedy about Andy Bergeron, who was waiting in the interview room.

"So I sat him down to get his statement," Kennedy started eagerly, "and he asked me about the girl. I asked him what girl? He says the one in the picture on the wall—the blonde girl. So I asked if he had seen her. He says he picked her up at the I-40 Exit 123."

"Our Tuesday Jane?" Patty asked excitedly. "I knew these things were connected!"

"Yes, and she drove with him just for a minute, he tells me, until they were onto I-40 eastbound heading toward Ash Fork, and she asked him about the smell. Well, he says I'm sorry about the smell. Then she says to let her out. To stop the motorhome. She can't stand the smell. So he says he stops the van and lets her out to walk. He says he drives off to Ash Fork, where he runs into engine problems and leaves the thing where we found it. Here's the clincher. He says she jumped out of the motorhome so fast she left her bag!"

"This is incredible," Patty said. "Look, get over to the yard and check out that motorhome evidence. I know there was plenty of stuff in that vehicle. We combed it for papers and identification but didn't pay much attention to all the clothing and supplies crammed in."

"I guess I'll have fun going through the garbage!" Kennedy replied.

Detective Malloy went into the interview room with Kennedy's notes. She brought a soda for Andy and a coffee for herself.

"Now, Andy, I'm very sorry about your mother," she said. "From what I understand, you were trying to find your brother Buck in Ash Fork to help you. Is that correct?"

"Yes, ma'am. I sure was looking for Buck."

"We are already searching for your brother. I have people looking through records to see where he may be. So we will find him."

"Buck will know what to do for Momma's funeral. We're gonna do right by her."

"I'm sure you will," Patty said. "Now, can you tell me more about the girl you picked up?"

"I seen her standing near that ramp. I was coming up from Williamson Valley Road, and I'm gonna turn for Ash Fork, and she was standing there, and she waved me down. So I stopped, thinking she needed help."

"She was a pretty young woman, yes?"

"I never paid much attention," Andy said. "But I seen her picture on the wall."

"Then what happened?"

"The girl started fussing about the smell," he said. "She wanted out. So I stopped, and she jumped out."

"How far were you from the exit ramp when you let her out?"

"A quarter mile . . . maybe a mile. I'm not too sure. The girl said she couldn't stand the smell. She wanted out. I was driving to find Buck, so I didn't care much about the girl. I was trying to get Momma to Buck!"

"Okay, Andy . . . so tell me about this trapping business. You're a trapper?"

"Yeah, my family has been trapping for a long while. Far back as anyone can remember."

"So Andy, the deputy told me you camp in the Prescott National Forest near the Bar-T Ranch?"

"That's right. Momma liked it in the forest."

"Do you still have a camp set up? That you left?"

"Yeah . . . there's a tarp tied up with some firewood and a latrine tent that we set up. And Momma's table. Some trapping supplies too."

"Back to your trapping, Andy. I often wondered, how is it that you euthanize animals that you find in your live trap? The bobcats and the coyotes?"

"Euthanize?" Andy asked.

"How do you kill these animals? Do you shoot them with a .22-caliber?"

"I don't have a gun. I've got me a club, and I've got me a snare," Andy said.

"You use a club and a snare?"

"Well, I usually put the snare pole in the cage, and they run their head right into it. I tighten real hard. Not much trouble."

"So you strangle them until they're dead?" Patty asked.

"Usually," he said.

"That's a pretty picture."

↔

"We've got two good suspects now!" Patty said to Kennedy as he approached her desk. "How do you like that?"

Kennedy confirmed that the forensic team at the yard found a duffle bag inside the motorhome, among several other bags and boxes of clothing. The duffle bag contained clothing in sizes similar to what the victim was wearing. Also, a toothbrush, other personal hygiene products, and a small bottle of Excedrin aspirin. And thirty-two dollars. Kennedy also left a hairbrush with the lab to compare to the victim's hair samples. Unfortunately, they hadn't discovered any identification or personal papers, as was noted previously. Nor did they find the girl's missing shoe in the vehicle.

"I suppose Sheriff Grady will want Bergeron here transferred over to HQ?" Kennedy said to Patty after discussing the evidence found.

"Well, let's wait for the hair samples before we run over to the sheriff. I want to keep him here as long as we can. But it looks like we'll need evidence or a confession from Mr. Bergeron."

"I double-checked with the coroner's office. Just as they told us the first time, no skin found under her fingernails, no signs of sexual activity or bodily fluids, no useful evidence they could find," Kennedy said. "Nothing."

"Did you know that Andy here strangles animals for a living? And we have a strangled girl with him at the approximate time of death."

"It's gotta be him, right? So we need a confession," Kennedy said. "Did you press him yet?"

"Oh no . . . I just buttered Mr. Bergeron up. I asked simple questions. Brought him a soda. I didn't even ask why he waited two or three days to bring his dead mother into town. But he's still stewing in the interview room."

"He said he was helping the foreman of the Bar-T Ranch with the fence mending. When he returned to his camp, his mother was in the same spot as when he left her sleeping. Only she wasn't sleeping. To think they didn't get her up to a doctor or hospital!" Kennedy said.

"Timmy, these are mountain people from way back. They don't trust our doctors! Also, this kid Andy seems a little touched in the head."

"For sure! But what about this Bar-T Ranch?"

"Right. We'll need someone to get over there to take down statements."

"HQ is on line two," Jerry, the desk sergeant, said to the detective.

"They couldn't know about Bergeron's connection to the victim yet," she said to Kennedy. "Maybe they've got something on your truck driver."

"Or, more likely, another useless lead from the tipline!"

Sheriff Joe Grady's staff at HQ took the baton on Deputy Kennedy's serial killer angle. They were looking into Rodney Russell Lee, whose physical description and modus operandi was a slam dunk match for their case. But unfortunately, they discovered from their FBI contact that Lee was back in custody in Oklahoma City and had been for over three months. So their I-40 trucker suspect was not Lee.

"Well, your serial killer didn't pan out," she said to Kennedy. "He's been locked up the past few months!"

"Took them this long to tell us he's locked up? That's efficient! So who's our truck driver? Back to square one on that side."

"Let's get a confession from Mr. Andy Bergeron; the trucker won't matter then!" Patty said, rising from her desk. "Any info on his brother, Buck?"

"Ah, yeah . . . that dude's in Disneyland!"

"You mean like metaphorically?" she said, smiling. "If he's anything like his brother—"

"Ha ha, good one! No, he's actually with his girlfriend and her kid in Disneyland. Won't be back for a couple of days."

↔

Sheriff Joe Grady was relaxing in a barber's chair across from the historic Yavapai County Courthouse. HQ was next door, and he'd run over to Floyd Burkham's barbershop daily for his old-style, straight razor shave. When walking down Gurley Street and seeing Floyd through the big plate-glass windows, working his razor on the leather strop, one would think it was 1881, and Virgil Earp was sitting in the chair.

The sheriff wanted to look good. His hair was always slicked back with pomade, his face glowing with a bright white smile, wearing his uniform perfectly pressed and clean. Grady was more politician than lawman. Most of his deputies disliked him, yet he was smart enough to let the good people of the department run things as they typically did. So he was more of a figurehead and less of an actual working sheriff, but things got done; crime was under control, he kept the budget in line, and consequently, during the most recent go-round, he was easily re-elected.

Floyd's television had the local news on, replaying the sheriff's earlier press conference regarding the girl's death. So Floyd stopped shaving the sheriff, and they both watched and listened. Floyd finished up with the sheriff's shave and said, "Sad business you deal in."

Sheriff Grady headed back to HQ and locked himself into his large office. His cute personal assistant Veronica, whose desk was outside his door, eyed him momentarily as he passed. Grady was a Casanova—lover of the ladies. His assistant Veronica was one of his most recent conquests, yet at that moment, he had someone else on his mind, and he locked his door so as not to be disturbed.

He picked up the phone and dialed. After a few rings, a woman answered.

"Lauren, I'm glad I caught you in," he said. "I've been thinking about you."

"I told you not to think about me."

"It's been a while since I've seen you. It's been hard on me," Grady said.

"Well, I've just seen you. On the television."

"Don't be funny!"

"You did look ridiculously handsome. I'll give you that."

"I'm glad you still think so," Grady replied. "You know, a funny thing happened. This morning my staff informed me about a certain someone's nephew."

"Oh?"

"This certain someone's nephew helped solve a little mystery we had in Ash Fork."

"Yes, he called me."

"He's also a witness on the big case we've got going on. So, um, he sure gets around!"

"I told him he should sign up with Patty Malloy," she said. "Make it official."

"Oh, thanks for the sketch work, by the way. The phones are ringing. Nothing solid yet, but it's helping."

"Yeah, it's been a while since I pulled the sketch pad out."

"Lauren, listen, I've got to see you again," he pleaded. "I miss you."

"You know how I feel about this."

"We could take a trip to Payson. Stay at the resort with a hot tub in every room. You know the place! You loved it."

"I can't . . . I can't do it anymore."

When Sheriff Grady hung up the phone, he reclined in the mahogany chair at his desk and considered his next steps to get her back. Nothing could dissuade the sheriff from attaining the things that he desired. And he absolutely desired her.

↔

Doc met Joe Grady at the five-year memorial for Sheriff Harry. The event became an annual fundraiser for the families of fallen first responders. Grady quickly worked his charm, and at first, she resisted but soon caved. Doc felt uneasy about dating the man who replaced her husband as sheriff. It was a pang of guilt that she harbored and couldn't shake. But she was fatally attracted to his movie-star looks, athletic physique, and passionate lovemaking. Like many other women before her and countless after, she fell under his spell, and only with utmost restraint and self-discipline did she pry herself loose. Nobody knew they'd been lovers. Doc kept the affair private. They usually went to a not-too-distant destination for an overnighter or the occasional weekend escape. Eventually, she broke it off. The relationship could never grow into more than just a flesh-fueled fling. He was a narcissist and a shallow man; a meaningful relationship could never be born between them.

She got a warm, tingly feeling while talking to the sheriff. She hated herself for letting him affect her like that. Self-control was easily preached but hard to practice. Doc had to get to a client's house by eleven. She hung up the phone and let Charlie out through the office slider.

Her eleven o'clock client—the wealthy heiress of the world's ketchup king—had been suffering from a systemic candidiasis infection. It was a stubborn case, and the oil of oregano, greek yogurt, and apple cider vinegar wasn't cutting it. So pau d'arco tea, oral antifungal meds, and creams were on the agenda. She disliked slapping on her allopathic medical hat and writing the traditional scripts, but at least she had the option. As soon as she started thinking about Mrs. Ketchup King's oral and vaginal thrush, the warm, tingly feeling that lingered from her conversation with the sheriff ceased. At times her job was the ultimate libido killer.

CHAPTER EIGHT

When Dolan arrived back in Sedona, his aunt was still on rounds. He was thinking about hiking Cathedral Rock. But first, he popped in on Red at his adobe casita.

"Hello, kid! Doc said you solved some motorhome mystery in Ash Fork this morning!"

"I didn't solve anything. The guy was panhandling at the gas station and decided to tell me about it after I handed him a few bucks. I got lucky. He would've told someone else."

"I don't know. It sounds like you may be a natural when it comes to working the law!" Red replied.

"Now that I'm back, I may do some hiking. Stretch my legs."

"I just got back myself," Red stated. "I bet you can't guess who I had lunch with today . . . well, me and six other folks."

"President George H. W. Bush?"

"That's a pretty darn good guess. It was old Jerry Atwater!"

"The ex-senator?" Dolan asked. "How in the heck do you know him?"

"I used to take him around, helping with his photography hobby back in the day. He knew I had some great locations, local knowledge and all, so he asked me to take him around. And once in a while, he came up to take shots of my favorite horse on the ranch. That was a funny thing. I thought he was a plain horse, not much different than any other, but he must've seen something that I didn't because those black and white photos of that horse came out pretty damn nice. Artistic-like. But I won't even tell you how I initially met Atwater."

Dolan waited for Red to continue.

"I used to handle the livestock for westerns being shot here in Sedona . . . mostly back in the '40s and '50s before they came and built all these damn houses. At any rate, my friend Duke Richards introduced us. Atwater came over to watch the filming, and that's where I first ran into him."

"Duke Richards? The old-time movie star?"

"Sure . . . The Duke. A nicer fella you would not meet! And when five o'clock rolled around, we'd pull the cork on some good whiskey, and he'd drink me under the table. What a man he was!"

A large bowl of apples was sitting on Red's small eating table near the kitchen. "Have an apple, kid," he said, pointing. "They gave me this whole bowl today after our breakfast, and I won't eat 'em all! They're from up Oak Creek Canyon."

Dolan grabbed one and polished it on his shirt.

"You know that Bar-T Ranch you told me about the other day? Does your buddy still own that spread?"

"James Tilly? No, old Jim died a while back. His son got the place and still has it."

"That guy with the motorhome mess said he does trapping for them. Fur sales and predator control, I guess. He and his mother lived on the Bar-T and surrounding area in that motorhome. Now let me tell you, Andy

Bergeron is one strange character. I'm pretty sure he may have a screw loose or two."

"After Jim died, plenty of strange characters hung around the place, so that ain't unusual. But you know, a lot of weird stuff happened at that ranch."

"What weird stuff happened?"

"When Jim's son was younger, he didn't want anything to do with the ranching business. Truthfully, he was a little light in the loafers. He didn't like gettin' his hands dirty and shirt sweaty. So he went off to California, mainly for college and what have you, but maybe to get away from the ranch. Well, one day, he came back, pulled his work boots back on, and got to likin' the place. So he made a go of it with his dad again, and Jim seemed happy. Probably for the first time since the wife runoff. But his son was just a youngster when his mother left, so that must've affected the boy." Red paused for a second. "Well, after Jim died, his son took over the ranch, and he had his boyfriend or partner—not sure what you call him—move onto the place. So you can imagine why they shut the ranch down to most visitors and didn't go into town much, wanting privacy, I suppose, but mostly not wanting to be targeted by the crazy haters—and there were a few of them. But anyway, the strange stuff started happening out there, with things disappearing all the time—a saddle, a salt lick, and a feed trough—you know, typical ranch stuff. A while later, they lost a dozen damn young steers born that spring. Every one of 'em disappeared off the range! No sign of them."

"That's weird," Dolan replied and took a bite of his apple.

"So my son Harry, the newly elected sheriff, looks into it, and they think it was the start of an elaborate cattle rustling scheme. So he started to inquire into all the neighboring ranches but never figured anything out. The steers were young, but they still weighed five hundred pounds or so. They were branded, castrated, weaned, and a few weeks later, all gone. Not like they could just vanish into thin air."

"I guess not!"

"But another crazy thing happened around the same time," Red continued. "A ranch hand was late one day, and his horse returned to the ranch with an empty saddle. No cowboy. So they go lookin' for him, my son and the deputies are out lookin' the next day too, and no sign of him. They reckon he had something to do with all the livestock that disappeared, and he was long gone. But no, apparently not what happened. Three days later, this cowboy came walkin' back into the ranch yard, buck naked, not even any boots on."

"What?"

"So he gets into the bunkhouse and gets a shower and gets dressed, and they get food into him and hot coffee, then he tells them this story about a big ol' bright light above him."

"Alien abduction story," Dolan says skeptically.

"Well, hell, they didn't know what was going on! My son figured it was a helicopter with a spotlight on him. Or then again, maybe there was never any light at all, and the cowboy hit his head on a low tree branch and knocked him silly off the horse. The cowboy said he saw the light and didn't remember anything afterward. Except walkin' in naked. Of course, having two gay cowboys runnin' the ranch, you can imagine all the jokes that came out of it!"

"You know, I remember reading about one of these bright-light alien abduction things in Arizona," Dolan said, musing.

"Right, that's what I was gonna say. Three months later—this is 1975—the same thing supposedly happens in Snowflake. This time it's a bunch of lumberjacks coming back from cutting timber. Supposedly they all see the light, but one guy gets taken. He comes back five days later. It was the same kind of thing. They even wrote a book about it. But most people thought it was a hoax or publicity stunt they dreamt up, probably after hearin' gossip about the Bar-T story."

"And nobody ever figured anything out?"

"A mystery, as they say. But it's funny that you brought all this up about the Bar-T Ranch now because none other than Senator Jerry Atwater started lookin' into all this alien UFO stuff. He believed the U.S. government had information that could set the record straight. So he asks to see a secret UFO information room, and they turn him down. Nope—it's top-secret, they say, 'need to know basis,' and you ain't on the list. So if Gerald T. Atwater can't get answers, we sure as hell ain't going to!"

"You know the things disappearing off that ranch . . ." Dolan started, "maybe that pretty little wife of James Tilly and the ranch hand didn't run off after all?"

"I never thought of that!" Red smiled.

Dolan heard a car drive up outside Red's casita, so he pulled the curtain back from the window and said, "Looks like a chubby lady in a gray Buick."

"The goddamn chocolate chip cookie lady!" Red said.

"Who?"

"She's a fresh widow-woman and is always baking up a batch of cookies for her next victim! Last month it was Bill Greeley across town. He finally told her he doesn't want her or her darn cookies!"

"You mean she's after you now? Ha ha! Great!"

"You're as bad as Doc!" Red sneered.

She knocked on the door. Red went over and partially opened the door, just enough that Dolan could see the woman's round, gray face and a big smile. Red ended up going out to talk with her for a minute. Soon he came back into the house with a defeated look and a plateful of cookies.

"She's got you now!" Dolan uttered. "You took the cookies!"

↔

Patty Malloy and her deputy made no progress on the confession extraction. However, while Malloy and Kennedy traded turns in the interview room, the forensic team confirmed that the hairbrush did belong to the victim. So the girl was indeed sitting in the motorhome with Andy Bergeron around the time of death. But, of course, he never denied this and came forward with the information himself, even disclosing she had left her bag in the vehicle. Patty had Deputy Kennedy contact Sheriff Grady's staff at HQ with all the information regarding Bergeron, and as suspected, HQ requested his transfer.

The St. Sebastian Church rectory also contacted the station with a reasonably solid confirmation that one of the truck drivers to their carnival matched the suspect. They took down the license plate number and description of the semi-trailer. Hours later, he was stopped near Santa Rosa, New Mexico, by the state police. The truck driver was fifty-five-year-old Billy Baker from Dayton, Ohio. Baker wouldn't admit he traveled through Seligman or knew anything about the victim. He said nothing. But according to his logbook, he rode through Seligman that Sunday evening and continued heading west toward Needles, California, where he stayed the night. He continued westbound I-40 to Bakersfield, where he picked up a stocked trailer for further deliveries to Albuquerque, New Mexico, for the St. Sebastian Church. Detective Malloy expected he'd be brought back the following day for questioning, so she needed Dolan around to make a positive ID.

"How are we going to make this work?" Malloy said to Kennedy. "From the way I see it, our Tuesday Jane and the cowboy trucker get in an argument, and she bolts then looks for another ride. Or she decides that she doesn't want to go all the way into California, which would be another day or so in the wrong direction, so she asks him to let her out again, still in Seligman. He drives off westbound for Needles. We know Bergeron picks her up for a short time, starting eastbound. So how do we put this Billy Baker back with her at exit 123?"

"Maybe he didn't leave right away. Maybe he was parked at the Tex-Gas station by the exit, and he was watching whether she'd get a ride or not," Kennedy says.

"Okay, so you think he stays at the Tex-Gas and watches her leave but sees she quickly jumps back out of the motorhome after a short ride down the exit ramp because of the stench from the corpse. So he rolls down the exit ramp and picks her up again. He drives another few miles to the old maintenance yard and pulls off. Perhaps he argues with her about going with him to California, but she won't come along, so he kills her and dumps her in a rage."

"Sounds possible."

"Then he'd loop back at Crookton Road, and now he's going back to Needles, California with only a twenty-minute delay or something? Reasonable, I suppose," Patty said.

"Also, what gets my goat is he could have told the New Mexico State Police that he did drive through Seligman and—whether or not he had the girl with him—kept going to California. But no, he says nothing. Won't say anything. So this makes him look guilty as hell," Kennedy said. "So he's gotta be back to being our number one suspect."

"I don't know, Timmy. Some people are pretty smart and understand it's best not to say a damn thing to the police. Maybe he's got other skeletons in the closet. But we have two suspects now and have to make something stick. And we have 48 hours to do it. So tomorrow, I'll pull Deputy McGraw off patrol duty and give him a special assignment with us. I don't want to ask for anyone from HQ. Deputy Smith and Gonzalez can work patrols."

↔

Dolan left Red's casita and hiked his way around Cathedral Rock. He went off the main Cathedral Rock trail and worked around to the far side of the majestic formation, descending in elevation with each step to the lower riparian area, where Oak Creek meandered through a lush green paradise. Vintage grapevines and lively raspberry bushes tangled beneath the massive canopy of cottonwood and sycamore trees. The creek dropped off uneven red rock steps and made a relaxing waterfall sound that echoed through the canyon. He sat on a reddish sandstone ledge that abutted a pool of water below. He kicked his boots off and dropped his feet into the cool water. He could think of no other place where he'd ever been that was as close to paradise as this exact spot in Sedona. Dolan made a full circle: he had been to hell, and now he had arrived in paradise.

He was eight thousand miles and seven months beyond the worst hell of his life. While in Saudi Arabia, preparing for the liberation of Kuwait from Iraq, he received heartbreaking news in a letter from back home. The letter shook him up. Ironically the military wasn't getting much mail through. All the other guys were complaining. They moved over sixty million pounds of mail to Saudi Arabia in February. It was piled up at the depot, waiting for delivery to the troops. Still, somehow, his letter slipped through.

As fate would have it, he had little time to dwell. The ground war had begun, and he and thousands of others pressed across the Saudi/Iraqi border. At the time, he believed the fight would take his platoon of Bradleys all the way to Baghdad to knock out Saddam Hussein. Of course, they never got that far. Still, during the 100-hour operation, as the gunner, he fired the 25-millimeter cannon sporadically and, during the final mission, relentlessly.

On day one of the operations, they rolled through the aftermath of the previous night's aerial bombardment and witnessed an endless caravan of mangled vehicles piled pell-mell across the landscape, blackened into oblivion, the bodies of countless Iraqi soldiers strewn, disfigured, burnt, and bloated along the way. The thick smoke that poured from the smoldering destruction combined with the enormous fires set across the oil fields; the sky, at first choked black with smoke, eventually yielded into an eerie orange-red glow as they pushed through the open, dusty desert; sandstorms would affect the workability of the equipment, as grit and sand particles messed up the operation of the various mechanisms. Then the rains came. On day two, they kept their gas masks on due to the threat of Scud missiles and chemical weapons. Dolan fired on an enemy transport vehicle and disabled it. The Iraqi occupants waved dirty white rags to surrender and were taken prisoner by infantry. Later, their Bradley crew felt tension and trepidation when they crossed a heavy minefield. Dolan joked to the others, "Well, it was nice knowing you guys!" However, the mine-clearing plows did an excellent job, so they went through the field without incident. His team's activities climaxed on day three when they arrived in a green and fertile river valley. There they intercepted dozens of Iraqi fighters who hadn't surrendered but instead foolishly decided to retreat. Most abandoned their armored vehicles and attempted to take cover across the marsh. The unit's orders were to use any means necessary to keep them from escaping. So he opened fire relentlessly. It turned into a bloody massacre. Death. Destruction. His remorse was immediate and long-lasting. He prayed it would end even while he was pulverizing them to pieces. His commander yelled, "Fish in a barrel, McBride!"

Dolan continued to exercise the Bushmaster cannon and its thundering pulse, causing absolute ruination and horror among the fleeing Iraqis. The commander of his Bradley Fighting Vehicle merely stated: "If these Ali Baba bastards didn't want this ugly and unmerciful end, they shouldn't have gone and gang-raped the women of Kuwait. I ain't sorry for this! Neither should you be!"

President Bush announced a ceasefire that day. Thankfully, Dolan wouldn't take another life—in the desert or elsewhere. It'd been four days since he read the gut-wrenching news from home. Four days, but it seemed like a lifetime had already passed.

CHAPTER NINE

Patty left a message on Doc's machine. She wanted Dolan to call her back. The trucker suspect would arrive in the morning, and they needed him to make a formal identification. His aunt handed him the phone when Dolan got back to the house. He called and let Patty know he'd be there. The detective also softened up about letting him get more involved with the case.

"We have a ride-along program where anyone from the community can sign a non-liability form and sit in the passenger seat with a deputy. So I'll let you sign a form, and you can ride with my deputies or me. But I imagine you may want to give us input here and there. So this is if you're still interested."

"Yes! Great! I'll see you in the morning!"

Doc made a big salad at the counter for dinner, and Dolan was seasoning up a boneless chicken breast and a nicely marbled ribeye steak to throw on the grill.

"She's gonna let me help with the case."

"I thought she'd come around. Our Patty is one smart cookie!" Doc said.

They sat on the patio to eat. The sun was getting low; the top of Cathedral Rock was bright orange, and darkness shaded its base.

"That view doesn't get old," he said. "Changes every time you look at it."

"Cathedral is an uplifting vortex. The energy rises and can help lift your spirits," his aunt said. "It's also feminine energy. It helps a person feel compassion and understanding. It can help you connect to your past experiences and thoughts. It is quite peaceful."

"I was down below Cathedral today, at the creek. It was the most peace I've felt in forever. So I'll try not to be my normal vortex-skeptic self!"

"It's okay to be a skeptic, especially if that's your nature. But everyone should try to keep an open mind. No harm comes from being open and understanding. Or at least trying to be. It takes much more energy to be contrarian and skeptical. But, on the other hand, if you open your mind and let the world wash over you, taking it all as it is, you will become enlightened and refreshed with almost no effort whatsoever. It's the same with meditation."

"That's a nice concept. But this wine also helps!" Dolan said as he poured a little red into his aunt's glass and his own.

"Just what the doctor ordered," she replied and lifted her glass to toast.

↔

They had six men in the police lineup. Detective Malloy explained to Dolan that she wouldn't say or do anything that could alter his judgment regarding the suspect or point him to the correct person. She said they would walk into the room and ask if he saw the man who was with their victim on Sunday night at the Blue Ox Saloon. He did, and he pointed to the truck driver. She noted a positive identification of the suspect, Billy Baker. They escorted him to the interview room to wait.

Patty brought the deputies together around her desk, along with Dolan. She started to hand out the assignments.

"McGraw, I want you to head to Seligman. Talk to some of the folks over at the Bar-T Ranch. Confirm that Bergeron was mending fences with the foreman while his mother was dead for two days in the van. And anything else they can tell you."

"Okie dokie."

"On your way back, stop at the Tex-Gas station at exit 123. See what view you have near the ramp. I want to get an idea of how far you can see. There are no trees, just grasses, so I bet you can see a mile or two down the road." She turned. "Kennedy, what's the tipline looking like on the victim's identity?"

"I've got one to follow up on this morning. A college student called in and thinks he may have driven the victim up to Flagstaff from Cordes. She was hitchhiking and wanted to be dropped off at a truck stop in Flagstaff, and she was heading east."

"Good, get on it," Patty said. "You know, I can't figure out why this beautiful sketch of this girl isn't getting leads out of Indiana. We know they have been getting air time. It doesn't make sense."

"Maybe she hasn't been there in a long while. Maybe since she was a little kid, so nobody would recognize her," McGraw said.

"Possible."

"You know," Dolan said, "I've been thinking about the girl. No ear piercings. No rings or jewelry of any kind. She had no makeup at all—no nail polish. I knew a girl like that from school. She came from a deeply religious family. Fundamentalists of some sort. The parents were whacko, and she ended up running away."

"Kid . . . you may be onto something!" Patty said. "Isn't there a large population of Amish and Mennonite in Indiana? I don't think they watch much television! So that could explain the lack of response."

"Sounds like a long shot," Kennedy said.

"Yeah, you're probably right. But how about you get in touch with the Indiana State Police again and see what they think about getting posters out in those communities."

"McGraw, take Dolan here with you to Seligman on a ride-along. If you want to go," Patty said, turning to him.

"Sure. I'd like that."

"Let's go then, partner," McGraw said, and they walked out of the station.

↔

The Bar-T Ranch headquarters was fifteen miles south of Seligman down a dusty dirt road. They pulled up to an electric gate with an intercom.

"Who is it?" A voice came from the other side of the speaker.

"Deputy Shane McGraw of the Yavapai County Sheriff's Office."

The gate started to open, and he drove the Crown Vic into the ranch compound. Inside the fencing was a sizable cedar-sided home with a wooden shake roof and an extended covered porch. A bunkhouse, a tack shop, a feed shed, and a small corral was visible from the entrance. A horse stable was near the corral.

Built to the side of the stable was a lean-to structure with several animal pelts hanging and drying.

As they walked toward the main house, a nice-looking man of about forty stepped off the porch.

"I'm Jimmy Tilley," he said. "How can I help you?"

"Hello, Mr. Tilley. Are you the foreman or owner?"

"Oh, call me Jimmy . . . But I'm both right now. It's a slow time of the season, so the bunkhouse is empty, and my foreman went off to visit relatives."

"I'm here to ask you about Andy Bergeron. He says he traps for you and was here all last weekend, helping you mend fences."

"Sure, he was here. He brought pelts up too. I'll show you."

They walked toward the stable.

"I'm Shane, if you didn't hear through the intercom. This is Dolan, on a ride-along with me."

Jimmy turned and shook each man's hands as they walked. He pointed over at the lean-to.

"Two beautiful coyote pelts here . . . and a gray fox and a bobcat," he said. "This is what Andy brought last time over."

"He was around here Friday through Sunday?" Shane asked.

"Oh sure, he used up three wire spools, so he spent a good amount of time on the fences."

"Did you know about his mother? Unfortunately, she passed away before the weekend."

"Oh no. No, I didn't hear. I wonder why Andy didn't tell me?"

"That's what we're trying to piece together. Bergeron took her body with him in that motorhome on Sunday night to Ash Fork and ran into engine problems. I wonder why he didn't come up here? To ask you what he should do."

"He may have. I went to Kingman on Sunday night. Didn't get back until late," he said. "So Carolyn passed away? We figured it would happen, though. She was sick, and we couldn't get them to go to a doctor or anything. She went through a bottle of that codeine cough syrup every week."

"Nothing unusual about it?" McGraw asked.

"I'm surprised it didn't happen sooner, to tell you the truth."

"Well, thanks for your time. I guess that should do it."

Tilley turned to Dolan and asked him if he was training to be an officer.

"I suppose you could say that," he replied. "Do you know Red Halleran?"

"I haven't heard that name in a while," he said. "Yes, he was a friend of my father way back."

"Yesterday, he told me about all the unusual occurrences you had. Back in 1975, I think he said."

He laughed.

"Oh, that was just a bunch of misunderstandings. Nothing really."

Shane quickly turned towards Jimmy Tilley and asked: "Who was that?"

A muscular man with a long black braided ponytail ran from the gate when he saw the sheriff's vehicle.

"That's Hualapai Johnny. I don't know why he ran like that. You'd think he'd seen a ghost."

"Hualapai Johnny?"

"John Mohon. He's from the Hualapai Reservation up near Peach Springs. He hunts mountain lions for the ranchers around here. He does odd jobs too."

"Why the heck did he run like that? I suppose he's got a warrant," McGraw said. "Let's go! He can't be going far. Thanks for talking to us."

"No problem," Jimmy said. "But I can't imagine Johnny being in any trouble! The guy is like a saint."

McGraw radioed to the Northern Division for a warrant search on John Mohon of Peach Springs. While they sped down the ranch road, they searched for a parked vehicle they assumed Mohon was running to. They didn't find one. Outside the fencing of the ranch complex, the land's topography was hilly and dotted with juniper and shrub. Mohon became invisible and could have been anywhere on a thousand acres of ground. McGraw pulled out to Williamson Valley Road and headed north. A cloud of dust floated behind them.

"What? Did he hike all the way over to the ranch?" McGraw asked aloud. "No vehicle?"

McGraw looped back down the ranch road again and stopped about a hundred yards from the Bar-T entrance.

"He's sitting behind a bush laughing at us," Dolan said.

"I imagine!"

They got a negative on the warrant search. The only record the office could find was a speeding ticket on I-40 issued by DPS six years previous.

"Screw it!" McGraw said and left.

They drove fifteen miles north until the road changed from dirt to pavement. They went over to the Tex-Gas station to examine the freeway exit and the visibility from the parking lot, as Patty asked them to.

"How about I go get us a couple coffees?" McGraw said and walked toward the entrance.

Dolan stood at the edge of the expansive gravel parking lot, large enough to service all the big semi-trailers that rolled off I-40 and parked. He examined the canopy above the fuel pumps. He was surprised to see a security camera. McGraw walked to the cruiser, set their coffees on top, and lit his daily cigarette. Dolan walked over to him and pointed up at the camera.

"What the hell! That wasn't there last week. I wonder when they installed it? Are we gonna catch a lucky break?"

Four cameras had been installed and operating since the previous Wednesday. One was behind the cash register, the second on the building facing the fuel pumps, the third on the canopy facing the large gravel parking lot and road entrance, and the fourth showing the foot traffic entrance coming through the door to the building. A super-slow time-lapse Sony VCR performed the recording. Each VHS kept twenty-four hours of footage. The videotape was to be changed each morning at opening. They had seven tapes in use, and after each week, the tape was recorded over again, which would erase the previous week's recording. Luckily the Sunday tape was still the original recording.

Ben, the pimply-faced kid, working in the store, was very excited about the technology and thoroughly explained how to play the tape back and watch the footage. The four camera views fed into a quad screenshot, so one could see all the images simultaneously while monitoring the playback.

"Do you think I could take the Sunday tape back to our station to watch on our VCR?" Shane asked him.

"I think the quality would be bad. Unless you have a time-lapse VCR to watch it back on."

McGraw wasn't sure, so they sat in the maintenance room where the VCR and monitor system was kept and started the tape. They fast-forwarded until the evening portion. They were surprised by what they discovered.

CHAPTER TEN

Patty Malloy began her interview with Billy Baker. The interview room was small and tight, with empty beige walls. Fluorescent lighting in the ceiling flickered and buzzed annoyingly.

"Hello, Mr. Baker. I am Detective Malloy. I want to chat with you for a few minutes if that is okay?"

She pressed the button on the recording device.

"This interview is being recorded."

Billy stared at her with a suspicious grin. From the time he was seen in Seligman, he had shaved his beard. He seemed like he wanted to speak his mind. He twisted his lips and took on a severe expression. Patty could sense he wanted to talk.

"Mr. Baker, I only want to help you here. Clear your name. The problem is you were the last person our victim was seen with around the estimated time of death, so it's not looking good for you here."

This statement wasn't exactly true, but withholding facts and outright falsifying events or evidence was par for the course in the interrogation room.

"Don't you want to clear your name? Tell us your side of the story?"

He glanced at the adjacent wall and back at Patty.

"She was such a nice girl, my witnesses tell me. Pretty young woman. Such a shame."

"Her name was Josie," he said, breaking his silence.

Patty was surprised that he spoke up so soon. She wrote the name on her pad.

"Thank you for that. Unfortunately, we didn't have a name for the poor girl. Did she give you her last name? Can you tell me anything more?"

"Just Josie. She was a good kid. She was standing out at the America Travel Stop in Flagstaff. I couldn't believe she was alone. She was too nice and trusting to be out alone. So I bought her dinner. We ate at the restaurant in the truck stop. She wanted to go east, but I told her I had to go to Needles, California, at the western Arizona border. It was going to be my last drop; they had a little carnival and needed supplies. Then I was going to head back home to Ohio. Maybe pick up a load on the way back. But I could take her all the way home. Right to her doorstep in Indiana."

"So she was going to ride along, out of her way, to Needles with you?"

"Yes, she thought that wouldn't be bad. I even told her she could hang around Flagstaff if she wanted, and I'd pick her back up on my way east. But she said she'd rather ride with me. So we get near Seligman—it's half past seven—and she gets a bad headache. Like sharp pains coming and going. She said it had happened to her before, and aspirin seemed to help every time. So I pulled off at Seligman. But the gas stations and stores were closed. The fuel pumps were on if you have a credit card, but the stores were closed. So we drove through town, and then I saw the bar. I've stopped there before, so I figured we'd try it. So I get a drink, she gets aspirin from a kid, then I hear my beeper go off, so I look at the number."

"Your pager?"

"Yes, and I know the number. It's the dispatch guy that gets me all the good hauls. So I have to call him back. So I go back and use the payphone over at Tex-Gas. So he tells me he needs me to pick up a loaded trailer from Bakersfield. His other guy's rig broke down, and he needed me. Two fairs were starting up, and they needed full supplies. So I tell Josie I've got to go to Bakersfield. It'd be another day or two out of the way. She smiled, wished me good luck, and said she'd catch a ride from there. I didn't want to leave her, but she wouldn't go with me. It was a pretty well-lit spot. And a few trucks and cars were still coming and going, so I figured she'd get a ride. So I rolled off."

"You didn't see her get a ride?"

"No, she was standing in front of the pumps when I left. So two days later, I'm dropping this load off in Albuquerque. Afterward, I stop and fuel up. I see a TV on, so I watch for a minute, and the next thing I know, my face is on that TV. It was a sketch of Josie and me. I damn near puked. That's when I started thinking—I did this! I did this!"

"You did this?"

"Of course! If I hadn't brought her to Seligman, that little girl would've been fine. I practically killed her with my own hands. I started thinking I was doomed. No way I was going to get out of this. You say I did it. Well, nothing I can do. So I shaved my beard and got rid of the hat. But they picked me up in Santa Rosa."

Patty liked it when a guy who previously wouldn't talk suddenly spilled like that—poured himself all out on the table. The problem for Patty was she believed him. He wasn't their guy. But that was just a hunch, so she still pressed him.

"So isn't it true that you didn't drive off from Seligman? That you waited around for her to get a ride. You were worried for her and wanted to ensure she got a ride before you left. So you sat parked in that lot until you saw her leave."

"No. But I should have."

Patty clicked the recorder off and stood up. "I'm going to go get a coffee. You want one?"

"Water if you could," he said.

"Oh, did she tell you what town she lived in? Where did she want you to take her to in Indiana?"

He turned his eyes up, trying to think. "She did tell me. I had never heard of it. It was a weird-sounding name. I think it started with an *S*, but I can't be certain."

"Thanks. I'll get you a map of Indiana, and maybe you can pick out the town."

She walked out of the interview room, and Deputy Kennedy dropped the phone and waved her over, acting excited.

"I've got a name for the victim! First name anyhow—"

"Josie," she said before he did.

Kennedy threw his hands up, looking exasperated.

"The trucker told me," she said. "But what else do you have?"

"Pretty much the same thing they got on the tipline. This college student, Tom Harkin, says he gave her a ride up I-17 heading north from Cordes Junction, and she asked to be let out at the America Travel Stop in Flag. She said she'd get a ride from a trucker heading east. Her name was Josie. He dropped her off and then went to NAU."

"My truck driver is talking now, and that confirmed part of his story; I don't think he's our guy."

"So back to Andy Bergeron? Not sure if they are getting anywhere at HQ with him," Kennedy said.

"We need a break here. I don't know. I'm not seeing it."

↔

Dolan and McGraw were watching the footage. McGraw had grabbed a bag of caramel popcorn and was vigorously munching as they eyed each frame. Of the quad-view captures, only the gas pump shot and the parking view in front of and adjacent to the pumps were helpful after store closing. They got excited when a female climbed from a semi-truck.

"That's her!" Dolan shouted.

The trucker walked to the payphone and back. He went and hugged the girl, hopped in the rig, and drove off. She was standing alone, with her bag, near the front of the pumps. A car came to fuel. The girl walked up to the driver while he was pumping gas, and he pointed in the westerly direction. She walked back to the front of the pumps. A minute later, she must've seen a vehicle approaching from Williamson Valley road, so she drifted a little closer to the eastbound exit ramp near the front of the parking lot.

Mcgraw started eating his popcorn even faster.

"There!" Dolan said as the motorhome pulled up in the frame, and she jumped in.

"Now we have to pay close attention to any other vehicles coming and going," McGraw said.

They waited for another vehicle, but one didn't come. A few more minutes of frames went by, and still nothing except a motionless shot of the parking area and road. They were getting a little discouraged.

"Don't tell me that's it!" Dolan said.

McGraw stopped eating the popcorn and watched and waited.

"She came back!"

The girl came into the frame walking from the exit ramp.

"No bag!"

She went closer to the fuel pumps and stood in the light. She was alone and vulnerable—a perfect target. Dolan was uneasy, knowing something bad would be coming. He took a couple of deep breaths and continued watching.

"Look—a pickup truck pulled in!" McGraw said to Dolan, who started to walk away from the monitor.

The girl turned toward the pickup but didn't walk over. A moment later, someone came walking toward the parked pickup truck from out of nowhere. She looked over at the pickup again but didn't approach them.

"Where did this dude come from?" Dolan asked.

Someone jumped out of the pickup truck. There was a confrontation on the far side, but the vehicle mostly blocked the view.

"Are they fighting?" McGraw said.

Suddenly the driver popped back in the pickup, and they fishtailed away. The individual that walked up earlier was lying on their back, holding their stomach. The girl turned to the injured person, ran over, and knelt closely. Suddenly the same pickup truck came racing back into the frame. The girl jumped up and started backing away. The vehicle rolled directly over the individual on the ground, crushing them.

"My god!" Shane exclaimed.

The truck fishtailed back around toward the girl. It came close to hitting her but did not. As they slowly circled, the girl was crouching. The passenger opened the door, grabbed her by the sweater and arms, and pulled her into the truck. The next frame showed the pickup truck rolling away.

"Terrible," Shane said. "I guess they didn't want a witness!"

Dolan stepped back and took a few deep breaths. His heart was racing; he felt sick. He walked away toward the employee bathroom. Shane continued watching.

"This body wasn't there in the morning . . . So?" he said aloud and kept watching.

A minute later, Dolan walked back to watch, "Anything?"

"No, the body is still lying here," he said. "Wait—"

Another person appeared out of the darkness. The individual wore a hoodie and sweatpants, all black or dark in color, moving like a ninja. They moved fast. The time-lapse recording only showed them contained in a couple of frame shots. They squatted, lifted the body over their shoulder with a kind of military move, and went off the camera's view.

"Well, that was crazy," McGraw said. He pressed the eject button on the VCR and pulled the tape out. "Patty will want to see this right away. I imagine Sheriff Grady will, too!"

"Should we call it in now?" Dolan asked.

"Good point. I'll call the office and let 'em know. And let 'em know we'll be releasing our two suspects pronto!"

↔

Patty was surprised when she heard about the cameras and footage. She was looking for a break, but this wasn't what she expected. They already set up a time-lapse VCR in the office brought over by Rob, the audio-visual technician. They were waiting for them to get back with the tape.

Patty popped up from her desk when Shane and Dolan walked in.

"Did I not ask you yesterday if they had cameras at that Tex-Gas?" she said to McGraw.

McGraw tilted his head with slight shame as he handed her the VHS tape.

"They only put the cameras in last Wednesday," Dolan interjected.

"Uh-huh," Patty said. "Stick the tape in there!"

The detective, deputies, and other office staff watched the footage. Patty turned to the audio-visual technician.

"Any chance of making this video clearer to see a face or a plate number?" she asked. "Get still images?"

"I doubt it . . . but I know a guy with an analog to digital converter, so I could let him play with it," he said. "We could put the digital data on a computer with image-enhancing software."

"Make at least two copies of this tape first. I don't want it lost or destroyed."

They were halfway through the relevant portion of the tape.

"So both Andy Bergeron and Billy Baker told us the exact truth. Now here's the girl back all alone, no bag," Patty said. "And here's the pickup truck you were telling me about. I'm assuming this is our second victim walking up now?"

"Yes. The perps attack the guy here," McGraw said.

"Pause this!" Patty instructed. "So he's holding his stomach. Was there a gunshot? I didn't see a flash."

"Possibly stabbed," Kennedy said.

"Okay, hit play," she said.

A collective gasp filled the room when the truck ran the victim over. And again, when the passenger yanked the girl into the vehicle.

"What's the make and model of this pickup truck?" Patty asked.

The desk sergeant Jerry said it could be a Dodge—late 70s.

"Dodge Power Wagon, maybe," Dolan added. "Looks like a 4x4."

"So we're looking for a 1970s Dodge 4x4 pickup truck. Possibly a Power Wagon. Dark in color. It could be black, dark green, or dark blue—you get the picture. Try to narrow down the model—McGraw?"

"Yeah?"

"Get a forensic technician up there to see if they can find blood or evidence on that gravel lot—shell casings, anything. Also, grab the rest of the videotapes. Maybe that truck and those guys were there other days. Maybe they walked straight toward that door camera," she said. "So we have another victim too. Kennedy, check with the hospitals in Kingman, Flagstaff, and Prescott."

"Could this person be alive?" Kennedy asked.

"Probably not, but perhaps this hooded guy carried the victim off and brought them to a medical facility. Doubtful—but check on it. Remember, this is Sunday night when inquiring."

"What happened here?" Dolan asked.

"Good question. A drug deal gone awry? Intentional hit on this guy? I don't know, but I'm pretty sure they took the girl Josie because they didn't want a witness," she said. "I suppose he could have said something to her when she knelt beside him. At least the guys in the truck seemed to think so!"

"Josie?" asked Dolan.

"That's our Tuesday Jane's name, as confirmed by Billy Baker and a tipline caller.

But we don't have a last name yet," Deputy Kennedy said.

"Okay, people, it looks obvious we're crossing Andy Bergeron and Billy Baker from the list. We're starting from scratch," Patty announced. "We need to recall the sketches of Baker and get one out on this pickup truck. Please go through our car and truck image book and find this model. You know the routine."

"You think they were sending a message here?" Dolan asked, "I mean, why did they leave the body of this other guy but take the girl away . . . Then dispose of her in a well-hidden spot."

"I don't think they cared about the guy they killed one way or another. They grabbed the girl because she saw too much. Then, killed and dumped her," Kennedy said.

"We didn't watch this whole tape," Dolan said. "It should run to the store opening on Monday morning when they would have switched the tapes out. So maybe this Dodge will come back in later frames? Or maybe it was at the store earlier?"

"Jerry, please watch the tape since you'll be sitting on your bum the rest of the day. Fast forward through all the spots with no activity," Patty said, "Then get it over to Rob so he can make copies and do his analog/digital thing that he was talking about for the computer."

"That's fine," Jerry said, "but while I'm sitting on my bum, you or one of the deputies can drive up to the Kaufmann Ranch near Ash Fork and take a report on stolen items. They called and wanted to make a report."

"Maybe McGraw could stop on his way back . . ." she said but hesitated. "No, no, I suppose I could run up there. God knows I don't have anything better to do!"

Jerry laughed. "I'm just the house mouse, remember?"

"Hey, kid," she said, turning to Dolan, "you want to go on a little ride-along with me, or are you done for the day?"

"Sure, I'll go."

CHAPTER ELEVEN

Dolan sat in the passenger seat of Patty's full-size Bronco. She looked funny driving such a big truck. She held herself close to the steering wheel, and her head didn't rise much above it. They took State Route 89 north toward Ash Fork.

"I wanted to talk with you," she said. "From the little bit you've been around so far, I can tell that you'd make a big difference in our office. So I do hope you're thinking about going through the academy."

"Yes, I'm considering it."

"Good."

"I have loose ends to tie up back in Michigan. And other decisions to make. But I'll let you know soon after that."

"I'm from Minnesota originally," she said. "I came out here for school in Tucson, The University of Arizona, and never left the state. I didn't have much to go back to, so no big thing. You know, crazy family and all. I wanted to get away from that bunch!"

"My family is pretty decent as far as families go. So I don't mind them."

"Well, I don't know about your folks back in Michigan, but your Aunt is my best friend, so I'll agree with you," Patty said.

At Ash Fork, they hit westbound I-40 and drove to Crookton Road. It all started to seem like an old rerun Dolan had seen on TV a dozen times. Hereford cows were standing with the same young black and white-faced steers. The same Black Angus bulls wandering solitary along the same fence line down the same lonely stretch of Route 66.

"This is all Kaufmann land," Patty said. "So technically, we're already on his ranch. I had to go to their ranch headquarters for a domestic issue a while back. Joseph Kaufmann's girlfriend Tina ran off and took most of the cash from their joint checking account! Not much he could do. That's the thing about joint checking accounts!"

"Seems to happen a lot around these parts!" Dolan replied.

"How's that?"

"Well, you know old Red? He was telling me about the Bar-T ranch the other day. Of course, at the time, I didn't know I'd be heading out there with McGraw. Anyway, he told me the owner's wife ran off and left him with a son to raise. This happened way back when. But supposedly, she ran off with one of the ranch hands. Speaking of the Bar-T, were you around in 1975 when all the crazy stuff went on?"

"No, sir. I was cleaning up crime scenes down in Tucson. That's how I first got involved in law enforcement—using bleach spray to clean the blood off sidewalks and other fun stuff! But no, I did hear things when I started in '76. Aliens and UFOs and whatnot!"

"Yes, well, here's a strange one for you. When we were out at the ranch, I asked Jimmy Tilley about the weird things back in 1975. He casually replied that it was a bunch of misunderstandings."

"Sounds like a man who wants to bury the past," she said.

"Could be. And what did you think about the character McGraw called in about this morning? Hualapai Johnny? He split right off that ranch when he saw us. We weren't able to find him. Just disappeared."

"His record was clean, though."

They pulled onto a perfectly straight gravel road north from Route 66. After about a mile, they ended up right in the lap of the ranch headquarters. It was wide-open flat ground. The buildings were all freshly painted white. All the roofs had reddish shingles. It appeared to be an immaculate and well-organized ranch.

"Here's Joseph now," Patty said. They jumped out of the vehicle. A tall, dark-haired man started to approach the Bronco.

"Hello, Detective Malloy," Kaufmann said, "I see they took my call seriously! Sent out the boss!"

"I've even brought an assistant," she said. "This is Dolan McBride."

Dolan shook Joseph Kaufmann's hand. Patty held her clipboard with a pen in hand.

"What shenanigans do you have going on here?" she asked.

"Oh, it's quite sobering," he started. "Very special items have been stolen. You may know that we are one of a few kosher-certified beef suppliers in the state. Granted, we are a small boutique operation. But, to be certified kosher, we use special *chalef* knives and follow rigorous standards and slaughter practices. Unfortunately, it was the *chalef* knives that were taken."

"Are these knives valuable?" Patty asked.

"These knives were specially made by the rabbi who trained me personally as a *shochet* and granted my certificate of *kabbalah*. He gave this set to me. The value could be in the hundreds of dollars. Even a thousand, I suppose, but the monetary value is meaningless to me. I want these knives back. I will pay a reward or repurchase them from the thief."

"Can you show us where the burglary took place? And the approximate time this happened?" she asked.

"Follow me," he said, and they walked toward an outbuilding. "I only noticed them missing this morning, but they could have been taken at any time in the previous week or so."

"What exactly is a *shochet*?" Patty asked as they walked.

"A *shochet* is a person authorized for the ritual slaughter of animals in my faith. We do so with respect and compassion for the animal. We attempt to minimize pain. Also, we must inspect the animal; it must be clean and free from abnormalities or defects to ensure the meat is kosher."

They entered a brick building painted white like the other buildings on the ranch. The floor was polished concrete and slightly slippery. Stainless steel rails were hanging from the ceiling that appeared to be meat hangers. At one end of the room was a roll-up metal door—the access point to the animal chute. At the other end of the room, a water hose was mounted on the wall; the adjacent flooring contained an open steel grate for water drainage. Finally, Kaufmann pointed to a shiny stainless steel work table in the corner.

"They were here," he said.

"So, could anyone walk in?" Patty asked.

"No, no. Here, I will show you."

They walked to another entrance door at the rear. Kaufmann pointed out where the thief pried the jamb with a tool. It was a steel door, and the frame was also steel and therefore took an abundance of effort to pry.

"So no one noticed the damage on this door?" she asked.

"No, it was closed, and we only entered the building this morning. We noticed the pry marks and the missing *chalef* knives."

"And nothing else was taken?"

"No, which is curious because we have a small office attached to this building. I can show you," Kaufmann said and started walking out. "The office has a wooden door which, I admit, could be easily opened. Inside the office is a small safe containing hundreds, sometimes thousands of dollars in cash. Firearms hang from a rack on the wall. We have two .45 revolvers, two 30-30 rifles, and a 12-gauge shotgun. So it is bizarre that they went through this effort to steal these knives but not touch the office."

The office file cabinet contained an eight by ten photo of the *chalef* knives as well as his certificate of *kabbalah*. So, the picture would be helpful.

"What amount will the reward be?" Patty asked.

"I will offer five thousand dollars to anyone bringing the knives back. No questions asked."

"Holy buckets! That should get some response," she said. "Your ranch hands?"

"Yes, I thought you may ask that," he said. "I have two hands right now, Luke Staley and Billy Espers, and they both have access to the keys for all the buildings on this ranch. So why would they break in like that?"

"Perhaps for that reason . . . Because you know they have access. So they try to make it look like an outside job."

"It doesn't make sense. I don't think so," he said.

"Well, Mr. Kaufmann, I will take this information and announce the reward. I'm assuming everyone with any old pair of knives may try and come forward for the five-grand! But we'll get it rolling for you."

As they drove back down the long and straight gravel road from the ranch house, Dolan said: "They were at the Blue Ox on Sunday night . . . Luke and Billy."

"Yeah, I know they work here for Kaufmann but didn't think much of it."

"And now?"

"Nope."

"I'm not sure—more strange stuff and more coincidences. That's all I know," Dolan said.

"Sam, the bartender, has attested that those two were still at the Blue Ox. They left an hour after Billy Baker and our victim did. So they couldn't have been at the Tex-Gas, if that's what you're thinking. At least not according to the bartender."

"True," Dolan said, pondering. "But the bartender also said we stayed at the bar for only a couple minutes after the girl and Baker left. It was more like fifteen minutes. So not sure the clock in his head is all that reliable!"

"I don't know. I suppose we could check on that timeline again. Also, this five-grand reward sure seems like serious overkill. Makes me wonder."

"Yep, and now I'm thinking of something else. I'm sure it doesn't have anything to do with this, but anyway," he started, "I knew a girl back in high school that was a member of a militant animal rights group. Her older sister was the actual member, but Sandra, the younger sister, was involved too."

"Like PETA?"

"Yeah, similar but a lot crazier . . . more militant. I think it's called the Animal Freedom Front or AFF or something. I remember she was vocal about the veal/calf process and kosher slaughter techniques. So this group made propaganda videos about these atrocities, as they called them, and used examples from around our area. Exposé-type stuff."

"And?" Patty inquired.

"Well, there was a farm north of our town. As you drove by the place, there were dozens of little black boxes that you'd see lining the road. In each box, a newborn calf was taken from its mother and force-fed by a tube. They had one calf in each tiny box so that they couldn't move. They don't let them move, or they might toughen the meat. So they live their short life trapped in a tiny dark box and then sold as veal. Look, I'm a proud meat eater, but this stuff makes me sick," he said and paused. "And south of town was this meatpacking facility. It was also a kosher slaughterhouse. They claimed that using these sharp knives is a humane way to kill animals. Slice their throat clean through. So one day, somebody snuck in to take an undercover video. They put that video out to the public; it was like a damn horror film! They shackled the animals by the rear legs, hoisted them up, and hung them by chains, the animal struggling the whole time. Not very nice."

"You're not saying this could be an activist-type ploy?"

"Nope. But it made me ponder on it. Activists would spray graffiti on the walls and do other things. Leave messages and destroy property. Not break in and steal two fancy knives. I suppose Kaufmann won't be able to properly butcher any meat until he gets another set of knives, though. So that's an angle."

"Did anything ever happen with that farm or the packing facility?" Patty asked.

"Someone burned the farmhouse right down to the ground. Not sure if anything changed at the meatpacking place."

"Jeez, Louise!"

"Nobody was hurt, but yeah . . . nuts."

Patty headed east down Route 66, and onto I-40, instead of making the loop toward Seligman. So they wouldn't pass the crime scene again. They went through Ash Fork and turned south on Highway 89 toward Paulden. Dolan thought about Josie. He was glad that they were making progress. At least she wasn't technically a Jane Doe anymore. He liked the name, Josie. It was a cute name—perfect for her face and smile. But he turned glum thinking about her. Luckily, he was momentarily distracted when a few trophy-sized pronghorn antelope meandered along the rolling grass hills covered in golden-yellow wildflowers. Dolan pointed the antelope out to Patty. She nodded. Finally, they approached a sign: *Welcome to Chino Valley*.

Back at the Northern Division Office, they found the sergeant finishing up with the video. He fast-forwarded through all the empty frames throughout the day and plenty throughout the night. But he saw nothing unusual or the Dodge again.

"Okay, get the tape over to Rob so he can play with it," Patty said to the sergeant. "And Kaufmann is offering a five-grand reward for anyone returning these slaughter knives."

"Wow!" he said, looking at the photo of the *chalef* knives.

Deputy Kennedy stood up from his desk and walked toward Patty.

"Our parking lot victim never made it to any hospital. I checked all of them," Kennedy said. "I also spoke again with my contact at the Indiana State Police. Local police departments have already started plastering the sketch of our girl in every Amish and Mennonite town. So if that's the angle, it should pay off."

"Good. Did you guys figure out what model that Dodge is we're looking for?"

"We are going with the 1974 to 1978 Dodge W100 4x4."

"Good. Now you can go down to ADOT and get vehicle owner records!" she instructed.

"Jerry and I are getting a pizza delivered. If you don't mind, I want to eat a slice or two before I run off!"

"You betcha! I'm not going to starve you to death, am I?" Patty said with a wry smile.

A familiar face entered through the office's clean glass panel doors. The man resembled the portrait hanging next to the U.S. and Arizona flags on the wall behind Patty's desk. Jerry sat up a little straighter as the man approached him.

"Good afternoon, sir," he said to him.

"Jerry—how are you doing? How's the wife and kids?" the man asked.

"I'm still married, and the kids haven't gotten expelled yet! So pretty good, I guess! Thanks for asking, sheriff!"

"Hello, Detective Malloy," Sheriff Grady said while approaching her. "So we have new twists on your Jane Doe case, they tell me."

"Yes, we ended up with video footage that changed everything. I'm having two extra tapes made if you want to watch one at your office."

"No, I've been briefed. I'm sure you're handling it all fine."

"Sheriff, this is Dolan McBride. The nephew of Sheriff Harry," Patty said, turning to introduce them.

"Hello, sheriff," said Dolan.

"You know, I've heard a lot about you already!" The sheriff said. "I'm even hearing that you're considering a career in law enforcement out here."

"Yes, sir."

"Well, it's good to meet you, son."

"You as well. Thank you!" Dolan replied.

"Look, I'm getting a bite at the Chinese joint. Can I buy you lunch? Late lunch, I suppose. Unless you're busy here," the sheriff said to Dolan, looking at his watch.

"No. That'd be great!"

"Well, take care, detective," the sheriff said. He and Dolan walked out to the parking area.

CHAPTER TWELVE

The sheriff drove a shiny black unmarked Ford Mustang SSP. It smelled brand new like it had just rolled off the Detroit assembly line. The sheriff wore a perfect, crispy white, long-sleeved dress shirt with a red tie. Dolan figured his sidearm was a Sig-Sauer 9 mm, semi-automatic. He didn't ask.

"You'll like this Chinese place," he said to Dolan.

"Yes, I will," he replied. "I ate there the other night."

"Oh, we could get a burger or something instead."

"No, I like Chinese food. I could eat it every day!"

They pulled into the paved parking lot of the Golden Chopsticks. The newer standalone building contrasted the older, western-looking wood buildings lining the street. Dolan felt a little anxious as they walked to the door. It was like attending a job interview. He wasn't sure why the sheriff took an interest in him, which made him curious. Probably because of his uncle.

The restaurant host met them near the entrance, smiled, and shook the sheriff's hand as they walked in. The host was the owner, Sam Ho, who loved the presence of law enforcement in his establishment. He brought them to a table adjacent to the noodle and soup bar.

"You must know I love your Wonton soup!" the sheriff said to the owner. "You always put me right next to it!"

They started with the soup as the sheriff explained to Dolan the need for active recruitment in law enforcement.

"A lot of guys and gals—kids mostly—think they want to be cops. So they go through the training, even get hired by a department. But then they don't make the grade and don't grow into the job. It's a tough career; you have to be cut out for it. So the point is they may only last a short time. Then they're gone," he said while slurping the soup. "I want to be active when it comes to recruitment. So when I see someone I want, someone we need, I go after them."

The sheriff carefully wiped his lips with the white cloth napkin, folded it back, and placed it next to his bowl.

"And we spend lots of time and money on the academy and proper training. Most recruits pay their way through the academy and classwork, but they're reimbursed once we hire them, so we do pay for it. We also recommend criminal justice degrees, so that's an additional cost." The sheriff paused for a moment. "I want to set you up here with a grant. We will pay your way through all the training and classwork, and I'll set you up with an apartment in Prescott, right next to the college. You won't have to worry about anything except showing up. What do you say?"

Dolan was listening to the sheriff talk. He understood the need for recruitment efforts and the outreach that the sheriff discussed. But the sheriff's offer was surprising. It was strange that the sheriff never asked a single question about his experience or anything at all. Like why he wanted to be in law enforcement, or make a good cop, or even anything about his military stint (if the sheriff even knew Dolan was in the military), or if he even graduated the eighth grade. This was the best job interview ever. But something was going on here that he wasn't seeing. Detective Malloy must've spoken to the sheriff. But he did not know.

"Thanks for this offer, sheriff. I told Detective Malloy that I had to go back to Michigan to get things in order. Then I will head back out here."

"Sure, sure. You get your life in order and anything you need to do," the sheriff said and pulled a card out of his wallet. "Here is my card with my direct line to my office and carphone number. So give me a ring when you're up in Michigan and have everything straight, and I'll set you up."

↔

Dolan went into the Northern Division sans the sheriff. Kennedy stood next to Patty and said: "Eighteen-year-old Josie Jane Yoder of Shawneetauka, Indiana. That's our girl."

"She's Amish," Patty added. "They will see about dental records and send any over if possible, but we're quite certain."

Dolan smiled lightly. It was bitter-sweet hearing her name. A family in Indiana was coming to grips with a tragedy. So he couldn't gain much satisfaction.

"Thanks," he said. "That's something anyway."

"Her sister Hannah was at the Shawneetauka Police Department when they called over," Kennedy said. "I spoke with her for a minute. Hannah said that Josie went to Los Angeles six months ago. I asked if she had run away from home, and Hannah said she just left. That was her choice, her sister said. So they went to a local thrift store one morning, and she got English clothes, she says, and other items, then left."

"What are English clothes?" Dolan asked.

"Apparently, anybody that's not Amish they call English. So normal clothes for us."

"So another pretty young woman went off to the City of Angels thinking it was the land of milk and honey," Patty said. "Half of them end up in prostitution and pornography. Not quite the Hollywood dream they had in mind."

"Shawneetauka to Los Angeles? On her own? She must've been one fearless girl," Dolan said.

"Foolish is a better word, I think," Patty replied.

↔

Deputy McGraw was out at the Seligman Tex-Gas with two members of the county forensic team. When he arrived, he taped off a portion of the gravel parking lot around the estimated area of the crime scene. A decade's worth of antifreeze, power steering fluid, motor oil, globs of joint lube, chewed-up and spit-out tobacco, chewing gum, disintegrated prophylactics, and god knows what other types of organic or inorganic materials existed. The forensic team did find thirty-seven cents in change.

After he was there a few hours, and they were ready to wrap it up, a woman who worked at the convenience store came out and signaled to McGraw, so he went over.

"I only work two days a week, so I assumed somebody already took care of this," the female worker started saying, "so I forgot about it. But one of our customers brought in a wallet the other morning. Found it around back. So I put it in the lost and found. I figured if the owner didn't claim it, we could mail it back to them, considering the address on the driver's license."

"I'll take care of it," Shane said. "People turn in wallets to us all the time."

He flipped it open and pulled out the driver's license as he walked away. *Fred Mohon - 1022 Route 66 - Peach Springs, Arizona.*

"This means something," Shane said aloud. He called into the Northern Division and got Deputy Kennedy on the line. He explained how a customer found a wallet around the back of the gas station the other morning. "Yes, Mohon—like Johnny Mohon, the Hualapai Johnny character that took off when he got spooked seeing my patrol car out at the Bar-T this morning! His brother?"

"Well, how about this for coincidences . . . I'm going through the list from ADOT of 1974 to '78 Dodge W100 pickup owners, and guess who's on that list? Fred Mohon of Peach Springs!"

"Wait . . . so was Fred Mohon the scumbag driving the pickup? Doesn't it make more sense that he was the poor guy that got rundown here? Or maybe even the guy that carried off the body? The wallet must've fallen out around the back, not in the middle of the parking lot!"

"Does it contain cash?" Kennedy asked. "What if someone found the wallet in the parking lot, emptied it, and threw it around back?"

"Forty-seven bucks in it. So I doubt it!"

After a brief conversation between Kennedy and Detective Malloy, the detective got on the line.

"McGraw, you should get back down to the Bar-T and see if they know where to locate Johnny Mohon and if they know anything about Fred Mohon. In the meantime, we'll call the Hualapai Police, and hopefully, they can tell us something."

"So can we check at this Fred Mohon's house in Peach Springs?"

"Not without the FBI. It's reservation land. That's across the Mohave County line, anyhow. No, we'll ask the Hualapai Police to see about picking up Fred and his brother. If that's who John Mohon is. Unless, of course, his brother was the person in that parking lot, now most likely dead. Then it's only Johnny we're looking for!"

↔

Kennedy contacted the tribal police in Peach Springs, while Patty called HQ and put out an all-points bulletin for the dark green 1976 Dodge Power Wagon W100 with license plate DHB156 belonging to Fred Mohon of Peach Springs, Arizona. Deputy McGraw pointed his patrol car down Williamson Valley Road and headed south towards the Bar-T Ranch.

Dolan was staring at the sketch of Josie Jane Yoder of Shawneetauka, Indiana, thinking he wasn't doing much around the office anymore.

He should take off. Perhaps he could be more beneficial to the operation by driving his Jeep around the back roads of the north country, keeping his eyes peeled for the dark green Dodge. At least he'd be doing something active and possibly productive. When Patty finished her calls, Dolan explained that he'd like to be an extra set of eyes and ears up north. So he was going to head out.

"Wait . . . If you happen to see that truck parked somewhere, do not approach it! Instead, just note the location and call the office. Understand?" Patty insisted.

"Yes, ma'am."

"Here. Take a look at this backcountry road map of our patrol area. Since you have a Jeep, you may want to take some of these roads drawn in red."

"Red roads?"

"Yep, they are four-wheel-drive access, so if you're only going out for a joy ride, you may have a little fun and not drive as many miles. For instance, you could cut straight west down this road and make it over to Williamson Valley near the southerly sections of the Bar-T and only drive about thirteen miles. It sure saves the trip of going around on the pavement."

"Nice. I guess I'm off to go sightseeing!" Dolan said.

"Also, please don't get any ideas about heading northwest toward the Hualapai Reservation."

"Is that a problem? Riding reservation land?"

"Uh-huh. Officially, yes. Maybe not for you. But still . . ."

↔

When McGraw got down to the Bar-T Ranch, Jimmy Tilley was heading out on a brown and white Paint. The deputy walked over and talked to him while Jimmy was in the saddle.

"That's a nice-looking horse," McGraw said.

"This is Annie. She's one smart and gentle animal."

"So, where can I find Johnny Mohon?"

"Last I saw him, I was with you this morning," Tilley said.

"Is Fred Mohon Johnny's brother?"

"Fred? Yes."

"We have reason to believe that Fred Mohon may have been involved in a homicide or even the victim of one. So please tell me if you know the whereabouts of Johnny Mohon or his brother," McGraw said impatiently.

"He was killed?"

Tilley hopped down from Annie; she grazed alongside the steers near the road. He leaned against the patrol car.

"I've been worried that this would all get out of hand. Johnny said he would deal with it, but obviously, it's way beyond fixing now."

"Okay, you'll have to tell me what's happening here!"

"I can show you. Can you ride a horse?" Tilley asked.

"It's been a while, but if it can help clear this up, go get me one!" McGraw said.

"If Johnny's down where I'm thinking, horses will be the quickest way of getting there."

Jimmy Tilley went back and saddled up Blackie. He told McGraw to ride Annie because she was easy to handle.

"Giddy-up, Annie!" Shane shook the split western reins. Blackie led the way.

They trotted down the road until turning south onto a lightly used trail. McGraw and Tilley meandered between large alligator juniper trees with cracked-gray bark squares covering their wide trunks and piñon pine that jutted along a rocky ledge. A ranch fence came down the rocks and ridge, continuing along flat ground. They rode along the fence for a few hundred yards until they reached a gate. It was tied shut with rope, and Tilley got off his horse to get it opened. They walked the horses through the open gate into a thick forested piece of ground. There were tangled manzanita bushes with shiny red bark and thick green leaves that grew over ten feet high and formed a bough you could walk under. They proceeded through this strange manzanita forest until coming back to a stand of Rocky Mountain juniper so thick it didn't seem possible to enter. Tilley came down off his horse and told McGraw to do the same. He tied up both horses to tree branches by the leather reins.

"Here. This way," he said, squeezing between heavy green juniper branches. McGraw followed while patting down his .357 Smith and Wesson revolver to ensure it was still available. The juniper they brushed against smelled like gin-laced cat urine. As the limbs snapped back, McGraw lifted his hand to shield his face. Finally, Tilley pulled a few more branches back and maneuvered around. The last juniper was concealing an opening at the base of a hill. Tilley pulled a small flashlight from the inside pocket of his brown denim jacket and entered the now dimly illuminated crevice. McGraw followed, descending a slope and entering the hillside behind him. It resembled an abandoned mine adit, like those he explored around Prescott's gold country as a kid.

"Well, Mohon isn't at this one. The light is still here," Tilley said and picked up the battery-powered lantern that lit up everything in front of them. McGraw couldn't believe his eyes. It was a magnificent underground cavern, with sparkling stalactites hanging from a cavity over twenty feet high and one-hundred feet wide. It seemed to go back forever, beyond what the light could reach.

"Holy shit!" McGraw said, looking into the stunning underground world. They accessed the cavern through the narrow gap of dirt and vegetative roots that opened into a vast limestone room. McGraw touched the lower portion of the ceiling and walls as they entered. It was smooth and wet.

"They call that moon milk," Tilley said of the creamy-white rounded limestone substance formed as a precipitate from the mineral waters that still dripped through from the upper surface. As the cavern expanded, the huge stalactites hung from the ceiling like massive icicles of varying sizes and colors.

"Don't touch the stalactites. Some are fragile," Tilley said. And they didn't walk in any deeper.

Tilley explained that this cavern and another one, a quarter-mile on the other side of the same hill, were discovered in 1975. However, only a few people associated with the ranch knew they existed. They'd been working with a nature conservancy group for the past two years in secret, attempting to form a public-private partnership with the Arizona State Park system, which would eventually take over control and ownership of the 640-acre section they are within.

"But here's the sticking point," Tilley said as he moved toward the narrow, earthy entrance and shined his lantern on the dirt ceiling and walls. "See all these white root clusters? This is the visible portion of what are called truffles."

"Like those expensive things that rich people eat in France?" Shane asked.

"Not quite, but similar. These are special fungal masses that certain Indian tribes use for spiritual and religious purposes. Colloquially they are known as magic truffles, like mushrooms, only rarer. They contain hallucinogenic compounds."

"Like a psychedelic drug?"

"Yes. Hualapai Johnny supplied many tribes with these truffles for spiritual ceremonies. Just so you know, we don't get compensated. It has been a silent agreement between this ranch and the various tribes, with Johnny as the facilitator. In the meantime, the tribes have petitioned the federal government to legalize natural hallucinogens—like mushrooms and truffles—for religious practices. Indigenous groups have already received an exemption for peyote cactus for use in sacred ceremonies, so we are hopeful. However, if they are unsuccessful, we may have to destroy all evidence of these very rare fungi to close the deal with the conservancy group and the state park system. That isn't our desired outcome, as it would greatly disappoint these native peoples."

"But what does this have to do with his brother Fred?" McGraw asked.

"Fred fell into gambling debts and stole the last truffle shipment from Johnny. I believe he planned to supply the truffles in exchange for the debts."

"Now it's starting to make sense!"

They proceeded to the north entrance and found it empty. Tilley was unsure where else to look. They found no evidence that Mohon had been to either cavern. "Maybe he's up on the reservation," he said.

They headed back through the rugged section of ground, then went on horseback to the ranch headquarters. Jimmy Tilley couldn't think of anything else that could help at the moment. Deputy McGraw would head out and contact Patty. Tilley did say that Johnny had an enduro motorcycle. It was a black Suzuki 400cc. He also had a 1967 El Camino. It was midnight blue. Tilley thought he stored it in town but wasn't sure. So at least they had more vehicles to look out for, which was helpful. At that point, McGraw agreed with Tilley. Mohon most likely slipped off to the Hualapai reservation. It made sense, anyway.

CHAPTER THIRTEEN

When the Hualapai Tribal Fire Department volunteers arrived, the family had already burned the tiny house off Route 66 to the ground. The close relatives of Fred Mohon assembled around in brightly colored garments, chanting prayers with their gourd rattles shaking. Johnny wore face paint and dressed as a traditional Yavapai Fighter with a buckskin loincloth.

Nobody called the fire department because Johnny and his family intentionally transformed Fred's body, home, and worldly possessions into ashes, as was the ancient practice of the Hualapai. So the fire station volunteers stood back and watched the ceremony without interference.

As Fred's belongings changed to smoke and drifted up to the sky, Johnny Mohon had already been preparing his plans to make things right, and although bloody revenge would be sweet, his plans would only use force and violence if necessary. At least, that is what he told his friend, the chief.

The Hualapai Tribal Police Chief was standing next to Johnny. The Yavapai County Sheriff's Office had already contacted Chief Elijah Watahomigie's department regarding Johnny and Fred's whereabouts. But Chief Watahomigie knew the circumstances surrounding Fred Mohon's death and that Johnny intended to make things right and even encouraged him to do so. So the chief advised Johnny to take his motorcycle through the rugged country trails east of Peach Springs so he could carry out his plan back in Seligman. He told him to stay off Route 66 since the sheriff's men would undoubtedly be patrolling for his return.

When the funeral ceremony was over, and the family dispersed, the chief headed back to the tribal department office and instructed his sergeant to contact the Yavapai County Sheriff's Northern Division. Detective Patty Malloy got on the line.

"Hello, sir. You have something for us?"

"Yes, Patty. I hope you are doing well. Unfortunately, Fred Mohon, the brother of John Mohon, is deceased, and the family carried out a traditional funeral today at his home on the reservation."

"Okay. We believe someone may have killed Mohon in Seligman, and therefore, we'll be requesting the body for examination here."

"That won't be possible, as the family burned his home and body."

"Burned his body? What? Wouldn't your office, or the feds, investigate a suspicious death? I'm confused," said Patty, getting frustrated.

"The family said nothing about a suspicious death. They chose not to have a modern ceremony. Instead, they performed an ancient fire ritual. They burned all of his belongings and his home."

"That seems rather extreme," she said. "I thought you had an annual ceremony to burn the clothing of all the deceased instead of the old ways?"

"Yes, that is true. But a few families have done this over the years.

"Does your office know the whereabouts of his brother, John Mohon?"

"He was at the ceremony and left with the others."

"I see. I don't suppose you could find Mohon and hold him for us?"

"Do you have an arrest warrant, Patty? Are you certain that someone killed Fred in Seligman? Maybe he died here in his sleep, as his family said."

"We need to question John about his brother's death. We don't know if the perpetrators are native or not, but this incident occurred outside of the reservation, regardless. And, um, no, we aren't one-hundred percent confident it was Fred Mohon killed, but we're gathering evidence."

"Patty, if we see Johnny on the Rez, we will question him and contact you as a courtesy. I will also send someone over to the family home. Perhaps they know his whereabouts," the chief said. He knew Johnny was no longer on the reservation.

"Well, okay. But one more thing, chief. We believe this incident and the death of Josie Jane Yoder—our body from Tuesday—are connected. The same perpetrators."

"I see. My men put up those posters throughout Peach Springs."

"Thanks for that. Look, what I'm saying here is we need your full cooperation. If we bring the feds out, they'll turn your reservation upside down. It'd be a real circus, so—"

"You have our cooperation. If you want to come up to the reservation, please stop at our department office first, and we will jointly pursue your lines of inquiry."

"Thank you. Then I'll be seeing you very soon."

"Also Patty, we all know Fred's green truck. We've seen him driving it over the years. So we are following up on your APB. My men are looking."

The chief dropped the phone. The perpetrators were not on reservation land. He also knew his friend Johnny Mohon would take care of the problem in his own way. But he didn't want the feds fumbling around his reservation. So he'd work with Patty and the sheriff's office in a limited way.

↔

Deputy McGraw contacted Patty and gave her the details regarding Fred Mohon's involvement with the stolen hallucinogenic truffles and his gambling debts.

"I'm thinking the suspects were driving Fred's Dodge truck. Maybe he let them have it for collateral on the debt he owed."

"Or they took it," Patty added.

"Right. And maybe that's why the perps were supposed to meet Mohon at the gas station, so he could get the truck back plus give them the drugs," McGraw said.

"Possible. And Mohon gets run down by his own truck?"

"Yep."

"So we need to locate that Dodge pickup, the El Camino, and Johnny Mohon. He's the only one who can provide any clarity here. He must know who these guys are," she replied. "Find out where he's storing that El Camino in town. It could be in one of the warehouses along the railway. If you find the car, possibly you can find him."

"Okie dokie."

"Unless, of course, he's still up on the reservation. But Chief Watahomigie has assured me they will be looking for Johnny and the green truck. So at this point, we'll have to trust they are doing their job up there. And we'll do our job down here. But if we're still empty-handed by tomorrow, we'll all be going to the reservation. Today we trust; tomorrow we verify."

"I think Abraham Lincoln said that," McGraw said, joking.

"It was Reagan!"

McGraw rolled his patrol car along the side streets in Seligman that abutted the BNSF railway line through town. The buildings were mostly in shambles. The Harvey House—a once glamourous railway restaurant and hotel—had been sitting empty for forty years. Behind the decrepit Harvey House were two wooden garages. McGraw got out his flashlight and peeked into the windows. He stood on a milk crate and shined his light through the opening. They were empty.

The deputy drove farther down the alleyway until he got to a Quonset hut warehouse. It, too, was derelict looking and also empty. Across the alley from the warehouse was a row of shack homes. Two tiny houses had a standalone single-car garage that faced the alley. A little pinkish home had its garage door lifted, with a vehicle inside covered by a gray tarp. The shape was correct—long and low. McGraw stopped near the open garage and got out. He'd knock on the pink door and ask the owner about the vehicle instead of just walking into the garage.

A little elderly woman answered. Her face was contorted and sunken from a lack of teeth. Her name was Martha Moriarty.

"Are you coming to arrest me?" she said, "I'm sure I did it. Only I forgot what it was I did, officer!"

McGraw laughed, "No. Just wondering if that would be a blue El Camino parked back in your garage?"

"It's one of those cars that looks like a pickup truck. And it's blue."

"That sounds right! Does John Mohon live here?" McGraw asked.

"Hualapai Johnny? He don't live here. He keeps his car here. He pays me two hundred dollars a year. I tell him I'd let him use it for free, but he pays me anyway. He's the best man around. Yes, that Johnny, he sure is."

"When was he here last?" McGraw asked.

"I think he was here a few nights back. I think I heard that motorcycle that he rides come up. Sometimes he leaves the motorcycle and takes the car. Sometimes he puts the motorcycle on the back of the bed and takes them both. He said he had to fix the spring on the garage door. Last week he said it broke, and he couldn't close the door, so he'd be back to fix it."

"It isn't fixed yet. I'm assuming that's why the door is open."

"Why are you looking for Johnny?" she asked.

"Just want to ask him a few questions. He may have information regarding a crime, is all."

While they were talking, a tea kettle must've been heating up on her stove because it was whistling louder and louder.

"You've been a great help, ma'am. Say . . ." he started to pull a card out of his wallet, "could you call us if he stops by again?"

"No phone," she said. "I'll let Johnny know you're looking for him. How's that?" She took the card.

"Much obliged. I'll let you see to your tea kettle!"

"You can stay for a cup!"

"I'm good! Thanks for the offer!"

She closed the door, and he walked to the front of the garage, where he'd parked his patrol car. The way the row homes were situated directly behind the garage, she couldn't see him, so he went into the garage to get a peek under the tarp. He pointed his flashlight into the vehicle. On the passenger seat were a few metal hooks and looped-up lariat ropes, like cowboys use on their horses, two long skinny knives in leather sheaths, fence wire cutters, and other items you'd see used on a ranch. A pair of cowboy boots, jeans, and a hat sat on the floorboard. The bed of the El Camino was empty.

He radioed in and let Patty know he found the car, but it wasn't much help. Hopefully, Martha Moriarty would get the message to Johnny. But he wasn't so sure Johnny wanted to talk with them. He was pretty damn sure he didn't.

↔

Dolan drove his Jeep over the rugged country from the south of town. He kept his eyes peeled for that dark green Dodge pickup but hadn't seen much besides beautiful wilderness and wide-open rangeland. It was getting late in the day when he pulled into Seligman. A patrol car was parked at the Shell station on the west end of town. He pulled in, and Deputy McGraw walked out. They talked. Shane explained what he found out down at the Bar-T and about the El Camino. Dolan let him know that Patty sent him through the backroad country. He didn't see the pickup. So he was thinking about driving the 4x4 roads north of town marked on the map. Cover more ground.

"Hell, it may be in a garage like the El Camino was. It was a fluke that I located that," McGraw said. "And how do we even know these guys are local?"

"I'd say they're local. I don't think anyone would come out here, to the middle of nowhere, to loan this guy cash or however he got indebted."

"Gambling."

"Well, they're either Nevada mobsters, or it's a local thing. They'd get nabbed if they're stupid enough to drive that pickup on the highway. So I'd say they're local, alright. That truck should be in the area," Dolan said.

"I'm supposed to be off duty now. It's after five o'clock. But I'll leave my patrol car parked and drive around with you for fun."

"Cool. Let me take a leak and get a pop from the gas station first. You want one?"

"A pop?"

"You know . . . a Coke or something. What you call soda! You want one?"

"Sure."

They took rough roads north of Seligman, heading east to the Kaibab National Forest area, close to Ash Fork. They looped around treed buttes, went through deep canyons, crossed prairie and meadow, ended up back into thick pine and juniper country, drove near rocky basalt outcrops, and crossed into grass prairie again. It was nearly dark, and turning back south, down one of the other roads on the map, would get them back to Route 66. Occasionally they'd come to a lightly used two-track path that shot off the main road, taking it for a while to check out the area before turning back. Most dead-ended at the base of a butte or stopped near a cliff. One two-track had a ground blind constructed out of sticks and tree branches where the trail ended. A hunter must've set it up. Finally, they took another two-track that came off the main road, only a mile from where they were supposed to intersect Route 66 again, and that's when McGraw made a grunting sound and said: "Look!"

Dolan hit the brakes.

Stuck between two large alligator junipers was the dark green Dodge with Arizona license plate DHB156. They jumped out of the Jeep and walked toward the Dodge through tall, dried grass. Dolan noticed a sticker on the left side of the bumper. It was round, and as they got close enough, he could see it was the tribal seal of the Hualapai Nation; two native faces were staring at each other with the Arizona flag in the background. Upon seeing that seal, a little memory flashed in his head.

"This!" he said.

"The Hualapai bumper sticker?"

"Yes!"

"I'm not following you," Shane said. "We know he's a member. They are pretty common."

"It just reminded me that I'd seen it somewhere. And it shouldn't have been where I'd seen it!"

"Where?"

"On Sunday night, Red Halleran and I were walking into the Blue Ox, and two pickup trucks were parked on the side. It was dark, and I wasn't paying much attention, but when I glanced down as we walked by, I saw that sticker on the bumper!"

"No Native Americans were in the bar that night!" Shane said.

"Only those Swedes that rode in on the rented motorcycles, Sam the bartender, and the two ranch hands from Kaufmann's place! It could have been this pickup."

"We're like two miles from Kaufmann's headquarters right here," Shane replied.

Dolan reached to open the driver's door to look inside.

"Don't touch it!" McGraw yelled. "Prints!"

They didn't have a radio, so they needed to get to Kaufmann's place to call it in. It was dark, but they got back to Route 66 in only five minutes. They headed east a couple of miles until Kaufmann's straight gravel road intersected Route 66, and Dolan turned left.

"How the heck do you know where Kaufmann's ranch is?" Shane asked. "I barely remembered the turnoff myself."

"I was here six hours ago," he said, "with Patty."

"Wait. Stop driving. — *Why?*"

"He called in a B & E. The theft of two knives they use for kosher slaughtering."

"Could Kaufmann be involved in all this?" Shane asked, musing aloud.

"No way. That guy is deeply religious, but more importantly, why would he call the sheriff's office if he was?"

"Okay, but we can't be sure Kaufmann isn't involved. Also, if we think that the green Dodge was one of the pickup trucks outside the Blue Ox Sunday night, then we have to assume that these two ranch hands are the bastards we're looking for. And they could be out here at the ranch!"

"Luke and Billy?" Dolan said. "Yes, I'm hoping."

"These two are most likely the cold-blooded killers from the tape!" McGraw shouted. "Patty would kill me if I strolled in without backup!"

"I can be your backup. I've got a .38-special hiding under my driver's seat!"

"You're lucky that's legal in Arizona!" the deputy replied. "But no way!"

"So? What now?"

"Head over to Ash Fork. We're not far. I'll call it in, and Patty could have that place surrounded!"

Dolan did a u-turn and started driving toward Ash Fork.

"It won't work out that way, I bet," Shane said.

"Why?"

"All we have is that you think you can place that Dodge over at the Blue Ox on Sunday night. We don't have any real evidence yet. I bet Patty will want to have the forensic team examine that truck at the yard tonight before she lets us do anything!"

"Damn, that seems inefficient!"

"It's called building a case! We can't blow in with guns blazing. Not if we don't have any hard evidence against these guys!"

"I guess this police business may take getting used to," Dolan said.

CHAPTER FOURTEEN

By the time they called Patty, went back to Seligman for McGraw's patrol car, then back to secure the area around the abandoned Dodge, it was ten o'clock. When the flatbed arrived to take the pickup truck to the evidence yard, Dolan rehashed all that happened that day. It felt like a week had passed since he did the police lineup first thing in the morning. Then he went out to the Bar-T with McGraw, discovered and watched the surveillance footage at the Tex-Gas station, went out to Kaufmann's place with Patty and back to Chino, had lunch with the sheriff, and finally drove all those miles in the backcountry looking for the truck. They accomplished a lot, and all the pieces were coming together, but he was dead tired. A hot shower at a cheap motel in Ash Fork was waiting for him.

"Did you hear our girl's family came forward today in Indiana?" Dolan said, turning to Shane.

"Nope. Patty didn't tell me."

"Her full name is Josie Jane Yoder. She's Amish, originally from Shawneetauka, Indiana. According to her sister, she had been in Los Angeles for six months."

"Weird, isn't it?"

"What is?" Dolan asked.

"It's weird that I forgot the girl is the reason we're standing here loading this pickup on this flatbed. And I haven't even thought about her since we watched that tape. Damn, I must be getting jaded!"

"To be fair, it seems like she was only collateral damage in all this mess. An innocent bystander."

↔

The hot shower was still working nicely at the Ash Fork motel. Perhaps too well because when Dolan jumped out into the steamed-up bathroom, he was wide awake, feeling good, and now hungry. Like other small towns, the problem with Ash Fork was that there was no place to eat at eleven at night. He couldn't drop down to the local Mcdonald's because one didn't exist. The diner opened at five in the morning, but that was a long way off for an empty stomach. Gas stations were closed, so he couldn't even grab a candy bar or bag of chips. When he came through earlier, he saw a hole-in-the-wall Mexican cantina near the other end of town. He'd walk over and check it out.

The street lights in town were sparse and barely illuminating. The concrete sidewalk along the main street was buckling and broken in most places, so you had to watch each step. The tiny houses that lined the road looked abandoned and decrepit, only they weren't because Dolan could see an occasional light or television through the windows. The town reeked of poverty. It was just another town, like many across America, destroyed when the progress of the interstate highway system put Route 66 out of business.

He approached a small building with a neon sign that flickered BAR. He crossed the street. A few youths were hanging around the door. They passed a bottle in a brown paper bag while laughing and pushing each other. Dolan nodded to them as he walked by, but they just made stupid faces. He entered the dimly lit cantina. Candles were burning at a few tables, and two bare incandescent bulbs were hanging above the bar top. Quiet mariachi music played on the radio behind the bartender. Three men stood at the bar. They stared at Dolan as he walked in.

The bartender must've been about eighty years old. He had a big white flowing mustache. He smiled when he saw Dolan and slid down the bar.

"Tequila and a beer, please!" Dolan said to the man. "And I'd like to eat if you have something."

"You want to eat? Go sit," he said, pointing to a table and turning toward the back. "Maria! A young man here wants to eat."

Maria emerged from the backway as he sat at the round pub table. The men at the bar stopped staring at Dolan and watched lovely young Maria navigate the fold-up bar top. The bartender set a Dos Equis down on the counter and a shot of tequila. She stepped back for the drinks and then came to his table.

"You want to eat?" she asked.

"Yes, I could eat," he said.

"I made the tortilla fresh. Do you want a burrito or fajita?"

"Yes, both."

"I'll bring you a big plate," she said, smiling. "Beans and rice too. Do you want beef or *pollo*?"

"Make the fajita chicken, I guess. Beef burrito." Dolan said. He was getting hungrier thinking about it.

Maria went back to the kitchen to cook his order. The beer was nice and cold, but he'd wait to drink the tequila until he got food on his stomach. The three men were tired of staring at Dolan and quietly talked amongst themselves in Spanish. The bartender, who seemed fastidious in his area, busily wiped down the counter, then he turned his attention to the brass along the mantle where he kept his bottles.

Maria came back with a large platter stacked with food. The men eyed her again as she flipped up the bar top and served Dolan at his table. Seeing his beer bottle empty, she grabbed it and got him another.

"This burrito is great," he said to her after taking a bite.

"Thank you," she said.

"Who taught you to cook? Your mother?"

"My mother is a bad cook. My father and grandfather are great cooks," she said and pointed toward the bartender. "That's unusual for Mexican men. Most won't go into a kitchen."

"Your grandfather?" he asked while nodding toward the bartender.

"Yes. My grandfather mostly taught me."

Dolan felt like talking. So he kept asking her questions, and she kept answering and adding details. She stood by him while he ate his burrito and half of his chicken fajita. He drank his shot of tequila, but he declined another when she asked.

The entrance door to the bar opened, and one of the youths stuck his head in.

"When will you be off work?" he asked Maria.

"I have to finish cleaning the kitchen." She was leaning next to the table, facing Dolan. "A couple more minutes!"

The grandfather objected to the youth sticking his head in the bar and told him to get out, which he did. The kid was maybe sixteen—eighteen at the most.

Maria went away, and she disappeared into the kitchen. He finished up his fajita, went to the bar, paid her grandfather, thanked him, left a nice tip at the table, and then walked out the door to the parking lot.

The youth who popped his head through the door was standing just outside. Without notice or provocation, he clocked Dolan across the face with a quick fist. Dolan stumbled. The other youths laughed and cheered. Dolan was normally not quick to violence, but they put him in an uncomfortable position. Considering he was a trained boxer with some talent, he immediately retaliated with a fierce right hook that knocked the youth to the ground. The other boys stopped laughing and decided to try their luck, but their luck was not good. Dolan took each one apart with a series of combinations. When the first youth, who instigated the action, stood back up and moved in, Dolan took him down again with an uppercut. The other two grabbed his legs to tackle him. At this point, the noise must've stirred the inside crowd, and they came out. The old bartender had a broomstick and started knocking the boys with it while shouting obscenities in Spanish.

After the dust settled, the bartender apologized to Dolan and gave him a napkin for his nose. It was bleeding from the initial sucker punch. He also instructed the boys to apologize, which they all did, and they shook Dolan's hand before he left. It was a good fight, he told them. The youth who instigated the action separately said he was sorry to Dolan and admitted he was always hot-headed and jealous. They shook hands again without any animosity.

Dolan went away and walked back down the uneven, broken pavement, through the dimly lit streets, until he reached his hotel room, where he collapsed on the bed and slept soundly until morning.

↔

Patty ran the office's overtime clock wild that night. She practically had the entire forensic team over at the county property and evidence yard by midnight. She wanted that Dodge torn down and stripped and every fingerprint lifted.

Luckily for Patty, one of the ranch hands, Luke Staley, had been arrested for disorderly conduct, and his fingerprints were on file. She had already provided the file to the forensic team for a quick match if and when needed. Patty was worried they wouldn't find any evidence or prints. They had the video of the Dodge but no way of putting Espers or Staley inside the vehicle. They had the alibi, so she needed to place them at the scene, in the vehicle, or prove the alibi false. She contacted

Rob, who was handling the VHS tape. He and his friend were working to enhance the clarity of the faces on the video. She woke Rob, but he said they had no luck so far. Rob's answer wasn't the news she wanted to hear.

Patty left the property and evidence impound yard and was back at the office. She was at her desk drinking a black coffee with sugar. She was hoping to make an arrest in the morning and needed to coordinate with Sheriff Grady, HQ, and the SWAT unit. Staley and Espers had access to loads of weapons at the Kaufmann Ranch, so she wasn't taking any chances.

Her phone rang. It was Leslie from the property and evidence yard. "Detective Malloy?"

"Leslie! You have good news? I hope—"

"We found your missing shoe. Size seven Keds white canvas. It was jammed up under the passenger seat."

"Great. That puts our victim inside the vehicle, so that's beneficial."

"We've got a thumbprint on the driver's door handle and steering wheel. It's a Luke Staley match."

"Bingo!" Patty exclaimed. "You guys are the best!"

"Should we head home and finish up during normal business hours?"

"Yes. That's a good idea. We should all get home now. Goodnight, kid!"

Patty hung up the phone. She was satisfied. Finally, all the hours and work paid off. Now she'd be able to sleep like a baby, preferably in her warm bed, not at the desk. She headed home.

CHAPTER FIFTEEN

Dolan woke up with a headache and unfortunately, the steamy shower didn't help as much as last time. He headed to the diner and ordered a light breakfast of over-easy eggs and toast with a coffee. He was going to stop at coffee, but he could always eat.

He thought of the cute waitress from the bar and her jealous young boyfriend and the workout in the parking lot that left his nose sore and his knuckles more so. He laughed. He'd only been in one other fight like that. After his 20th birthday, he and a few of the guys from Fort Riley went to a strip club. It was one of those clubs that charge admission to see pretty females pole dancing. But most dancers would get friendly with the customers for an extra fee. They didn't sell beer, but they let you bring your own, so it was a rough and rowdy place. The building was a converted barn located far outside of town.

On this outing, Dolan was interested in a young woman named Angel. Some other guys had already bought her time for a private party, and when they started taking her away, he didn't understand. He tapped one of the guys on the shoulder to ask what they were up to, and the guy gave him a friendly shove in return. So consequently, he was engaged with four guys within a few seconds, and Angel ran for the bouncer. It turned into an all-out brawl when his Army buddies got involved. The place was wrecked. Somehow he and his friends made it out in one piece. He laughed again and shook his head, thinking about it.

After breakfast, he called the Northern Division to hear the plan for the day. Jerry, the desk sergeant, answered.

"Having a big briefing here in a few minutes," he said. "The sheriff, SWAT, and all our team here."

"Can I speak with Patty?" Dolan asked.

Jerry got Patty on the line.

"Hello, kid," she said. "It's all looking good for us taking down Espers and Staley for this.

So thanks. You and McGraw did fine work yesterday. The whole team did."

"I don't suppose you would let me be around for the arrest?" Dolan asked, knowing the answer.

"You should go back to your vacation life. Go fishing! Or go back to Sedona and meditate with your aunt," she said. "I would if I could!"

"Well, I'll stick around the area for a little while. Maybe I can talk to you guys afterward."

"Suit yourself," she said. "But fishing would be more fun!"

He called his aunt to let her know what was going on. He wondered what Red was up to. It was Saturday, clouds rolled in, and rain seemed likely. It was the first time the sky wasn't pure blue since he'd been in Arizona.

↔

The Yavapai County Sheriff's convoy rolled down Route 66 and veered onto Kaufmann's straight gravel road. The sheriff's black mustang was the last vehicle in line. Patty's Bronco led the caravan, and Deputy McGraw was sitting in the passenger seat. They were wearing kevlar vests.

"Kaufmann will think we're going all out on his burglary and theft!" Patty said in a cheerful tone.

"So what exactly was stolen?" McGraw inquired. "Dolan was telling me about it."

"These," she said and grabbed a folder off the dashboard. It had black and white copies of Kaufmann's long-bladed *chalef* knives. "Five thousand reward! Not bad."

"Um . . . I think I saw these yesterday," McGraw said.

"What? Where?" Patty asked.

"With all the cowboy gear in Hualapai Johnny's El Camino!"

"Johnny Mohon stole the knives?"

"At least he had them."

The ranch gate was open like the first time Patty drove up, which was a plus. They decided earlier at the briefing to roll their vehicles into the ranch compound and spread around buildings if the gate was open. If closed, they'd spread out along the fence line.

The caravan rolled into the compound one by one, and Patty turned her Bronco sideways at the back entrance to the bunkhouse. It was nine a.m., and Patty was concerned that Espers and Staley could be anywhere on the ranch.

"Here's Kaufmann," Patty said to Shane.

Joseph Kaufmann came out of the main house. He approached Patty's Bronco, and she got out. The tactical officers were leaving their vehicles to spread out around the buildings.

"I was just going to call you!" Kaufmann said.

"What happened?" Patty asked.

"Luke and Billy must've robbed me during the night. All the cash from the office is gone, as are some firearms—our two .45 revolvers! They must've run off before light, but I didn't hear them leave."

"What are they driving?"

"Our white Chevy pickup. It's gone," he said. "They emptied their stuff from the bunkhouse too."

Patty signaled everyone to come together.

"We will be going through all your buildings, Mr. Kaufmann. Just to be sure one of them isn't hiding out."

"That's good," Kaufmann said.

"Any other people in your house or on the property?" she asked.

"Nobody."

"Clear all the buildings! It looks like Staley and Espers have left the ranch, but confirm. They are driving a white Chevy pickup!" she shouted, then turned to Kaufmann, "I'll need the year and plate number for an APB."

"Yes, I'll go look for the registration papers."

"Staley and Espers are armed and dangerous," she shouted again.

Sheriff Grady parked near the gate and walked over.

"I think someone may be disappointed they won't be getting a photo-op," McGraw whispered to Patty.

"A little bad luck here, sheriff," Patty said.

"They could run anywhere now. Out of state? Vegas? Mexico?" he said, clearly disappointed. "How did this happen? Weren't they here?"

"We had Deputy Gonzalez staked out at the ranch entrance all night. Nobody drove through. They must've gone out on one of the back roads."

"Damnit!" the sheriff shook his head.

"Kaufmann is getting the plate number for that white Chevy. I'll sit down with him to try and get a clearer picture of everything going on here," Patty said. "He may know more than he thinks. Also, Johnny Mohon's name is coming up again."

"How so?" Sheriff Grady asked.

She went on to explain the stolen knives.

"I'm sure you'll piece it all together," the sheriff replied. He walked toward the outbuildings.

Patty turned to McGraw and said: "You have to admit, our sheriff is pretty easy to work for!"

"That's true!" Shane replied. "As long as he gets all the glory."

The vehicles that made up the convoy were all gone, except Patty's Bronco. She and McGraw went to the main house with Joseph Kaufmann. They sat at a round oak table in the bright kitchen. A large rectangular window behind the sink and counter provided natural light. The view was east. Bill Williams Mountain was in the far distance. The sky beyond was gray and dark. Mr. Kaufmann offered them coffee and set out pastries that his lady cook had baked the previous afternoon. McGraw was happy.

"So, has Johnny Mohon spent much time at your ranch?" Patty asked.

"Yes, he works predator control for us. He is a hunter and has killed cougars. He also assists in our slaughter when my sons are away. He is good with the livestock and seems to have a calming effect on them. It's an innate ability with him."

"Does it make any sense why your knives would be in his possession?"

"Johnny has them? I can't believe he stole them. That isn't in his character," Kaufmann insisted. "He's a very moral man."

"We will be getting in touch with him soon, so we'll get an explanation. Perhaps he retrieved them and was planning on their return."

"That makes sense."

"Have you ever met Fred Mohon? Johnny's brother . . ."

"Never. The first time I heard his brother's name was when I learned of the attack and death this morning from the sheriff," Kaufmann said.

"Tell me about Espers and Staley. Does it surprise you that they could be involved in all this?"

"Well, yes, I'm surprised. They came over when we moved the herd from the summer to the fall pasture two months ago. The other hands left, and they stayed, and I began to trust them. So yes, I'm surprised."

"Did they ever mention where they're originally from? Did they speak of any family?"

"Not that I recall, but I know they previously worked on a ranch in Wickenburg. So I called the old foreman for their references. He didn't have anything bad to say. So I hired them."

"Could I get that ranch name and number if you still have the information in your files?" Patty asked.

"Yes. I will go check."

Patty ate a pastry while she waited for Kaufmann to return. Shane ate two.

"Let's head over to your lady friend's place in Seligman. Martha Moriarty, is it? Maybe she'll let us take a peek in her garage. We'll get those knives back for Kaufmann. But more importantly, we need to find Mohon. I have this strange feeling that he knows everything we don't know! Does that make sense?"

"Yes, ma'am. I think it does—possibly!"

"We'll take a trip up to Peach Springs and talk to Chief Watahomigie afterward."

Kaufmann returned with the Wickenburg ranch phone number written on scrap paper.

"How is it that you know Johnny has my *chalef* knives?"

"A tip we received," she said, cutting off McGraw before he could say anything. "We'll get them back for you."

"Perfect," he said. "My sons will be returning to the ranch in a few days. I certainly can use them now!"

"We'll be in touch," Patty said, and they walked out the door.

When they drove out onto Route 66, Dolan was sitting in his Jeep on the side of the road. Patty pulled alongside and informed him they were heading into Seligman.

"I'll meet you there," he said.

"You're not going to ask about Staley and Espers?" Patty inquired.

"Deputy Kennedy already told me when he went by!"

It was raining when they got into Seligman. Fog floated along the hills and through the valley. Dolan parked his Jeep at the east end of town and jumped into the back seat of Patty's Bronco.

"I'm not sure I like this very much," Dolan said while putting his fingers through the partition cage.

"That's so you can't attack us. You look dangerous," Patty said, peering through the rearview mirror.

"Turn left here," McGraw said. "It's just beyond the old Harvey House."

As they approached the tiny pink house of Martha Moriarty, the rain got heavier. Her garage door was open, but there was no car, only a motorcycle.

"The El Camino is gone! Damn!" McGraw said.

"Well, go out and see if your friend Martha is home. Ask her if she knows where Johnny went off with his car," Patty said. "Try not to get too wet!"

McGraw moved relatively quickly to her house. Standing on the porch, he leaned in underneath the overhang of the eave and knocked on the door. The little old lady opened the door. She pulled McGraw inside. The rain was coming down, and the noise of the drops hitting the fiberglass top of the Bronco was annoying.

"I've never seen a 4-door Bronco," Dolan said to Patty.

"What about the Bronco?" Patty replied as the rain was loud.

"I didn't think they made 4-door Broncos," he said louder. "This is a beast!"

"That's because it's a special model. They're conversions made by a company called Centurion. They could've done all the extra police stuff too. Like that dog cage that you don't like!"

"Nice. I'm used to sitting in a metal cage, though. I was the gunner on a Bradley Fighting Vehicle."

"Is that like a tank?" Patty asked.

"Pretty much. But lighter and a little faster. Much smaller gun. We could transport troops too." Dolan replied.

McGraw leaped back into the Bronco. He wasn't too wet.

"Anything?" Patty asked.

"Martha got new dentures," he said. "But aside from that, she didn't even know the car was gone or Johnny stopped by."

"Gosh darn it!" Patty exclaimed. "We missed another chance!"

"Wait . . ." Shane said and jumped back out of the vehicle. He went into the garage and knelt next to the motorcycle. He came out and leaped back into the Bronco.

"Well?" Patty asked.

"It's not warm. So who knows?"

"You're getting better, McGraw. So he was here and gone during the night or very early morning."

Patty backed up the Bronco, pulled around, and headed toward the main street. She turned right instead of left.

"Aren't we heading to Peach Springs to speak with the police chief . . . Chief Whatshisname?" Shane asked.

"*Watahomigie!* We will, but I just remembered we need to talk with a certain bartender regarding a false alibi! What's Sam's last name anyway? If he's not at the bar, we should pay a little visit to his home. He may be more involved than only a false alibi!"

"Not sure. I'll radio in and have Jerry look him up," Shane said.

The rain was letting up as she pulled into the empty Blue Ox parking lot. She pulled around the backway and then suddenly slammed on her brakes. Dolan almost flew face-first into the cage.

"Holy Toledo!" Patty exclaimed.

Mohon's blue El Camino was parked next to Kaufmann's white Chevy pickup truck around the rear. She swerved onto the side road and backed the big Bronco up until it was out of sight from the building.

"Forget calling in on the bartender! Get SWAT out here *ASAP*!"

CHAPTER SIXTEEN

Back on Wednesday night, when Johnny Mohon was creeping slowly around the outbuildings of the Kaufmann property, the only thing on his mind was vengeance. The moon was black that night; not even a sliver showed in the sky, so he was invisible, even to the cattle lowing in the distance. Mohon was well acquainted with the ranch. He knew each building and what he could find inside. But first, he entered the slaughter room. He had a plan for Luke and Billy and wanted to use the special knives. Perhaps those knives were too good for them. After pulling one from its sheath and inspecting the perfectly sharp razor blade, he thought of that. Maybe a rusted piece of sheet metal would be more appropriate for carving those two up. But it was the fear he wanted to inflict more than the pain. It was the terror he was after, and it seemed appropriate to use the slaughter knives to evoke such a reaction.

Johnny's younger brother Fred wasn't a perfect man. His mind wasn't balanced. He constantly wrestled with demons from the underworld that twisted his spirit. He gambled. He drank. He spent many nights at the adult detention center on the Hualapai Reservation. But he was never violent, and he never physically harmed another soul.

Fred was easy prey for Staley and Espers. They let him win at the pool table the first three times they played. They didn't gamble for much—drinks at first, then a few dollars here and there. Then they got him confident and reckless, and he started losing. Fifteen hundred big ones. But it wasn't the cash they were after. There had been whispers about his brother's secret hoard of psychedelics, which he supplied to various tribes around the American West and Mexico.

They didn't just want the lousy $1,500 worth to pay off the debt he owed; they wanted the entire supply. Fred eventually let his brother Johnny know what a mess he was in. He also thought Staley and Espers had an accomplice back in Wickenburg who had been behind the idea that got him trapped. This information worried Johnny. His supply of ceremonial psychedelics was no longer safe.

Johnny discussed the situation with the tribal police chief, Elijah Watahomigie. The white man law couldn't help with the mess since much of what Johnny had been doing was illegal. At least according to the letter of the law.

Watahomigie was sympathetic but had no ideas to assist him. He didn't know. Johnny assumed the location of the cavern system was still unknown. He went out of his way to keep his movements secret. He traveled at night when he could, used various vehicles, mainly stayed on backcountry trails, and visited nearly all the ranches in the area to not appear to spend any extra time on Bar-T ground. Of course, the operation would be changing significantly. The caverns could be opened to the public as a state park. Because of this, he attempted to transplant several of the white roots to a new location on the reservation. He was trying to grow them on similar soil that was damp much of the year, along springs that fed the Grand Canyon on tribal lands. Transplanting was a backup plan if the Bar-T didn't reach a formal agreement with the nature conservancy and the state park system. But even still, Johnny didn't trust them since so many past agreements with the whites were not worth the paper they were printed on.

But he wasn't thinking about this while crawling around the Kaufmann Ranch with the knives in his possession. When they killed Fred, everything changed. Johnny was out for blood and would have cut them up in tiny pieces had he found them in the bunkhouse that night. But they'd live another day because Johnny didn't find them when he entered that building. They ran off to Wickenburg and wouldn't return until later that morning.

But after the ceremony—after Johnny and his family burned Fred's body, belongings, and home—the absolute rage waned from his soul. Earlier that day, he spent time in a sweat lodge to purify and heal his spirit. The desire to annihilate the responsible men lessened when he emerged from the heat. Police Chief Watahomigie also convinced him to use the law to bring justice and make things right. However, Johnny wasn't sure how to use the law.

"You will figure out the way," the chief said. "You will make things right."

↔

Inside the Blue Ox Saloon, three men were hanging upside down. John Mohon had thrown lariat ropes over the round log beam spanning the ceiling. He fastened each rope to the brass foot rail along the bar's base after he pulled each of them up so their heads barely cleared the bartop. Those three men were Luke Staley, Billy Espers, and Sam Mills. Johnny did his best to get them to talk throughout the early morning hours. Up to that point, they were sitting on the bartop with hands tied behind their backs, legs crossed, and ankles bound. Propped up against a stool was the sawed-off shotgun he had previously wrested from Sam. He had a small tape recording device on the bar; he had kindly asked each of them to tell their stories about the night someone killed his brother Fred. But they did not talk. So finally, Johnny lost all kindness and patience and roped them up one at a time. While hanging upside down, he told them he'd fantasized about various torture methods.

"My ancestors would stake a man out on the top of a large anthill and pour sticky cactus juice all over his naked body. They would let him agonize in the hot sun, eyelids pinned back, while the fire ants devoured him, one little bite at a time! That was one of my favorites, but as you can see, I do not have an anthill available." He paced between them. "But my next favorite . . ." he started, and pulled the *chalef* knives from his bag, "was when they would string a man onto a post and start cutting. First, they made many tiny incisions across his body. Just small ones because they did not want the man to bleed or die too soon. Then, of course, they'd start pulling out tricks: like rubbing salt in the open wounds, cactus needles under the finger and toenails (before they ripped the nails off completely), and hot coals around his feet. But this was just the caressing stage—the warm-up period of torture. Everything was slow; this needed to last a *long* time. Days." Johnny pressed the flat blade of the knife against each of their faces, one at a time. As Luke Staley twisted his face away, the edge made a small nick across his ear lobe, and a single drop of blood fell to the bartop. "Unfortunately, gentleman, time is not a commodity I have in abundance this morning. So I will skip to the best part. You will like this. My ancestors' last act was to carefully and methodically slice the man's—Wait! You know what, gentleman? Instead of telling you, I will show you! *Show* is so much better than *tell*! Who will volunteer to be first?"

Sam was the weakest link, so Johnny started on him. As he reached for Sam's belt buckle, the young bartender whimpered immediately. Johnny pressed the button to record.

"Stop! Please! I didn't do anything. They told me to say they were here when it all happened. So I did! That's all I know!"

"That is good," Johnny said. "But I am sure you did a little more than that! Did you not?"

He reached for the man's belt buckle again. His face had changed to blood red from being upside down.

"They were gonna give me cash! That's all! When they got the big score!"

"Shut up, idiot!" Luke Staley said from his upended position.

Billy Espers was soft too. He'd be the next to break down. Johnny gently pressed the knife's blade against his thigh and began to slice the denim material of his jeans so that his bare, pink skin was visible through the torn gap.

"I see you are going commando! That will make my job easier!" Johnny said.

"I was there, but I didn't do anything!" Billy shouted. "It's Luke! He's goddamn crazy!"

"Now, what did our Luke here do?" Johnny said and raised the knife again, placing the flat cold blade against his thigh.

"He stabbed your brother! In the gut! Pulled that little stiletto blade out of his pocket and stabbed him!"

"Shut up! Just shut up!" Luke shouted.

"He drove that truck right over him! I couldn't believe it! Why?" he said, his voice starting to break with emotion. "And he yelled to get the girl! Grab the girl! So I pulled her up into the truck. She was sitting with me. She barely fought or anything. She was gentle. The next thing I know, Luke pulls off the highway, comes around to my side, and pulls her out. He grabbed her by the neck and choked her until she was dead! I couldn't believe it! Why? —Why did you do this?"

Johnny lowered Sam and Billy down from the ropes. He assumed Luke would not say a word, so he turned the recorder off. He rewound it and played it for all to hear.

"Means nothing," Luke said.

"Legally? That could be true," Johnny said. "I do not know much about the law. But to me, it means plenty. Also, I am sure that since your friends here did not commit the murders, they will be happy to tell this to the authorities, just as they told this tape recording machine. Should they not?"

The bar's phone rang. Johnny had been expecting it to ring, and he answered it.

"Thank you for calling the world-famous Blue Ox Hair Salon. This is Johnny. How can I help you?"

"Um . . . Is this John Mohon?"

"Yes, it is. How may I be of service to you?"

"This is Deputy Tim Kennedy from the Yavapai County Sheriff's Office. Are Luke Staley and Billy Espers with you?"

"They are."

"Good. I want you to know that I am outside the bar, and our SWAT team has surrounded the building. Everyone needs to come out with hands in the air. Will you do that?"

"Yes. I will bring everyone out. But their hands are tied. I will not untie them."

He hung up the phone and quickly cut Staley down; his head slammed the top of the bar with a thud.

"Oh, sorry about that," Mohon said with contrived compassion.

↔

Patty stood next to the SWAT commander. They had the rear door covered. Two SWAT deputies were around the front. Kennedy put down the commander's car phone and stood alongside Patty. They all tensed up while the door opened, and one by one, the suspects appeared with their hands tied together. Johnny Mohon was last in line.

"Down . . . Down!" The SWAT commander shouted as he approached with his 12-gauge pump-action shotgun pointed at their faces.

"Drop that," he said to Johnny, who had the tape recorder in his hand. He pressed play as he laid it on the gravel parking lot.

"What is that?" Patty asked and walked up to Mohon.

Billy Esper's voice recounted how Staley killed the girl.

"You've got yourself a confession tape!" she said to Johnny Mohon. "You can stand up."

"Thanks. I will"

"Could you play that again?"

While Patty listened to the tape, Kennedy went inside the bar, and McGraw started rummaging through the white Chevy pickup. He found a large leather bag filled with clothing, cash, and two Colt .45 revolvers.

"Looks like stolen items from Kaufmann's place!" McGraw shouted over.

"How did you manage all this?" she asked Mohon. "Tying them up like this."

Johnny responded facetiously: "I snuck up on them, very quiet-like. Only an injun can sneak up on people like that!"

Dolan started coming up from the road and walked over. Patty made him stay back in her Bronco while the action was going on.

"Congratulations!" he said.

"Thanks, kid. Looks like we've got them hooked, and we'll get 'em booked! Special thanks to John Mohon, here."

Another patrol car pulled into the parking lot. It was Deputy Ed Smith—a bulked-up, sandy-haired young man.

"It's Eddie!" Patty said in a friendly yet still patronizing tone. He was the low man in the office, and she liked to mess with him. "Did you run out of tickets to write?"

"My cherries and berries have been flashing plenty, ma'am!"

"Good boy! One of these days I'll have you running down case leads! But you've got to put in your time first," she said and looked at Dolan. "You see, if you join us, you'll give guys like Eddie here a chance!"

Patty turned and asked Johnny Mohon if he'd come down to the division office with her. She needed many items cleared up and wanted his statement. He agreed without any issues.

The SWAT commander had the suspects loaded into the vehicles, one in each patrol car, and read them their rights. Patty yelled to him: "Bring 'em all to Northern Division! I wanna question them before HQ takes over!"

Deputy Kennedy walked out through the rear door of the bar holding a large clear plastic evidence bag. It contained Kaufmann's two *chalef* knives, which he held high for Patty to see.

"You may have to explain those," she said, turning to Mohon. He shrugged.

CHAPTER SEVENTEEN

When Dolan arrived back in Sedona, his aunt was on the phone in her office, so he went onto the back patio and sat on the outdoor couch under the covered porch. It must've rained off and on most of the day; the red rocks were dark as the sandstone was still wet. A misty fog floated around the base of Cathedral Rock in a surreal way. The damp pine and juniper gave the air a pleasant cedar-like smell: clean, fresh, and renewed.

Doc's cat Charlie appeared from the patio's edge and ran to Dolan. But instead of jumping onto the couch, he stopped a few feet shy, sat down on the pavers, and stared with those big round eyes. He was a funny-looking cat.

Doc's glass patio door slid open on her balcony. The cat looked up.

"Hello, Aunt Lauren!"

"Are you staying this time, or will Patty make you run off again?" she asked.

"We brought the suspects in this morning! At least Patty and crew did. It was that guy I told you about, Hualapai Johnny! He had them all tied up at the Blue Ox Saloon in Seligman."

"They killed his brother?"

"Yeah."

"I was just on the phone with Sheriff Grady," she said as she came down the steps.

"Did he fill you in?"

"Yes. Mostly I think. But Grady called me for other reasons."

"Yeah?"

"Look, Dolan, I want you to know that I'm afraid the sheriff may be attempting to use his influence a bit—"

"How so?"

"I'm a little concerned that he's offered you the apartment and schooling for other reasons than only wanting a good recruit. He can be manipulative and scheming."

"I'm still not following you. What does the sheriff want from me?"

"Not from you . . . but me," Doc replied hesitantly. "We had a relationship once, and he said he wants me back. I've told him how I feel! I'm afraid that what I may say or do now will affect you, and I don't like being in that position! I needed you to know."

"You and . . . the sheriff?" Dolan said, wrapping his head around that picture.

"I kept it quiet for the most part."

"Don't get me wrong. I'm not judging you or anything. The sheriff's a good-looking, prominent man. And you're an amazing and gorgeous, *single*, professional woman."

"But it was a mistake," she insisted. "I want you in the loop so that you know the sheriff's motivations may or may not be what they seem."

"I understand. And you don't have to worry about me. You could call ol' Grady back right now and tell him you wouldn't take him back if he were the last man on earth and all that! But please, don't have any worries on my account."

"Perfect. We don't have to say another word!" Doc said, "How about lunch?"

"Well, cat?" Dolan asked, looking down at the funny-looking long hair. "Are you hungry?"

"I'll call down to Red's and see if he's in," Doc said. "He doesn't like to miss a meal either!"

Dolan had a morbid thought as they went into the house. "So when a person dies far away from where they live, how does the family usually get the body back home?"

"Funeral homes have agreements with trucking and airline companies for this. It's a common practice."

"So when they release a body . . ."

"First, it would go to a funeral home for embalming," she said. "Next, the health department would issue a permit; then someone could move the body across state lines."

↔

When they got him in the interview, Luke Staley immediately asked for a lawyer. He was a smallish, thin guy with tight-set eyes and fidgety hands. Patty didn't expect much from him anyway and quickly ended the interview. Next, it was Billy Espers' turn. Espers spilled so much information that Kennedy needed an extra sheet of paper to take notes.

He started by saying the actual murders took him by surprise. He had no idea Staley would snap like that. He couldn't believe it had all happened. It was like a dream or more like a nightmare. He described the events just like on the tape recorder. However, Espers admitted to keeping Fred Mohon's truck hidden near the ranch on the forest land. He and Staley took it from Mohon a few days before the night of the killing. They held it in lieu of payment for the debt until he got them the psychedelic truffles. They told him to meet them at the Tex-Gas parking lot at eight p.m. on Sunday in exchange for the stuff. They would bring his truck. However, the plan was to get information on the location of the entire stash. Convince him to become a partner in the enterprise. Let him know it could be worth tens or hundreds of thousands. But he didn't give up any information on the rest of the stash; he didn't even bring the shipment he stole to hand over. Staley went berserk. He pulled the little stiletto out of his pocket and jabbed him in the gut.

"Who came up with this whole idea anyway? To trap Fred Mohon in debt to get at his brother's supply," Patty asked.

"Luke's girlfriend over in Wickenburg. She knew Fred before, and he told her things. He would get drunk and tell her things. She's the one who let us know about the work over at Kaufmann's place. That's how we found out he needed two ranch hands."

"What's this lady's name?" Patty asked.

"Tina . . . Tina Albright."

"The same Tina that got involved with Kaufmann and drained their joint checking account?" Kennedy asked as they left the interview room and walked toward Patty's desk.

"Yes . . . one and the same," Patty replied, then referring to Kaufmann, "There's no fool like a lonely old fool!"

"Looks like we get to take her down for conspiracy this time!" Kennedy said. "That should make Kaufmann happy!"

"Get an address for her! I pray to God she lives on the north side of Wickenburg in Yavapai County, so I can personally put cuffs on her! Otherwise, call the Maricopa County Sheriff's Office or Wickenburg Police, depending on the jurisdiction."

"Will do!"

"Also, escort Johnny Mohon to the auxiliary interview room so I can get his involvement in all this puzzled out."

↔

When he got to the division office, Johnny Mohon contacted Jimmy Tilley by phone. He let him know what went on that morning at the Blue Ox. Tilley was concerned that the ranch would be susceptible to thieves and curiosity seekers with the caverns being made public and the information regarding the rare truffles leaked out. He would now need to hire 24-hour security personnel at great expense. So Tilley told Johnny that he wanted all the mushroom and fungi material removed from the hillside and cavern openings. He imagined that if he dried them, he could have an enormous supply lasting years for the various tribes while keeping the dried product safely on the Hualapai Reservation. But in any case, he wanted them off the ranch.

"But the mushrooms can grow all over the hillsides, and hidden below ground are the sclerotia. Only the roots and sclerotia near the cavern openings are visible. It would be difficult to remove them and could cause ecological harm. I strongly suggest not being too rash here, my friend," Johnny replied. "I will personally be involved with the section's security and get other tribal members to assist."

"That would be helpful. But I still want the truffle and root material removed. I can no longer risk this interfering with the transfer to the nature conservancy. You know I want to turn the cavern system over to the Arizona State Parks, and it's always the mushroom issue coming up."

"Perhaps you should contact Denson before we do anything hasty," Mohon answered.

Jonas Denson was Tilley's attorney who also assisted the various indigenous tribes with their federal lawsuit involving the ceremonial use of hallucinogens.

"I suppose that would be prudent. I will call Denson today and get his feedback on the matter," Tilley said.

↔

Mohon was getting hot and sweaty, sitting in the tiny room waiting for Detective Malloy. He disliked being cooped up indoors, especially in tight quarters. He took his black hooded sweatshirt off and placed it on the chair. He drank from the water bottle the deputy gave him.

Patty finally entered the room with her clipboard and a pen and apologized for keeping him so long.

"Crazy day," she said.

"Yes," he replied.

"So I want to ask about Sunday night at the Tex-Gas station. You came and carried off your brother's body from the parking lot? You were there all along?"

"Fred came to me. He let me know his mess and the deal he had made with Espers and Staley. He had to pay off gambling debts. He told me that he took the product harvested for the tribes. They convinced him to do this. But he wanted to give it back. He made a terrible mistake. He wanted my advice at this point. So I decided to give him fifteen-hundred cash. To pay off his debt."

"So then you went up there?"

Mohon waved his finger, not yet finished with his story.

"For a minute, I considered letting him give the mushrooms in place of the debt. Just to make them happy and be done with it. But that could be a serious crime. Not to mention I could not allow these redneck white boys to take a sacred item from us, from our people.

Instead, I gave him the cash and drove my brother there. I waited for him around the back and parked inside the old warehouse behind the Tex-Gas. I waited for him and had no reason to believe anything was wrong with the arrangement. He would get his truck back, drive around the rear, and tell me how things went. But it was taking longer than I expected. This worried me. Eventually, I went around the building to check on the situation. I found him spread out on the gravel. So I carried him back to my El Camino. I was not sure if his spirit left him. So I drove to Peach Springs to the medical center. But by the time I was halfway to the Rez, his life was gone, so I brought him home. I placed him on his bed. Then I found the fifteen-hundred cash still in his shirt pocket. He might not have been dead if he handed it over."

"I'm sorry about your brother," Patty said. "You told Chief Watahomigie about these events?"

"I told him nothing," Mohon replied, clearly protecting his friend, the chief. "Later, my family found his body and announced that our brother died in his sleep, and they would carry out a funeral ceremony at his home, like the old way."

"And instead of contacting your tribal police or us, you took matters into your own hands to get a confession out of them?"

"I wanted to kill them. I wanted to destroy those two. But that was not what the Great Spirit intended, so I came to my senses. I wanted to confront them. To get the truth."

"Espers and Mills claim that you threatened them with those knives. That you were planning harm."

"No comment," Mohon said.

"And the knives? Did you break into the building at the Kaufmann Ranch?" she asked.

"I have nothing to say," he replied. "Don't make me call my lawyer. I do not like him."

Patty tried not to laugh. She tossed her clipboard over to the empty chair.

"Now I'm going off the record . . ." she said. "Tell me what happened at that ranch in 1975 . . . I heard you were around then."

"You mean the UFOs?" Mohon said with a partial grin.

"Yes."

"Off the record?"

"As I said," Patty responded.

"Well, it all happened when the area got much rain for several weeks. It was rainy or damp all the time. Not like the usual weather. So one of the ranch hands—Tom Plinkin—went out to check on the fencing a few sections south. He never returned, but his horse did with an empty saddle. There was a search in the area where he was working and along the trail, but we found no trace. Remember, this is a big ranch. Twenty thousand acres. There was standing water all over. Hard to track. When everyone else gave up, I went scouting on my own in different, more rugged areas. I ended up at one of the more wild sections of the ranch. This ground was not very good for ranching but seemed like a good place for a man to be lost. I stayed out searching. That is when I saw him crawling through the brush. He was picking mushrooms when I came up to him. All the recent rain caused the mushrooms to sprout again in the undergrowth. I turned my flashlight onto Tom, and he got jumpy and crawled into a narrow opening in the hillside. I thought it was a cave. I followed him inside. He had a small fire burning that lit up the chamber. It was the first time I entered the caverns, and I could not believe my eyes. It was like a whole new world—a secret world. The rains must have caused the earth to open and expose the entrance, which was how Tom found it. It was a miracle. My ancestors talked of such a place. They discovered a mystical place on their spirit walks but never found it again. The tribe assumed the ancient talk referred to the Grand Canyon Caverns, now well-known near Peach Springs. But others disagreed and insisted there was another place too, and it was the gateway from heaven to hell—a mystical place where shamans came to know the Great Spirit and could speak with demons and the dead. When I entered, I thought this could be that place. I recognized drawings on the walls and ancient symbols from other sacred settings. Other drawings looked like mushrooms. I had never seen anything like that. Tom was sitting by the fire and did not even notice I was there. He ate the mushrooms, and I watched him. I understood what they were right away. This cavern was the place where the shamans had been. They must've used mushrooms in ancient times. So being curious, I, too, tried the mushrooms. And that was the day I found religion. I communicated with the dead and the ancient spirits. I could see and hear the demons. The shamans allowed me to see the hidden world that others could not see. So I sat and watched the story unfold. As time passed, the fire grew dim and started to burn out. I aimed my flashlight toward the dim fire and lit Tom's face. He looked terrified. His face was frozen, his eyes were wide, and he did not blink. I called out his name, but he did not move. He was paralyzed by fear or perhaps the power of the mushroom. I am not sure. He was sitting naked. He had taken off his clothes and burned his shirt in the fire. I flashed the light in his face again, and he seemed to move a little. He seemed to thaw from his frozen state. Then suddenly, he leaped at me like a cougar on prey. He ran right through me, and I watched him go. I stayed in the cavern the rest of the night. I did not want to leave. But eventually, the next day, I returned to the ranch house. I heard Plinkin's story of the great light beaming down from the UFO. He thought an unknown force swallowed him and spit him out a few days later. He did not know what had happened to him. He did not remember anything."

"Your flashlight? That was the light," Patty said.

"Possibly. But I was thankful that Plinkin remembered nothing about the place. So I went back and covered up any tracks leading to the cavern, hoping that would prevent anyone else from investigating the area. I also found where the fence wire was lifted high enough that the smaller livestock could slip underneath. I believe those young steers got under the fence to eat the mushrooms.

Something drew them in any way. I'm not sure what else it was. So I followed up around the north section of the hill. Now, remember, this is rugged ground. I had only been in that section to hunt lions. It was ground only a lion would call home—thick with brush and rugged and dangerous. I went around the hill, and I found a sinkhole and fissure. Again the rains must have caused this. A crack in the ground fell straight down into the earth. I held a juniper branch to avoid falling in, leaned over, and shined my light. The livestock must have fallen into the fissure, and the earth swallowed them up."

"Mystery solved?" Patty queried.

"I would say so."

"You know, this is all pretty crazy. I wouldn't have believed a word you said had one of my deputies not been out there today with Jimmy Tilley."

"I do not expect you to believe it. But you asked."

"I heard many other items went missing. Things from all over the ranch disappeared. Any explanation on that?"

"No. We assumed it was a thief or a prankster. We never found the stolen items."

"So Tom Plinkin never remembered about the cavern? Whatever happened to him?"

"He drifted to other ranches as many cowboys do. I heard he was in Wyoming. Whether he ever remembered anything, I do not know."

"I'd like to visit these caverns!" Patty said.

"That may be possible."

Patty picked up her clipboard, looked over what she wrote, and asked: "So help me understand these truffles. Are they a dehydrated version of the mushroom?"

"I will tell you," he started. "Soon, the mushrooms all dried up and disappeared. That is when I noticed what was growing in the ground beneath them—the mass of white roots and truffles. They grow like a potato would grow in the ground beneath their green plant above. They are a food store during the dry seasons—a dormant state. These are what scientists call sclerotia. They contain the chemical psilocybin, which, you may know, is a hallucinogen that is also in the magic mushroom. For some reason, this variety of mushroom has potent truffles. Also, these are extremely rare, from what I can tell. I do not think they exist anywhere else. So I feel these mushrooms and truffles are sacred and should only be used by native peoples during rituals and for healing and medicinal purposes. I strongly believe they belong to my people alone. Indigenous people. The same with peyote. These are Holy Sacraments. We believe that consuming peyote and other traditional hallucinogenic compounds is legal under the American Indian Religious Freedom Act for use in ceremonies and healing."

"We think so, too," Patty said. "I've discussed this with the sheriff and the county attorney. They have no issue with the religious use of these plants or potions; however, no written law exists, so the next sheriff or county attorney may not agree. Also, the problem is when they end up in the hands of drug traffickers, dealers, and recreational users. Then we have to treat them like any other dangerous drug. For example, as a class four felony for possession or a class two felony for transportation or sale. But, of course, that is what we would've been dealing with had your brother handed over that stolen package like they were expecting. But you already know this."

"Yes . . . true," Johnny said. "Members of several tribes have brought lawsuits at the federal level to protect our legitimate rights. We believe an amendment will be made to the Religious Freedom Act to codify such rights so we can continue their use without fear of prosecution."

"Well, thank you, Mr. Mohon. This discussion has been fascinating. But truthfully, I'm disappointed no UFOs or aliens were part of your story!" She lifted her clipboard and rose from her chair. "How about lunch? We may get Chinese take-out. You want to eat before I have a deputy take you back to your car?"

"I have nothing against eating Chinese," Johnny said with a grin.

CHAPTER EIGHTEEN

It was the weekend, so Doc didn't have much work. She'd get an occasional call from one of her clients, but typically Saturdays and Sundays were relatively carefree. So Red nudged her to go bowling.

"I won't even make you eat a chili dog!" Red said. "But I love those chili dogs!"

Doc begrudgingly agreed, and they headed to the bowling alley. Dolan drove Red's Lincoln.

They checked out their bowling shoes, and each picked out a ball—Dolan helped his aunt find a nice ten-pounder that fit her slender fingers. They went to their lane and started a game. Red, standing straight and eyeing the pins, proceeded to throw a strike right down the center of the lane.

"What the hell!" Dolan shouted. "Am I gonna get beat by an eighty-year-old?"

Red laughed. Then he told Doc not to get too close to the foul line on the lane, or she could slip.

"Just throw the ball down that way," Red said to her, pointing to the bottom of the lane.

Doc released the ball; it made a loud thump and rolled painfully slow toward the pins. Finally, the ball miraculously hit the number one pin, and each of the other pins started tipping and falling, slowly, one by one, until none stood.

"Yay!" Doc yelled. "Strike!"

"Holy smokes!" Red said. "Good job Doc!"

"Nice, Aunt Lauren! Now I have pressure on me!" Dolan yelled.

Dolan approached the lane and raised his ball; his right bicep flexed into a bulge. His technique was perfect, and the ball made almost no noise as it was delivered quickly down the lane with an immense spin. It curved to the left, just at the last moment as he expected, but instead of hitting the pocket off the number one pin, it slid prematurely, missed altogether, and ended in the gutter. He dropped his head down.

"I knew this would happen!" he shouted to them.

"Better luck next time, kid!" Doc yelled.

His second ball looked very much the same. Except for this time, hitting the sweet spot, all the pins loudly crashed in unison.

"Your strike is a spare!" Red yelled. "But just as pretty to watch."

By the time they finished the game, the world order was back in alignment. Dolan bowled a 193, Red bowled a 131, and Doc more than likely bowled about 40, but they stopped keeping track after she handed them verbal instructions not to. She did enjoy a chili dog with the guys. They sat at a table near the bar.

"I'm afraid someone will catch me eating this!" Doc said, with big eyes, as she took another bite of the sloppy dog, with mustard, chili, and onions rolling off. "That makes me a hypocrite!"

"Your health-crazed vegan millionaire clients ain't gonna be hanging around this smoke-filled bowling parlor," Red said. "So enjoy that unwholesome tube steak!"

"I must admit, Red, this thing is as good as the coney dogs we have around Detroit! And that's saying something," Dolan said.

"I wouldn't lie to you, kid!"

"I'll eat your french fries too if you leave any!" Doc said to Red.

"You created a monster," Dolan said, looking at Red.

"Son of a bitch!" Red exclaimed, "Is the chocolate chip cookie lady coming at us?—Hide me!"

Red lifted the bar menu off the table and covered his face, pretending to read. Dolan and his aunt were laughing. His ever-present cowboy hat was all that was visible atop the menu.

"His eyes are so bad he can't drive, but he can see the cookie lady across the way!" Doc said and grabbed a few more french fries off his plate while he hid behind the menu.

"The coast is clear, Red," Dolan said. "She went into the gift shop!"

"My lord," he said. "Let's get the hell outta here!"

They walked out to the parking lot and were still ribbing old Red.

"What's wrong with her cookies anyway?" Doc asked.

"She's a three-time widow, and no sooner than the latest victim drops dead, she's out looking for her next! And she's one whale of a woman. Have you ever seen her walking from behind? Her rump looks like two pigs wrestling in a gunny sack!"

"I like her cookies," Dolan said. "Tasty!"

"I'll tell her that next time she comes around!" Red yelled back at him.

"Between all your cookies and chili dogs," Doc started, "you should be ready for a nice healthy fish and vegetable dinner tomorrow! Because that's what I'm making. Also, how about a hike in the morning?"

"Well, I darn know you ain't talking to me about hiking!" Red said. "But I'll eat your fish and vegetables."

On the ride home, Red told a few old stories. He must've been thinking about his wife; all the stories related to her in some respect. Betsy died in 1968. He still missed her.

↔

The trip to Wickenburg wasn't as long and tedious as Patty had expected. She drove the Bronco, and Deputy Kennedy sat shotgun. They were to meet two other deputies from the local Wickenburg area substation. Tina Albright's address was north of Wickenburg in Yavapai County. It was a low-elevation ranch country; saguaro and brittlebush dotted the landscape with sparse grasses and bare, sandy soil. Tina was shacking up with another older man, living in his big house on a few acres of ground. She made a habit of getting what she wanted from men. From the older men, she got money, comforts, and an easy life; the young men gave her excitement and all the other things a spirited woman craved and yearned for.

"Every girl and woman I've ever known named Tina has been bad news!" Kennedy said to Patty as they eyed the home's front door from the Bronco. Deputy Flanagan and

Deputy Martinez were heading around back to get staked out if she tried to flee. They waited for the deputies to be in position before approaching the home.

"I don't recall ever knowing a pleasant Tina either," Patty replied as they started walking toward the front. "I'll have to think about this. There must be one somewhere, right?"

The car Tina had been driving—a red 1990 Mazda Miata convertible—was parked in the horseshoe driveway, so they expected her to be home. They were not expecting the front door to swing open before they were even on the porch and for Tina Albright to be waiting with a nickel-plated over/under shotgun from her rich old man's fancy gun collection. But that's what happened, and the business end of the shotgun was pointed straight out. Kennedy didn't have his gun drawn, only his Miranda card. Kennedy pulled it out and was ready to read the lines during the arrest. But he inadvertently dropped the card and kept his hands high. Patty also had her hands raised. In addition to the over/under, they could see the pearl handle of a six-gun stuck above her belt.

"Don't do this!" Patty yelled. "Put the gun down!"

Tina was an attractive woman. She had long and bountiful brown hair with frosted highlights. However, her pretty heart-shaped face expressed intense, maniacal anger.

In front of the porch were two large stone pillars, columns to each side, which gave the entryway an impressive appearance but served a better and more practical purpose at present. Patty and Kennedy each stepped behind their respective pillars for cover. As they did, Tina discharged her weapon, and the impact of the shot exploded along the stone edge where Kennedy took refuge. He and Patty pulled out their handguns and were ready for engagement. Kennedy looked over to Patty and signaled that he'd jump around the right side of his pillar to take a shot. She shook her head no, but after Kennedy shrugged, wondering what she wanted to do, she got on the same page and signaled back with a whirlybird finger in the air. She'd also go around the far side of her stone column. So they both leaned around, Kennedy from the right and Patty from the left, and concurrently opened fire on Tina Albright. Martinez and Flanagan made it up front in time to see Tina collapse onto the flagstone porch.

"Stupid girl!—Why?" Patty yelled with emotion. "I didn't want this!"

Tina Albright was already deceased when the Wickenburg fire and ambulance service arrived. Patty was distraught. In all her years of service, she had never discharged her firearm, let alone take a life. Patty started to second-guess herself.

"We did what we had to do," Kennedy said to her. "She did this to herself! We had no choice."

"I was so gung-ho to slap those cuffs on her!" Patty said. "I didn't want this!"

The detective wiped away tears as she slowly drank from the bottle of water someone handed her. Kennedy looked at her as if wanting to say more. Maybe something calming or reassuring or comforting. But he turned his head down and bit his lip. He said nothing.

↔

"So aside from Patty, who else from the Northern Division should we invite to the party?" Doc asked Dolan as she sat at the kitchen table with her paper pad and pen. "How about everyone?"

"May as well," Dolan replied. "Of course, I'm sure at least two of the deputies will be on duty, so they won't be able to come."

"Right, so I'll leave it up to Patty. I'll tell her to invite whoever isn't working that day."

Dolan was putting the dirty lunch plates into the dishwasher. Doc had made a poached salmon and vegetable platter, and now they were talking about putting together an end-of-summer/fall barbecue for the following weekend. Red retreated to the living room and rested in the leather reclining chair. He was sleeping off Doc's lunch. Charlie was staring at him from the floor, looking like he wanted to join him.

"So, how much beer and wine do you think I should buy?" Dolan asked.

"I'm thinking twenty to thirty people."

"Well, if it were my Army buddies, we'd be talking kegs, not cases."

"Most of these folks will be wine drinkers. I have many bottles down in the cellar. So three or four cases of beer. Your choice what kind."

"If your fancy guests will be drinking wine, I'll just get Coors and Budweiser for us common folk," Dolan replied with a grin.

"I'm doing this barbeque for you mostly. A nice send-off. So you can get fancy beer if you like. I'm buying!"

"I don't even know what fancy beer is! In Michigan, we drink Canadian beer if we're feeling special. Labatt's, maybe! The snobs drink Heineken. I suppose, in Arizona, it would be a special *cerveza*, like Modelo Negro or Corona. Imports are the fancy stuff."

"Yeah, get Mexican *cerveza* and Heineken. My fancy friends may drink that. Especially the snobs!"

"What's all this beer talk?" Red's voice came from the living room. He was awakened from his *siesta*.

"We're figuring out what to buy for Dolan's send-off party next weekend," Doc said.

"Next weekend? Like in six or seven days? That's almost green banana territory for me. But you know I don't buy green bananas!"

"Says the guy who'll live to be a hundred!" Dolan chimed in.

"Thank you, son. I appreciate that."

The telephone rang, so Doc went into her office to answer it. Dolan went over to Red in the living room. He found the cat and Red in the middle of a staredown.

"This damn cat doesn't blink!"

"His eyes are as big as an owl's . . . He's one weird-looking cat," Dolan said. "Where the heck did my aunt find this thing?"

"He showed up one day at that back glass door. She let him in; he hasn't left the property since."

"Hey, you did the same thing!" Dolan said to Red, laughing.

"You son-of-a . . . !" Red shouted and threw a pillow from the chair at him. "When did Doc say you were leaving? You're gettin' too big for your britches!"

"After next weekend. But you'll miss me!"

"You know, kid . . . I never took you to any bull riding or rodeo!" Red remembered. "When are you coming back?"

"I'm hoping soon. When's the next time the bulls will be around?"

"December, down in Cave Creek, I think."

"Well, I better be back by then!"

"Sounds good! We'll go if I'm still bucking and kicking at that time. You know—green bananas and all."

Dolan laughed and turned as his aunt came into the room. She looked upset.

"That was Patty on the phone," she said. "She's not doing well."

"What happened?" Dolan asked.

"She and Deputy Kennedy had a shoot-out with Luke Staley's girlfriend in Wickenburg . . . Tina Albright."

"Damn. Are Patty and Kennedy okay?"

"She's shaken up pretty bad. They didn't get hit. They're fine. But they killed Tina Albright."

The room went silent. Red nodded his head. Doc flopped down into the chair next to him, and Charlie immediately jumped onto her lap.

Dolan almost forgot that it was part of the job and was a possibility every day. To kill or be killed. He could see his uncle's portrait from the corner of his eye. That's what Doc and Red were feeling—living that day over. James Earl Donahue was locked up for life, having gunned down his uncle in the street without cause. He did a plea deal to avoid a trial and the death penalty. He said he shot him for no particular reason; he looked like a nice target. Of course, the powers that be didn't believe his story. It seemed like a hit job. But through all the investigative work, the man-hours, they could never connect any dots to make it any more than it was: a random act of violence. He shot down a hero for no reason at all. He smashed up Doc and Red's world and darkened it for countless others.

"Maybe having the barbeque and inviting Patty and the deputies is not such a good idea," Dolan said, breaking the silence.

"That's what I said to Patty," Doc started, "but she immediately said she wanted to come. And she would drag Kennedy along and Deputy McGraw too."

"I can't understand it!" Red said. "That pretty little blonde girl and that Hualapai Indian both get killed . . . for what? Now this Tina woman? It's all damn senseless."

Dolan thought about that Sunday night at the Blue Ox when she first walked through the door, and he popped up out of his bar seat, looking to help the pretty damsel in distress. If only he'd known. All he did was get her aspirin. Within an hour, she'd be dead. The guys responsible were kicking back on a Sunday night playing pool. Even they didn't know it would happen.

Their moods had soured. Truthfully it shouldn't have bothered them as much as all that. Tina Albright was in it just as deep as the other two. It was her idea and conspiracy that got the ball rolling. But it was Patty that was suffering. Doc felt it the most, and they could feel it from Doc. It was a daisy chain of emotions passing from one being to the next. Empathy is a mysterious thing. To feel what another person feels and to understand it. That's what being human is all about.

Dolan made his decision long ago. He wanted to help people; he knew of no other way. He wanted to serve and protect. It was his calling. That would be his life's work. The war messed with his head, and he was convinced he had to think through things, think through the decision to become a cop. But that was just a momentary setback. After working with Patty and the others, he remembered again. He remembered the man he wanted to become.

He nodded and grinned as he turned toward the portrait of his uncle. It was only a plain canvas hung by a nail—no fancy gilded frame or adornment. It depicted a tough, gritty young man with a cowboy hat and a big Wyatt Earp mustache. He had an odd smile—a partial grin. His genuine smile was big and wide.

That's how Dolan remembered his face. He always had a big smile, no matter how bleak the world looked in front of him. The canvas showed a phony smile. Doc must've had him pose this way to look respectable or maybe enigmatic. But he was neither. He was just an honest, rugged cowboy ready to give away his last dying breath at a moment's notice for next to nothing in return. A genuine, bonafide specimen of a human being—*a real goddamn man*. A real hero.

So Dolan would be a cop too. Just like his idol. No doubt about it. He would make Harry proud. *He had to.*

BOOK TWO

An Amish Autumn

☒

CHAPTER NINETEEN

Josie Jane Yoder was the middle child of many. She had three older siblings and three younger ones. There were seven children altogether. Her sister Hannah was eleven months older, and her two brothers, Caleb and Jacob, were twenty and twenty-two. The family lived on a small dairy farm east of Shawneetauka, Indiana, in LaGrange County. Hannah was also employed at the Red Barn Cafe in town and had been since she was sixteen—starting as a dishwasher, then a food-prep worker, then the salad bar attendant, and more recently, as a full-time waitress.

She learned about Josie Jane's sketch at the Red Barn. Bob and Millie Smythe, who'd been regulars at the restaurant for years, approached her and said a picture of a girl on television resembled her sister. After the lunch rush, she went to the local police station to inquire. They just received posters from the Indiana State Police and were preparing to put them up around town. Hannah gasped and covered her mouth when she saw the sketch of the girl on the paper. The image bore a strong resemblance to her sister. When the Shawneetauka Police contacted the Yavapai County Sheriff and found out that their Jane Doe had been called Josie by two witnesses and was hitchhiking to Shawneetauka—according to trucker Billy Baker—it was most likely confirmed. Shawneetauka police would also send over dental records for maximum certainty (most Amish never go to the dentist, but Hannah was sure that Josie had a cavity filled and X-rays taken at Dr. Ludwig's office in town).

Later that day, Hannah broke the news to the family. Her mother, still taking down the wash from the outdoor clothesline, was calm and quiet after, and Hannah almost wanted to tell her again to ensure she understood adequately.

"I will gather the *kinder*," her mother replied with little emotion.

Hannah went to the dairy barn where her father and Caleb were supposed to be working on the afternoon milking. Her brother dumped the last milk from the pumping containers into the stainless steel storage tank. The black and white Holsteins were looking on.

"Where is *Dat*?" Hannah asked.

"Lena is sick, so he went to the phone shack to call the vet," Caleb replied.

Lena was one of their problem cows. She was stubborn and fitful when it came to milk production. But that day, she was shaking and had trouble standing.

"But what is wrong with *you*, Hannah?" Caleb asked.

She was strong up to that point. Hannah barely cried at the police station. But her strength was all but gone now, and her eyes welled as she stroked Lena on her back. She didn't look at Caleb.

"The vet said she may be getting the milk fever," their father announced as he came back into the dairy. "We will need to give her more calcium. If that doesn't help, he will come by."

Hannah pressed her face against the cow, visibly emotional.

"There is no reason to fuss now, Hannah. She should be fine," her father said.

Caleb had a perplexed look and walked over to Hannah and the cow. She looked up at him and said: "Josie is gone."

Her father and brother didn't understand. She'd been gone for months. Her father put his hand on her head, on her white prayer *kapp*, like he did when she was a little girl.

"She died in Arizona," she said through tears. "Someone killed her . . . Josie was coming back home!"

Her father fell to his knees next to Hannah. The news was a hard blow that he could never have expected. He held his daughter's hand, and Caleb held her other.

"Now, Hannah," her father started saying while attempting to hide his heartache and shock, "please tell us everything. Who told you this? Can we be sure this is true?"

Hannah stood up and wiped the tears from her eyes. She looked at her father and told him about her customers, Mr. and Mrs. Smythe, what they said about the sketch, everything that happened at the police station in Shawneetauka, and her conversation with the sheriff's deputy in Arizona.

"It is *Gottes Wille*," their father said as they all came together to form a little circle. He had tears coming down his rosy cheeks. None of the family ever saw such emotion from their father. "Let us pray to the glory of *Gotte*. Let's pray that our Josie is with him now."

Their mother and the three younger children came down from the house. Little Rachel and Anna entered the dairy first, and Aaron, who was eleven, walked in with his mother. Only Jacob, the oldest son, wasn't present as he was still at his job at the RV factory. All the others looked at their father as he spoke and led a prayer. When he stood, he looked over at his youngest son.

"Aaron," he said, "please take Rachel and Anna and go feed the calves."

They fed the new calves with a bottle, and the girls loved that job. As they ran to follow their brother, the white strings from their *kapps* dangled and bounced around their teary-eyed faces.

"*Dat*, the police would like you to come in and talk," Hannah said to her father. "I think they want your permission to send the dentist records to Arizona."

"*Jah*, I understand," he said, turning to his son. "Caleb, get Lena's calcium and bring the buggy around. I'll sit with *Mamm* for a minute before we leave."

He held his wife's hand, and they walked to the bench outside the dairy. Hannah stayed with Lena and stroked her back while waiting for Caleb to return with the medicine.

↔

Hannah, too, considered going off with Josie Jane earlier in the year. But unlike Josie—who had a quiet disdain for their mother, their way of life, the bishop, all the rules, and almost every aspect of Amish living—Hannah loved her family and the life they led. However, she did have a curiosity and a desire to enjoy the freedoms of life that the *Englischers* had. But, unlike Josie, she had a great fear of the unknown, which counteracted her curiosity and desires. So she may have thought of leaving with Josie, but it was only a fleeting and momentary thought, which vanished when the fear took hold of her senses.

Hannah and her sister were so different. Before working together at the Red Barn Cafe, they attended the same small, white-painted schoolhouse until the eighth grade, slept in the same bedroom at home, and sat shoulder to shoulder on the same pine bench at church every other Sunday. They were grown from the same stock. But all this sameness made no difference. Josie was still Josie.

Hannah was a year older but spent her rumspringa years less "running and jumping around" and more working and spending time with her family and extended family—along with traditional group singing after church and the occasional buggy ride with a suitor. Josie also got a job at the Red Barn when she turned sixteen, but the similarity of their experiences ended there: Josie preferred fast cars to slow buggy rides and rock concerts to Sunday night *singeon*. The family knew little about her interaction with *Englischers*, aside from what she told Hannah. But eventually, there were murmurings and whispers in the community and even a serious talk from the bishop before church one Sunday. The bishop never spoke with the parents about any other Yoder family member. Just Josie. It was the next day that she left.

Another waitress at the Red Barn, an English girl named Danielle, who was friends with Hannah and Josie, met up with them at the thrift store in town. Josie picked out clothes to buy. When Josie and Danielle drove off towards Middlebury, where Josie would catch her first Greyhound bus to California, Hannah cried as she walked back to the Red Barn Cafe. Josie was gone, and she'd miss her sister.

↔

Caleb and her father went off to town to the police station, and Hannah helped her mother with the table and the dinner for the rest of them. Jacob wouldn't be home until later, and his mother put aside a heaping of chicken and noodle casserole for him like she normally did, plus two extra servings, this time for their father and Caleb. The rest of them barely ate anything. Even Aaron, who usually had a voracious appetite, ate scantly. Consequently, her mother put all the servings back into the casserole dish to warm up for later.

Hannah helped her mother clean the dishes, but neither spoke a word. Afterward, the girls went off to the quilting room, and Aaron went to the neighboring farm to play basketball with his friend Samuel. Hannah liked working on the quilts with her mother. While quilting, she felt relaxed. The quiet harmony of the work helped her feel safe and comfortable.

Rachel and Anna helped for a while, then went to play. When Hannah and her mother were alone, Hannah periodically looked over at her mother to see if any emotion developed on her face, like she was waiting for tears to form in her mother's eyes. But none came. None came earlier when she first told her the news, and none came when she sat with their father on the bench outside the dairy. Josie secretly said many times that their mother disliked her, maybe even despised her, but Hannah could never believe such a thing. *How could a mother hate her child?*

So every time she glanced at her mother and saw no more emotion on her face than usual, it upset her. She wanted to say or ask something about Josie to see if her frigid expression would change. Hannah never wanted to think unpleasant thoughts about her mother, but that's what happened.

"*Mamm*, do you think the police will help arrange *her* return? Her body, I mean, for a funeral?"

Her mother looked up, continued to stitch, and replied: "Your *dat* will have to speak with the bishop about that."

"The bishop?"

"He may not allow a traditional funeral."

Hannah became angry. The bishop denying her sister a traditional funeral and her mother merely admitting the fact with no emotion, no considerations of her own, sickened her. Hannah was disappointed with her mother, but she held her tongue to avoid saying anything she could regret later. She stitched for a few more minutes, then excused herself and went outside to the vegetable garden. The girls followed. A little light remained in the day, maybe fifteen minutes more, and Hannah went through and picked the last of the red tomatoes and placed them in the bucket. The girls ran barefoot through the dirt rows and picked a few she missed. The first frost would come soon, and the family had already done most of the year's vegetable picking and canning.

Rachel and Anna ran up and down the adjacent rows of dried corn stalks. Just like her and Josie at that age—without a care in the world. Hannah wanted to snap her fingers and be six years old again.

They could hear the clippety-clop sound of a horse and buggy coming up the lane. Rosie, their chestnut mare, was returning with Caleb and their father. Rachel and Anna ran over toward the carriage shed to welcome them home. Hannah stood in the garden and stared into the distance; the orange and pink clouds glowed from the sunset. She felt strange. She wasn't angry anymore, just low and gloomy. It was as if the veneer of her perfect little world was peeling; underneath, nothing was as it seemed. She disliked what she saw and felt. Tears developed in her eyes again, and she slowly and hesitantly walked up to the house.

CHAPTER TWENTY

Danielle picked up Hannah in the morning, and they headed to work.

"Are you okay?" she asked Hannah as they drove toward town in Danielle's silver Oldsmobile. "You're so strong for wanting to go to work after this."

"I didn't cry yet this morning . . . so I'm better," she replied quietly. "And I have to work. I think it will help me. Doing my normal thing."

"I'm very sorry for you and your family."

"*Denki* . . . thanks. My father took it hard. And my brothers."

"And your mom?" Danielle asked.

"I got angry with my *mamm* last night. She acted as if nothing had happened. She showed no emotion. Nothing."

"Everyone grieves differently, I suppose. And is it true your people don't show much emotion?"

"Maybe in public. But this was my mother and me alone. She had no grief at all."

"From what Josie told me, they didn't get along," Danielle said.

"I guess I'm in my own little world because I never noticed. Josie did say that *Mamm* disliked her. But to me, our mother seemed to treat everyone the same. Also, I knew gossip about Josie was going around, but I didn't want to hear any of it. I didn't ever want to hear anything bad about my sister. She would have told me if she wanted me to know her problems. I mean . . . I know something happened with Noah Miller, the bishop's son. Josie told me she didn't want to see him again, but she never said why."

"Yes, all the horrible Shawnee town gossip. I know it's worse for your people. Gossip can get you into a lot of trouble with the community," Danielle said as she turned onto Van Buren Street.

"Josie never told me what people were saying about her. Instead, she implied it was bad but mostly untrue. But it never got to my ears, nor would I have listened anyway."

"I think Noah Miller was behind all the lies going around!" Danielle suggested.

"That makes sense," Hannah replied. "Of course, everyone would believe the bishop's son. Including Bishop Miller and my mother."

They pulled around the back of the Red Barn Cafe and sat in the car for a minute longer. It was a cloudy but warm morning, and a few raindrops fell onto the windshield.

"I shouldn't have said that about the bishop and his son," Hannah mentioned quietly. "I've been angry . . . At my *mamm*, the bishop, the people responsible for Josie's death. I know I'm supposed to forgive. That's what *we* do. But it's hard to think about forgiveness at this point. I go from angry to sad when I think about my sister and how much I've missed her. I've never felt like this."

"Well, talking helps," Danielle said.

"*Jah*, I'm glad I can talk to you," Hannah replied. "I don't think I could talk with anyone else. I have hundreds of people I can talk to.

Family, cousins, and so many in our community, and I do talk with them. But, with you, I can *really* talk."

"I'm here for you," Danielle said. "Almost every day, nine to five!"

"*Denki* . . . Oh, and here," Hannah replied, pulling cash from her little purse. "Gas money."

"Next time when I fill up, I might let you pay. You know I drive right past your farm anyway! So it's not like you cost me extra!"

"Are you sure?"

"I also know that you give most of your tips and earnings to your family, and you barely have two nickels to rub together. So keep your money." Danielle scrunched her face up with a playful seriousness.

They left the car and headed through the delivery entrance at the rear of the restaurant.

"I did want to ask you if I should go to the police station and tell them what I know about your sister," Danielle said. "Like why she went to Los Angeles and who she may have been with. I guess what I'm saying is, do you think they need to know about the people she lived with? Could they have had anything to do with her death?"

"Did you speak with her?" Hannah asked with a surprised look. "I don't understand."

"She called me a couple of weeks ago and said she was thinking of coming home. She said she didn't want anyone to know—not to tell anyone. So I didn't," Danielle said. "So anyway, when she first went out to stay with Sara Wilcox, she wasn't just staying with Sara. They were living with a bunch of guys from a rock band. Josie and the group's singer—a guy named Lance—ended up a couple. That's why I'm wondering if the police need to know about this guy and his bandmates."

"I don't know. The police said she was in the wrong place at the wrong time. She was a bystander. It couldn't have anything to do with her life in California. But if you think you need to talk to the police, you should." Hannah shook her head. She was disappointed that Danielle kept this from her.

Danielle's eyes dropped. "I'm sorry, Hannah, but you've told me you didn't want to hear anything bad about her. And Josie told me not to tell anyone anything. So I was between a rock and a hard place. I hope you can understand."

"No, no, don't worry. I understand. But . . ." Hannah started and paused, "I think we should have a good, long talk on the way home tonight. I think it's time I heard everything."

It was a busy day at the restaurant. Tourists filled up Hannah's section, even during the slow period between two and three in the afternoon. She hardly had time to stock the salad bar, but thankfully Mindy, the owner, had been there often and helped out too. Mindy mentioned to Hannah that she could take time off if needed. Hannah assured her that working and keeping busy was what she needed. Mindy was quietly relieved, as business was booming lately, and she didn't have anyone else to cover.

After the two evening shift waitresses arrived, Danielle and Hannah cleaned up their areas and hit the road. They stopped at the police station and spoke with Marshall Bill Platt and Deputy Jim Pickett. They were the officers that sat with Hannah the previous day and showed her the sketch of her sister.

Danielle explained to them about her call from Josie. She also explained how Josie went to California to meet up with her friends who had left the previous week. Her friend Sara and guys from a local band. They went to Los Angeles.

The marshall said it'd be best to contact the Yavapai County Sheriff's office and let them hear from Danielle. He acted confident it wasn't essential information, but the sheriff's office could decide. So he put his phone on speaker and dialed. Deputy Tim Kennedy took the call from the Shawneetauka Police. Kennedy told Bill he was glad he called because he intended to contact them before going home for the day. Kennedy wanted to let them know they had the suspects in custody, and the victim's family could rest easy knowing there'd be justice.

Platt picked up the handset and clicked the speaker off. He mentioned Josie's California connection to Kennedy, exchanged a few more words, said "I see" a few times, and then hung up.

"So, as you must've heard, it seems like it's all wrapped up in Arizona," Marshall Platt said to the young ladies. "They have the suspects in custody—they are locals—so the deputy said no worries about your California information."

"Thank you . . ." Hannah said quietly.

"I'm sorry about all this," the marshall said.

Danielle put her arm around Hannah's shoulder. She became upset once again with the news.

"Miss Yoder, we gave your father the phone number to the town's Amish Services Department. I am sure they'll assist you with the transportation and final arrangements for the body," the marshall said. "Here is their card if you want to speak with them directly about anything. They are there to help."

"Also, we electronically sent the dental images this morning to the Arizona lab. Your father gave permission last evening," Deputy Jim Pickett added.

Hannah nodded and accepted the business card. They both thanked the officers and then left the police station. As they got to Danielle's car, Hannah said: "Josie and this *Englisch* singer, Lance, were a couple out in California?"

"Yeah. For a time."

While sitting in the parking lot of the police station and on the ride home, Danielle began to tell Hannah everything she knew about her sister—from gossip to the facts. At least the facts that she got straight from Josie's mouth.

"Of course, you know about the parties on the weekends . . . mostly kids from high school and others. A few Amish youths doing the rumspringa thing. The normal teen drinking and promiscuousness—the typical teenage stuff, right?" Danielle started. "I guess Lance's band played at one of these big parties at a farm near LaGrange. Josie went there with her friend, Sara Wilcox. Anyway, Sara and Josie got to hang out with these bandmates. Sara hit it off with the guitar player. A week later or so, the bandmates all went to California. Sara went with them."

Danielle abruptly turned her Oldsmobile into the entrance of the Gas-and-Grab market.

"Do you want a Coke?" she asked.

"*Jah*," Hannah replied, still bracing from the quick turn.

"I'm buying a pack of cigarettes too. I quit for a month, but I can't take it anymore," Danielle said, exasperated and nervous. "I knew I'd need to smoke as soon as I started talking about Josie!"

Hannah handed her friend a dollar bill for her Coke and waited in the car. Danielle quickly ran into the convenience store as it was just starting to rain.

While waiting, Hannah remembered the only time she went to one of those teen parties. It could have been the same farm where Josie met her singer friend. It was also near LaGrange. She chuckled because the only time she went to a party, she didn't drink or smoke or dance with boys. Instead, she remembered spending most of her time sitting on a hay bale, playing with a few barn kittens. The other kids danced around the bonfire while she was content playing with cute little kittens. Eventually, the police came and broke up the gathering and sent kids running. She had never experienced another teen party. Josie tried to get her to go to a few other parties, but she wouldn't.

Danielle plopped back into the driver's seat, put two Cokes into the cup holders, and eagerly opened her pack of Virginia Slims. She pressed the cigarette lighter button, and when she pulled it out to light her cigarette, it glowed a deep red.

"Why did I try to quit?" she said while exhaling. She seemed instantly relaxed.

Hannah watched her smoking the long, delicate-looking cigarette and surprisingly asked, "Could I try one?"

"Huh? Well, you are of age, so I don't see why not." She handed her the pack. "You're going all rumspringa on me!"

Hannah laughed and used the car cigarette lighter as Danielle did.

"Now, don't inhale much, or you'll cough up a lung, then get dizzy and vomit all over my car!"

Hannah laughed again. Her friend always made her laugh. She was a comedian and didn't even know it.

"Okay then," Danielle said and started the Oldsmobile. "So this is when I think Noah Miller was spreading his gossip. Maybe he heard she was at that party. She'd been hanging out with Sara, the bandmates, and Lance. So you can imagine there was talk."

"*Jah*, maybe Noah was hurt. Maybe he thought they would become, you know, special friends."

"Well, when I asked Josie about him, she didn't say anything. Silence. That dude ticked her off!"

"I decided today that I want to forgive Noah for anything he may have said or did. I don't know, but I have to try and forgive. I can't be angry. It's not *gut!*"

"Forgive Noah Miller? —As if!"

"I want to forgive him and everyone else I'm angry with. I have to."

Danielle shook her head.

"Anyway, as you know, Josie decided to get on a bus that Monday."

"*Jah*, she said she would meet up with her *Englisch* friend, Sara, who left the week before. But I didn't know she was following this band too," Hannah replied while placing the hardly-smoked cigarette in the ashtray.

"When I drove Josie to Middlebury, to the Greyhound station, she told me about Lance and his band and meeting Sara."

"*Jah*, but what else?"

"Okay, so you heard what I told the police—about the phone call from Josie and what she said. But I left out personal stuff. I didn't think they needed to know. Now, this is stuff that Josie told me on the phone."

"Like?"

"She fell for this Lance dude. He was tall with that big heavy-metal hair. He was a real smooth talker—a poet, an artist. Good looking guy. Well, you know, he was like some kind of irresistible rock god . . . Well, maybe *you* don't know."

Hannah made a face but still smiled.

"But anyway, they became a pair out in LA. The band practiced a lot, did a few gigs, and lived together in a warehouse or commercial building. The way she described it, it sounded like a flophouse. People were coming and going. Drugs. Drinking. Artist types. Lots of other girls too."

"Other girls?"

"Right. She found Lance with another chick, and that was it. Last straw. Josie just left. I guess this Lance character is a real piece of work. Manipulating and controlling."

"Poor Josie . . . So she was coming home?"

"No. Not then. Josie knew these young people that were hanging around the beaches. Camping. Surfing. So she took up with them and had fun. She told me this the first time she called."

"She called you more than once?"

"Twice. The first time was a few months back and then a couple of weeks ago. But both times, she told me not to tell anyone. So I'm sorry."

"So the second time is when she said she wanted to come home?"

"Yes. Josie said she was drifting around at that point. She missed us and wanted to get back some time. But, you know, she never did say anything about her friend Sara. Not sure if she was still hanging with the band. I didn't ask her either."

"Did she seem sad? Or was she back to being the normal Josie?"

"Oh no, not sad. Nothing could keep her down for long. She missed her family, she said. But no, she had lots of people she was hanging around with, having fun. Loved the beach, she said. Even learned to surf!"

"For sure and certain, that sounds like Josie. I'm happy she was back to being herself!"

When Danielle turned into the lane next to their farmhouse, several black buggies were outside her home.

"You have lots of visitors," Danielle said.

"They've come anyway! Very nice," Hannah replied. "I was hoping everyone would start coming."

"Just remember that I'm here for you anytime you want to talk," Danielle said.

"*Denki!* You are a friend."

"I may not give you another cigarette, though!"

"Please, do not!" Hannah laughed a little. "I have no idea why I asked to try one."

"Well, I'll leave you to your visitors. I'm off to spend another Saturday night with Daddy!" Danielle said in a resigned tone.

"You are a good daughter!"

Hannah left the car and walked along the edge of the vegetable garden to the dairy barn. The rain stopped, but the air was damp and cool. It felt pleasant.

A few of her cousins were helping Caleb with the milking and feeding. Lena was standing strong and looking healthy. Hannah smiled and stroked the cow's black and white back.

"She's doing fine now!" Caleb yelled over to her.

"*Jah*! She looks good."

One by one, her cousins came over to her and offered their condolences. The community met any family death with assistance and mutual aid. The men helped with outdoor work or business, and the women brought food dishes and took over small jobs, chores, and gardening. Her cousins lifted Hannah's spirits. Finally, life returned to her beautiful face, and her blue eyes brightened. Her father came from the rear stalls.

"Hello, *Dat*," she said happily. "Lena is healthy now."

Her father walked up to Hannah and hugged her. He didn't seem to care that the others were around to see this. He never hugged his daughter or showed such affection in front of other people.

"I may be at risk of being prideful," he whispered, "but I can't help but think I have a perfect and beautiful daughter. More than a father could ever hope for."

"*Denki*," she replied, full of wonderment.

"I just want you to know," he said, showing a rare grin above his long, graying beard.

Hannah's bright eyes were close to tearing up again, but this time due to an overabundance of happiness that poured out of her heart. A day earlier, she was becoming disenchanted with her perfect little life. She was questioning her faith and family, and even friends. Her sister was gone, and that sadness and shock altered the perceptions of her long-held beliefs, and she started to see things differently because of it. She was searching for answers and blame, perhaps. But at the same time, she needed to forgive and forget. So that morning, when she woke, she prayed and asked for guidance. At first, it seemed no guidance came. But throughout the day, especially during the busy time at her work, she slowly started to see things clearly. She had to forgive. Forgiveness would cleanse her soul, and hatred and bitterness could otherwise eat away at it. She also saw Danielle for what she was—a true friend. It made no difference that she was an *Englischer*. Before, she felt apprehension about allowing her into her life. There had been that invisible dividing line between *her* and *them*. But Hannah broke the barrier, and she would never erect it again.

Her father tapped her on the head and started walking toward Caleb, but after a few steps, he turned to Hannah and said: "Your *Englisch* waitress must be smoking in her car again! You smell like a chimney top!"

"*Jah*!" she said, laughing. "I probably do!"

↔

With her identity confirmed, and all the paperwork and permits ordered, the town's Amish Services helped arrange with the local funeral parlor to bring her body home from Arizona. According to custom, they placed her body in a plain pine box upon arrival. The

Bontrager family—the neighboring farm and cousins of the Yoders—would help with the services. Benches for the regular church service had been loaded on wagons and arrived at the Bontrager farm because they were already scheduled to host services that Sunday. Each family in the church district held church services at least once a year, and it was the Bontrager's turn. Bishop Miller and the current home ministers would preside over the funeral with no issues or apprehensions.

The funeral took place the third day after the arrival of the pine-box casket. Nearly all of the one hundred and forty-seven members of the church district were present, along with several English, including Danielle, and her weak and ailing father, who she lived with and cared for. Mindy, the owner of the Red Barn Cafe, was present too. Hannah made a point of approaching young Noah Miller to welcome him warmly. Forgiveness was absolute.

The service was much like a typical church day, with sermons by the ministers and reading of the German Bible. Afterward, there was homemade bread and peanut butter spread, pickled beans and beets, ham, cheese, and pies, with fresh milk and punch.

Later, they placed the pine box on a horse-drawn hearse. The family followed in a procession to the cemetery a few miles down the road. The black buggies passed quaint farms and well-maintained homes with green lawns and fall gardens—fields of alfalfa and dried corn separated by stands of hardwood trees with orange and red leaves. It was a warm and sunny October afternoon. Hannah peered out the little window of the buggy. She was thankful they were given such a perfect day.

CHAPTER TWENTY-ONE

Dolan was driving along the Indiana Toll Road when he passed a billboard advertising Amish Country painted on the side of a barn. Curious, he turned off the highway and entered a park-and-ride lot near the exit. He pulled out his road atlas; Shawneetauka was only ten miles south. Considering the ultimate journey was almost two thousand miles, a mere ten miles out of the way would be like a blip on the odometer, hardly noticeable. He followed all the signs and billboards to Shawneetauka. He must've been close. A bearded man, wearing a blue shirt with suspenders and a straw hat, was sitting in a black buggy. The man and his brown horse were waiting at a stop sign for him to pass.

The town was charming. The buildings were mostly farm, barn, and country-themed. Hanging baskets overflowed with vibrant-colored fall flowers. Manicured trees, strategically placed pumpkins, decorative corn stalks, and flower patches lined the sidewalks.

Fried chicken dinner for $5.99 was advertised on a billboard and again on a marquee in front of a country-style restaurant. Dolan would investigate further; he was hungry, as usual. He parked his Jeep and walked into the restaurant. A hostess escorted him to a table next to a wall of windows that overlooked the flower garden. He laughed when he flipped to the back of the laminated menu. *Pop* was printed instead of *Soda* above the list of soft drinks available. That meant he was close to home. But he'd get a coffee instead and perhaps wake up a little. The road was starting to wear on him.

"Welcome to the Red Barn," the waitress said as she came up.

Dolan lowered the menu and saw her face. He saw *her* face and was speechless for a moment. He recollected his aunt's hand, drawing her big eyes and the nice rounded curve of her upper lip. Her sister—the girl he was now staring at—had a fuller face and was taller. But she was beautiful, and they had a similar look. He could see some light blonde hair hiding under the bonnet she wore. The oversized, plain black dress that draped to her ankles hid her figure as well as could be expected.

"Could I get you something to drink?" she asked again when he didn't respond the first time.

"Yes, I'm sorry," he said. "Coffee, please."

When she returned with the coffee and creamer, he said: "You must be Hannah?"

She seemed surprised.

"*Jah*," she replied, "I'm Hannah."

He grinned a little when he heard her faintly foreign-sounding accent. Josie didn't seem to have a noticeable accent when he spoke with her three weeks prior. Perhaps she practiced hiding it.

"I'm Dolan McBride. I was in Arizona, and I'm heading back to Michigan. So I thought I'd stop by Shawneetauka since I was nearby."

She tilted her head a little and didn't seem to understand.

"I'm sorry. You wouldn't know about me. I was helping the Yavapai County Sheriff with the case. Condolences to you and your family."

"Are you with the police?" she asked.

"At first, only a witness. Then I assisted."

"A witness?"

"I spoke with your sister . . . before it happened. I also helped with the identification and sketch."

Dolan felt bad. He had no intention of bringing up painful images. It was a sheer coincidence that he walked into her workplace.

"Did the Shawneetauka police tell you I work here? So you could speak with me?"

"No . . . I'm sorry. It was pure chance that I came in and sat down. I'd no intention of bothering you or anything. But, just now, I noticed the resemblance between you and your sister. So I knew."

"Oh . . . That is a curious thing," Hannah said. "Well, why don't I take your order first? Then I would like to talk to you a bit. Would that be okay?"

"Certainly, yes."

↔

She brought him his fried chicken dinner and more hot coffee. The evening waitresses arrived. He was her last customer. She had plenty of time to sit, ask questions, and talk since she had clocked out. Danielle left early that day; she had to bring her father to the doctor's office for an appointment. Mindy occasionally eyed them. She most likely wondered about the young man Hannah sat with.

Dolan explained his chance encounter with her sister in Seligman, Arizona. The headache, the aspirin, and so on. Hannah wasn't interested in anything else—such as what happened with the suspects, how Deputy McGraw discovered her body, or the actual crime. She only wanted to hear what Josie said. Her exact words. How she looked. Did she look well? What about her headache? Did she seem happy? Dolan assured her that she was in good spirits. Josie's happiness seemed essential to her.

"*Gotte* decided it was time to take Josie, and now we have to live with that," she said. "Of course, I'm still sad. But it has to be this way."

"You two were close, I imagine," he said.

"*Ach, Jah!* At least, I think so. Josie was very independent, unlike the rest of us, so it was a little hard to know what went on with her. But you know, as little girls, we were like twins. But lately, that changed. She was younger than me, but you would never know it. My friend Danielle—she works here too—said Josie was like thirteen going on thirty. I'm the opposite. So as we got a little older, she did her own thing—but we were still close."

Hannah was talkative. She loved her sister; Dolan could tell. She was a fine person with a kind heart. He no longer felt bad about stumbling unexpectedly into her world and resurrecting the images of her sister. She was grateful that he turned up—he could feel it.

"Well, I should go now. I have to call for a ride home," she said while standing up.

"I am pleased to have met you," Dolan said, and he stood up as a matter of politeness.

"I'm so glad you happened into our restaurant and not one of the others," she said. "It's a *gut* thing we advertise fried chicken on the billboard!"

"Yes, that was a great dinner!"

"Be sure to tell Mindy that you enjoyed her chicken. She's the owner, the woman standing in front of the cash register and staring over here," Hannah said. "She must be getting curious about you!"

Dolan laughed and said. "Oh . . . If you need a ride home, I'd be happy to oblige."

"No, I don't think I could let you do that."

"It's not a problem. I'd be happy to."

She hesitated a moment, turned, and said: "I'll get my handbag!"

When they got out to the parking lot, Hannah explained that transportation was a problem for her and others in the community, especially those working away from home, which was the majority of younger people around, because not as many young people were working on farms.

"I usually get a ride from Danielle, but I manage one way or another if she's not here."

"Who were you going to call for a ride?"

"Amos, the Amish taxi driver. It looks like rain, or I would've started walking. I usually get picked up by someone in our community before I get too far!"

"I got my first part-time job working at fourteen, way before I could drive, so I know what you mean!"

Dolan cleared the passenger seat for her. He tossed the road atlas and miscellaneous snack food bags into the back and helped her into the Jeep.

"*Jah*, I don't like driving the buggy. I mean, not in town or on busy roads. I don't mind down the side roads where it is nice and quiet. We've had horrific crashes around here. The trucks and cars make a mess of the buggies when they collide. It's been happening a lot."

"Not a pleasant sight, I imagine," Dolan said. "So you said your taxi driver is Amish? How does that work? Forgive me for asking a stupid question, but I didn't think your people drove cars."

"Oh, Amos is not Amish anymore. He never got baptized, so he didn't make a vow to follow the church. But we all trust him."

Dolan pulled to the main road and waited for Hannah to point the way.

"South, yes."

"So I may sound stupid again, but aren't your people shunned if they leave the church?"

"We have a choice after rumspringa to get baptized, make a vow, and stay with the church, or decide not to. You are not shunned or in the *Bann* if you choose not to. Now, if you make the vow, are baptized, and later decide to leave or get into trouble, that is when it is more serious. We would no longer be able to do business with this person or have relations."

"That's interesting. My people are Catholic—baptize you when you're a baby, so you don't have much choice!"

"*Jah*, that's funny. Little babies getting baptized!"

The Jeep rolled south, passing the remaining businesses with their fall decorations of dried corn stalks, orange pumpkins, pretty flower gardens, and manicured trees.

"You have a beautiful town," Dolan said.

"*Denki,* thanks. We have many tourists that come through to see our community. I suppose I'm used to it myself, but when we do go on longer trips and see the other towns and places, that's when I know we have a special place here."

"So is this rumspringa I hear about like an endless party for the Amish kids? Or is that not true?"

"It isn't true for most of us. I've heard about the television and movies that show such things. They show us kids being crazy and drunk and doing sinful things daily. It's true for some, I suppose, very few. —I did go to a teen party once!"

"Maybe I saw you on one of those *Amish Gone Wild* television shows!" Dolan said. She laughed.

"But really, rumspringa is the time we have to grow up a little, between when we get out of school and before committing to the church. It's the time to see what's out in the world, try new things, and possibly decide to leave and not come back. But only a handful of kids do. Most stay."

Hannah pointed out where he needed to turn onto the upcoming road.

"I suppose most of us are a little afraid too," she continued. "We know we have great people around us—in our families and community. So it doesn't make much sense to leave it. And we believe *Gotte* is here with us. Not so much out there. At least that's how I feel."

As he turned the Jeep onto the side road, he thought about what she said. That God is here with them but not so much anywhere else. For the most part, he doubted that God was around at all. "It does seem like your little community here may be more blessed than others I've seen," Dolan replied.

"That's a nice thing for a visitor to say."

"So you live on a farm?" he asked as they drove past alfalfa fields.

"A dairy farm. We have lots of cows to milk!"

"You work at both the restaurant and your farm?"

"*Jah*, but I love everything we do to keep things going. The chores aren't too hard—not chores at all! It's been a struggle financially, though, sometimes. My brother and *Dat* work hard, but it's tough with low milk prices. But things get better. They always do. I love our farm."

"So you've never considered leaving?" Dolan questioned, but it may have been inappropriate to ask. He instantly thought about her sister's fate when the question came out of his mouth.

"I've thought about it," she admitted. "As I said, that's part of what rumspringa is about. But, I mean, *jah*, you have to think about it."

Dolan briefly glanced over as she spoke and looked back to the road. She was so pretty—and so very Amish. Hannah lifted her hand and pointed to the farm they were approaching. "Here is our farm!"

"Nice place!" he said and pulled into their lane. A stacked stone wall along the drive separated the property from the next one over. Their home was an older, two-story farmhouse, painted bright white, with a covered porch along the front. The house was angled on the land, so the side faced the main road, and the long porch faced the huge garden. The big dairy barn was down a sloping hillside below the house. Various smaller barns and buildings were even farther back. One small, peculiar building, located near the entrance off the main road, appeared to be an outhouse. "That's our neighborhood phone shack!" she said, noticing Dolan's gaze. "We don't have a phone in the house, but it's okay to have one here."

"I thought it was an outhouse for a second!"

"*Jah*! Funny. But thankfully, our district allows indoor plumbing!"

He pulled up a little farther and parked near the side of the house.

"I'm happy that you stumbled into the Red Barn today! And I appreciate the ride," she said. "Also, I was pleased when you told me what you did for Josie Jane and everything after—helping the police and all. You are a good person."

"Thank you. I'm glad I got to meet you," Dolan replied. "Maybe the next time I'm driving past, I'll stop in for a chicken dinner and see you again!"

"Please do. That would be nice!"

Hannah jumped out of the Jeep and walked toward the farmhouse. She stopped shy of the door and turned to wave goodbye, smiling.

CHAPTER TWENTY-TWO

The next day Hannah informed Danielle about the unexpected customer who stopped at the restaurant while she was away. She didn't dare confess her true feelings; she would hardly admit them to herself. Hannah told her about the young *Englischer* and his involvement with her sister's case in Arizona. But, of course, she didn't tell her that he was the most handsome young man she'd ever seen in her life or how all that night after he dropped her off at the farm, she could think of nothing except his gentle, reassuring eyes and beautiful face. Hannah had never felt this way. It was a bad thing that could only bring her heartache because anything beyond the little fantasy spinning around her head was an impossible dream.

On the drive home that evening, Danielle looked over to Hannah and asked: "So, were you ever going to tell me that your *Englisch* boy is like a heavenly Adonis dropped from the sky?"

"What? My *Englisch* boy?"

"Mindy said he is gorgeous! You are keeping the best bits to yourself!"

"*Jah*, he could be considered handsome," she replied coyly.

"Does he have a girl? Is he married?" Danielle inquired excitedly and pressed her cigarette lighter button in.

"I would not know that!"

"You didn't ask?"

"*Ach*, no!"

"I know, but a girl can dream, right?" Danielle said and lit her cigarette.

"He's a nice young man. For sure and certain. But that's all."

"I'm just having fun with you! I know he'd be forbidden fruit!"

"I'm not so sure I like your biblical references," Hannah said with a slight smile.

"You would surely be exiled from Eden if you taketh that fruit," Danielle said, laughing. "Okay, I'll stop! But seriously, now, answer me this—why haven't you settled on one of your boyfriends? Let's face it, we all know you must be the most beautiful girl in Shawneetauka, and you could—and do—have your choice of young lads. I know you go on buggy rides after your Sunday *singeon*. So?"

"I don't know. I'm not sure. I've never felt comfortable around boys. Except for my brothers," she said and paused. "I get embarrassed and shy. And I've never been drawn to anyone."

Danielle turned her Oldsmobile onto the driveway at the Yoder's farm and parked near the house.

"So, were you embarrassed and shy around *him*?" she asked. "Your *Englisch* boy . . ."

Hannah smiled and didn't say anything.

"Oh my gosh!" Danielle shouted. She turned her head from side to side, probably wondering if anyone was close enough to hear. "You do like him, don't you?"

"It's stupid. I know. It's a bad thing too—"

"Bad?"

"Well . . . just impossible."

"Wait. What are you doing tonight? Nope. I know what you're doing tonight!" Danielle said firmly. "You are going to come to my house, and we'll sit and have a heart-to-heart! What do you say?"

"It is Friday night, so—"

"Exactly. Now go into the house and tell your family you'll be back later. Tell them you'll hang out with my old dad and me for a little while. He needs visitors, you know! It'd be like charity."

"I'll tell them!" Hannah shouted back, running to the house.

Danielle's home sat on considerable acreage. It was an operating farm, but they didn't work the ground. Instead, the neighboring farmer leased the land. This arrangement provided monthly income, and Danielle helped a little with the rest of the expenses. However, her father became physically disabled and relied primarily on Danielle for daily needs, so much of the home's upkeep was lacking. Still, Danielle did her best, and the place looked none the worse for wear, at least from a distance. The fuel oil furnace functioned, the roof didn't leak, and hot water came out of the tap; they could live with the small stuff, like the paint peeling off the window trim or the sticky latch on the screen door.

"Daddy, do you want a frozen pizza tonight?" Danielle asked from the kitchen. He was sitting in front of the television in the living room, watching a hockey game.

"Thank you, dear!" he said back.

"I've brought Hannah over to visit," she said.

"Oh, good. Hello there!" Danielle's father replied and turned to look over towards the kitchen at them. Hannah waved to him from the entryway.

"Who's winning?" Danielle asked.

"The darn Red Wings are losing to Winnipeg! Yzerman got a goal, though."

"Yay for Stevie!" she shouted back. "Pizza is in the oven! I'll make us a little salad too."

"Sounds fine."

Hannah and Danielle sat at the kitchen table, and Danielle offered her a wine cooler. Hannah unenthusiastically agreed.

"You'll like this strawberry flavor," Danielle said.

"*Jah*, it tastes . . . interesting."

"Here's to rumspringa!" Danielle said, toasting with her bottle, and Hannah laughed. "So, are you going to tell me how you really feel about your *Englischer* and what he's like?"

"His name is Dolan McBride. He has kind and gentle eyes. He's a *gut* person. And yes, I think he's the first boy I've ever loved!"

"Oh my god!"

"*Jah*, it's bad! It's terrible! And I know it's pointless. But I can't help it. He's all I can think about now!"

"Wow! I was only teasing you. I had no idea! I mean, I know you said you liked him!"

"I'm sure if I mentioned this to my *mamm* or one of my cousins, they would say that it's the devil that's grabbed my soul or something! Maybe bring me to the bishop! No good can come of this. That I understand."

"I don't believe that for a minute!" Danielle replied. "You are pure. You are kind. You are beautiful. If you love him, it can't be a bad thing!"

"You are very nice to me."

"Yes, *I am!*" Danielle said, laughing.

"It's possible I may never see him again. He might never come back here. So it's all just stupid. And even if he did come back—"

"It's meant to be!" Danielle interjected.

"But how?"

"That's easy! Just go with that thing beating in your chest!"

"What?"

"Your heart!"

"But I love my family and our community. These crazy romance fantasies only work in those books I read. In real life, not so much!"

Danielle smiled and pointed her finger at her heart. "You'll know."

Hannah took a drink from her bottle and made a funny face. "I'm trying to enjoy this."

Danielle smiled and drank the rest of her bottle until it was empty. She opened another right after.

"I'm twenty-six. No beau. And live with my dad. So I need a little something to help me through life!"

"What happened with your college friend, Tom?" Hannah asked.

"Oh . . . Tommy got a few other friends. Aside from me. So I told him that Daddy and I don't need him coming around anymore! He got the message because I haven't seen him in three months."

"I'm sorry."

"I'm not. I knew Tommy wasn't the one for me. I was buying time with him."

Her father seemed to get excited by the television.

"Probert is at it again!" he yelled over to them.

"Fight?" Danielle asked.

"He tried to check Shawn Cronin, and now he's pounding on him!"

"Bob Probert is the enforcer!" she said to Hannah as she rushed to watch the replay. "He punishes anyone that messes with his teammates!"

Danielle stood next to her dad and imitated Probert's punches while shadowboxing. Hannah giggled while watching her friend dance around the television, mimicking the hockey player's moves. Hannah's people didn't believe in violence and fighting. But it made sense to her that this Probert wanted to protect his friends.

The kitchen timer buzzed, and Hannah got up to check on the oven. Danielle came back, and they pulled the pizza out and sliced it on a giant wood cutting board. They ate in the living room with her dad and watched the hockey game together. Hannah never ate dinner in front of a television—she barely ever watched one—but everyone seemed happy and comfortable. So it couldn't be that bad.

"I forgot to make the salad!" Danielle remembered.

"It's fine," her father replied. "We don't need any of that rabbit food!"

Hannah laughed. She liked Danielle's old dad.

After they finished eating their pizza, while the hockey game went into its second intermission, there was a knock at Danielle's front door. It was almost dark, but not late. Who could it be? Danielle looked at Hannah and shrugged, then went to the door. A moment later, she returned to the living room and said to Hannah: "It's Noah Miller! He said your mom told him you were here!"

"*Ach! Jah!* I forgot I told him I would sit with him after dinner tonight," she said, flustered.

"Sit with Noah Miller? It's good he said he'd wait for you outside because I wasn't about to invite him into the house!"

Hannah whispered, "I think I was too nice to him when I decided to forgive and forget."

"Not sure how you could do it! Forgiveness? Him? So now it's going to be buggy rides and picnics? Your naivety knows no bounds!" She shook her head in disbelief.

"*Ach*, I know!"

Hannah said goodbye to Danielle's father and thanked her for being a good friend. She went through the door to see Noah Miller. After an awkward greeting, they jumped into his two-seater buggy and headed down the road toward the Yoder farm.

"Are you warm enough? I've got a blanket," Noah said to Hannah. It was a smaller, open-air buggy.

"No. I'm fine."

It was getting dark, and Hannah was afraid of riding at night. The buggy had a reflector on the rear, but she worried about car collisions. Traffic was usually light in the area, especially after dark. Of course, for some reason, several cars had passed them on this night already, perhaps because it was a Friday. So every time Hannah heard a vehicle coming from the rear or saw one coming from ahead, she inadvertently pressed closely against Noah.

Across the Bontrager farm was a small pond. Noah maneuvered the rig onto the lightly used road adjacent to the shoreline. He stopped at an open clear-cut that overlooked the water, away from the main road. Hannah suddenly got anxious. She disliked being alone with him. Especially there. What was he thinking?

"I've got to get something," he said, then twisted around and lifted the blanket from behind the bench. From beneath it, he grabbed a glass flask of whiskey.

"I need to warm up!" He drank from the bottle. "You wanna try some?"

"No," she said, waving it away, surprised that the bishop's son was drinking hard alcohol.

"Look at that," he said, pointing across the pond. The bright moon showed from behind clouds, above the trees. "Harvest moon?"

"That was last month."

"*Jah*, I guess you're right," he said, "But it's a nice reflection on the water."

He took a few more drinks from the bottle.

"You sure you don't want to be warmed up?"

"No."

"You know, you are a beauty," he said and pressed closer to her.

"Because it got dark," she replied, not knowing what else to say.

"No, you are the nicest-looking girl around. I talked to my friends last weekend, and they all said the same thing. They said whoever gets you for his girl would be the luckiest."

Hannah was irked and embarrassed that he and his friends were talking about her. But more definitively, at the moment, she disliked that he was pressing closer and closer to her, with his hot whiskey breath in her face. She pulled back. His huge, black Percheron horse got startled.

"Dixon is wondering . . . he's wondering why you're pulling away from me," Noah said. His speech was drunkenly slurred, and he pulled on the reins. "Whoa, Dixon!"

"We should go to my house now."

Noah messed up his mouth and removed his straw hat: "Not until you kiss me."

"What?" She pulled back. "No!"

He leaned in and grabbed her by the upper arm. He tugged Hannah toward him and forcibly kissed her.

"Stop!" she shouted and turned her face.

He did not stop. Instead, he pulled off her prayer kapp, placed his hands around her head, and pressed his face close to hers.

"Why are you doing this? —*Stop it!*"

She twisted and squirmed.

He pressed himself onto Hannah with all his weight and grabbed her with his big hands. He pulled himself toward her and touched her everywhere, grabbing and squeezing. She began to scream, but that was a mistake because he quickly covered her open mouth tightly while his other hand groped over her.

Terror and fear filled her eyes. This could not be happening!

He pulled and lifted her dress. She panicked as his hand moved along her thigh. She tried to push him away or pull away, but it was useless. His force and weight trapped her. She screamed into his hand, but no sound escaped her mouth. She banged and kicked her heels against the footboard. Her heart was beating hard and fast; he covered her mouth so tightly she could barely breathe. She continuously kicked and squirmed to try to free herself. She was terrified and losing hope. She kicked her heels against the footboard again, but only feebly as she slowly lost strength. She couldn't breathe. She was panicking. Finally, she used both hands to peel and pry his fingers from her mouth.

—*Air*.

She turned her head to take a breath. She almost cried out once more, but she thought better. He'd cover her mouth again if she did. She wanted to breathe, so she stayed silent. She didn't want to die. She only wanted to breathe.

That left both his big hands free to grope while he moved his open mouth over her face, lips, and neck. She twisted, squirmed, and resisted as he pressed harder and harder against her. She wouldn't be able to fight much longer—her strength was gone. She prayed, now begged—*Please, Gotte, make it stop!*

Her legs were tight and tense. Her arms went from pushing and pressing to flailing and thrashing. And then only dangling uselessly to each side. She was giving up and going numb—resigned. She barely noticed him pressing, pawing, and kissing. Tears came. She could only cry. She couldn't fight him anymore. Now she was sure the awful thing would happen. She couldn't stop him.

Her hand brushed along the seat. Hannah opened her eyes. The leather reins of the buggy were draped over the bench.

She stretched her arm to reach, then twirled and twisted the leather around her left hand. Gripping tightly, she lifted her arm high and forcefully snapped the reins across Dixon's shiny back using all her remaining strength.

The massive horse reacted by jumping, bucking, and kicking. The small buggy started to shake and jerk and was lifted into the air, bouncing around. Noah turned to grab the reins, and Hannah was free to leap from the buggy. Noah himself lost his balance, hobbled, and fell forward. He landed at the front of the hitch beneath the enormous black horse, even as the horse continued to jump, kick, and stomp. Hannah could hear him cry and moan in pain as Dixon trampled over him. She stood near but didn't move. As the horse continued bucking and jumping and stomping, she looked on. She didn't know what to do. Finally, his cries of pain ceased even though the horse continued its mayhem. Hannah circled the buggy and tried to look beneath the horse. Noah Miller was lifeless.

Hannah ran home, stunned. She thought of calling for emergency services as she went by the phone shack, but her brother was outside the house with a lantern, working on their buckboard wagon. She ran to him.

"Caleb! Noah Miller got trampled!" she yelled frantically. "His horse—"

"Where?" he asked.

Caleb was at the house earlier when Noah stopped by, so he must've expected them back shortly.

"By the pond," she said breathlessly and pointed.

Caleb didn't ask more questions. Instead, he started running with his lantern in hand. Hannah stood near the buckboard as he headed to where she came from. She went to the phone shack and reluctantly dialed 911.

The huge black horse had strayed approximately fifty feet from where Caleb found Noah. The horse was now calm and gentle. He set his lantern next to Noah and felt for a pulse or a breath. He felt nothing. The nearly-empty bottle of whiskey was lying on the grass. He tossed it into the pond. He went over, grabbed the horse by the reins, and walked him closer. Caleb lifted the body and placed it in the buggy. He found the blanket and covered him up completely. Hannah's prayer kapp and Noah's straw hat were lying in the grass, so he picked them up. He jumped into Noah Miller's rig and headed back to the farm.

Caleb returned with the body several minutes before the ambulance arrived. The police arrived moments later. However, Caleb had already told his father and Hannah that he was deceased. The paramedics confirmed this by placing the blanket back over the body and shaking their heads.

Their father stood by as the police officer asked Hannah the particulars.

"He wanted to stop near the pond to show me how pretty the moon looked across the water," she said, sobbing, if only because the adrenaline ran its course, and she felt low. "The horse got spooked and started going wild. I leaped from the buggy, and he fell. I started to run home . . ."

"Fine, you need not say more," her father said as her tears flowed. He turned to the police officer, shook his head, and waved him off to let him know that was enough for now.

↔

Hannah sat in the kitchen with her mother, who gave her a tall glass of meadow tea to drink. Caleb and her father remained outside, helping the police officer with his report. The red and blue lights from the patrol car still flashed near the road. The ambulance left.

"It's a terrible thing," her mother said. "That horse! That beast!"

Hannah nodded reactively and drank her tea. She couldn't tell them what actually happened.

It shamed her. No one needed to know what Noah did. That was between him and God.

But if it hadn't been for that beast, as her mother called the horse, she would have been violated by Noah Miller, and if so, she may as well have been dead too. The animal protected her from further harm. Dixon, the horse, was her protector. And now, of course, he was sure to die. They always put down animals that do harm to humans. Hannah started crying again when she pictured them putting the black horse down on her account. It was her own hand that instigated the action.

"*Ach*, dear child," her mother said. "Young Noah is now with *Gotte*. For sure and certain. No reason for tears."

As if, she thought in anger, borrowing one of Danielle's English phrases. She wasn't shedding tears for Young Noah.

Hannah left the kitchen; she needed to be alone. She went up to her room and lay across the bed on the quilt she and her mother had made together. She stared at the plain white walls and ceiling for a long while. Then, an idea occurred to her. What she experienced, or at least partially experienced, may have happened to her sister Josie in the springtime.

Suddenly it all made sense; maybe that's what finally drove Josie away. It couldn't have been Noah Miller merely spreading lies and gossip. It must've been more than that. And she wouldn't have given voice for such a thing, owing to shame and guilt. Yes, Hannah was sure of it. Noah Miller must've done terrible harm to her sister.

CHAPTER TWENTY-THREE

On the morning of Halloween, he stepped from the shower, shaved and smoothed his hair back, and put on his only good pair of dress pants, shiny black shoes, and a nice white, button-down oxford shirt with a loose tie. The tie was a gift from Bree on their graduation day so that he'd look dapper (her words). He hadn't worn it since that day or had occasion to. He grabbed his black and navy plaid sports coat and headed down the steps.

He went out the front door of his family's two-story log home and opened his Jeep to find the fishing vest still packed away. He grabbed Bree's folded letter from the upper pocket and put it away in his sports coat. He wanted to walk, but it was cloudy and misty and cold, so since the weather changed his mind, he jumped back into the Jeep and drove around to

Thompson Lake. He parked near the boat launch and walked to the benches and picnic tables that overlooked the water's edge. His watch showed it was ten minutes to noon. So he went onto the walking path that lined the lakeshore and the cemetery and continued until he reached the peninsula's tip. This was Bree's favorite spot. The view of the lake was panoramic, and across the way was a sandbar island with a few trees that made for splendid scenery. He sat on the bench under the big pine tree and pulled her letter from his pocket. Luckily the light rain ceased. A wispy mist moved along the trees of the island. It got colder. A few gray and white seagulls made noise near the shoreline. He unfolded the letter and started examining Bree's writing, remembering. The big dots above her i's, the occasional smiley face randomly inserted in a sentence. She was still a silly girl then. —He loved her.

It was a dreary day, and his mood mirrored it. The emotions and old feelings bubbled up. He got off the bench and started up the center path of the park cemetery. He went by several old headstones, barely legible, decaying, and a few newer polished ones. Finally, he stopped at the monument of her grandfather's grave. He died during their first year of high school. It was the middle of winter, and Dolan remembered standing next to the pile of freshly-dug dirt already covered by new snow. They lowered her grandpa's shiny casket into the grave, and the blizzard kicked up again with powdery snow and wind, shivering cold, and Father Murphy was thankful the committal service was over.

Next to his were two empty gravesites reserved for her parents, and Dolan walked by those; he came to the new, shiny, polished headstone at the end of the row.

There it was.

Our
Beloved
Daughter
BREE REGAN
May 5 - 1969
February 9 - 1991

When he read the words on the stone, he shook his head. He couldn't believe it was her name. Of course, his mother told him they buried her near her grandfather. But it didn't seem real. Her name could not have been chiseled into that granite. It was impossible. Yet here she was.

He got news of her death when he was in Saudi Arabia before the Kuwait liberation. He was stunned and kept reading the letter over and over. Two guys from his platoon saw him kneeling on the ground next to his Bradley. He handed them the letter, and they understood. Soon after, they rolled out and began the ground assault. He didn't have time to think about it, to mourn; perhaps it was a good thing he didn't.

Her death was an accident. Her agency in Lansing was giving an opulent industry gala for the talent. Several models and other guests were crammed out on the third-floor balcony, smoking and drinking champagne. A few of the girls were sitting atop the half-wall. Bree was there with the others smoking, sipping champagne, and laughing. The model to her right stated that Bree lifted her glass to make an announcement and suddenly slipped backward before saying a word. Bree slipped back and fell straight down. She landed on the walkway near the entrance some thirty feet below. She died instantly. A portion of the tile cap on the half-wall came loose, and when it broke away, she slid off.

Dolan stared at her headstone. He flipped up his watch, and it was noon. The family had placed a large concrete vase filled with flowers on her grave. He eyed the dry carnations and baby's breath; he should have bought fresh flowers. He tilted up the heavy flower vase from its base, and beneath it, he slid Bree's letter—a perfect place. He'd bring flowers around the next time he came. Maybe orange roses. She liked those best. He laughed a little when he remembered running around the day of the homecoming dance, trying to locate a flower shop that could make a quick corsage with orange roses since he forgot to order one in advance. He ended up driving to the far side of Brighton to pick it up.

Suddenly everything inside let loose. He fell to his knees. The dam broke. He steadied himself with one hand on Bree's gravestone. It all poured out. Pain and memories gushed. He hadn't shed a tear in over four years. But he did love her and never stopped loving her. So it all poured out.

But even when they were kids, he figured Bree needed to go out and conquer the world without him—to see Paris, London, and New York. He was a barely-educated country boy who'd never be more than a grunt or a cop in some small town. He was okay with that; he never had worldly ambitions or lofty goals. But she had big hopes and dreams; she wanted to see the world and do great things. He realized this early on and didn't want to hold her back. So he had to let her go.

Now every other buried emotion from deep within busted out. The guilt. The pain. The hurt. The Iraqi sons and brothers he had butchered during the three days of hell—cut in half with the 25mm cannon, pulverized to pieces—the burning flesh and bloated bodies.

The Army counselor assured him he was only doing his job and that it was part of war, part of being a soldier. He wasn't designed to handle it: death and loss. The counselor said he mixed up Bree's accident with the war and the killing and destruction. It was all mixed up in his head because, to him, it all happened at once. So his guilt and sadness were all blended in a strange concoction. But time would heal, they told him. The thoughts and nightmares would end. And so it all poured out.

And then there was Bobby Allman. It was a kick in the gut when Allman killed himself. Dolan was pissed—not sad, not mournful—just pissed. They grew up together and were pals, and he went and did a thing like that! So he never shed a tear for his friend. Not one. At present, he chided himself for not understanding. But how could he have? How could anyone? So now tears came for Allman.

Dolan recalled what he had written on that hotel's bathroom mirror with his girlfriend's bright red lipstick. —*Tell my mom I love her.*

That was the worst part—thinking about his parents.

Dolan kept his eyes closed and searched for calm. He tried to remember what she said. The secret words that could help. Then his aunt's voice came—soothing and serene. He remembered her words. He followed her instructions. Silence, quietness, and stillness slowly crept over. The inner storm was passing. It was happening. Calm was coming. And stillness. Doc's meditation was working.

Breathe in slowly. Now mind the gap—the nothingness—fall into the gap. Breathe out slowly.

He opened his eyes to bright white. It was snowing. He tilted his head to the sky. The large flakes cooled off his hot face and tears. It was a strange and pleasant thing to have a full-blown white-out as early as Halloween, not unlike the blizzard the day they buried Bree's grandfather, minus the wind. The snow was strange but lovely—calming and mesmerizing. Dolan stood for a moment over her gravesite. He smiled, brushed his hand along the cold slush on top of the headstone, and slowly went away.

He walked through the silent and gentle snow. A strange peacefulness surrounded him. The quietness and snow were like a buffer to all things external. He felt cleansed and reborn. He was glad he made it for Bree's day. Nothing could have kept him away. He drove back two thousand miles to be there on that day.

Dolan left the park.

Had it not been for the unfortunate accident, perhaps Bree would have been there too, on that snowy Halloween, standing near the entrance, waiting for him, with her bright and cheery face, while nervously fidgeting and wondering if Dolan remembered the silly idea she stole from Cary Grant and Deborah Kerr, only modified by time and their personal circumstances.

But *that,* of course, he would never know.

CHAPTER TWENTY-FOUR

The phone started ringing as Dolan returned to his family's home. He wasn't going to pick up; the answering machine would get it. But the caller-id box flashed an Arizona number. It was his aunt.

"Aunt Lauren?"

"Hello, kid," she said.

"What's up in Arizona?"

"Well, something big. Luke Staley escaped from the county lock-up!"

"What? How?"

"I just heard the news myself on the car radio. He was out in the jail's recreation yard and jumped up and grabbed the basketball net and rim. Then he pulled himself up to the top of the backboard and jumped over the high-security fence behind it."

"The guy is a crazy, murdering maniac, and they let him hang around in the rec yard. Nuts!"

"I'm expecting to see Sheriff Grady on the news any minute. It won't be his finest hour!"

"So the other two . . . Billy Espers and that bartender Sam, they must be in custody somewhere else. They're supposed to testify against him."

"Yes. The Camp Verde jail."

"Good."

"So other than this excitement, nothing much else is happening here in Arizona!"

"Wow. I hope they get him quickly!"

"Let's hope!"

"Well, how have you and Red been doing this past week without me?"

"We're lonely without you! But Pops had a visit from the cookie lady yesterday!"

"Funny!"

"But this time, she brought him chicken noodle soup! She must be getting serious!"

"Tell Red to hang in there because I'm gonna be coming back soon to rescue him!"

"Nice! How soon?" his aunt asked excitedly.

"Police academy starts the 22nd of November!"

"So it's for sure? Great!"

"I'll get a U-haul trailer and start packing a few things. I don't have much. Then I'll hit the road."

"Your fishing boat won't fit!"

"Nope. I'll let my dad use it. When he retires soon, he'll use it even more!"

"Doubtful . . ."

"No. My mom and dad are talking about retiring early and heading down to Arizona!"

"Seriously? Fabulous! He never said anything to me."

"Well, that's the talk around here! You'll have to convince Uncle Bill to come down too, and we'll have the whole crew down in Arizona!"

"Probably won't happen. But we could try!" she said.

"I just got back from visiting Bree's gravesite," he said in a severe and subdued tone.

"It's hard . . . to lose someone."

"Yeah. You would know this."

"Well . . . she was a good kid," his aunt said.

"We hadn't seen each other or talked much since, you know, around graduation. But we were still friends. Crazy that she's gone."

"We had fun when you two drove out back then, didn't we?"

"Oh, yes, we did. Thanks for calling, and hopefully, I'll see you soon!" Dolan said.

"Okay, great, and I'll keep you informed on the manhunt!"

"If he's still on the lam when I get to Arizona, I'll join the posse."

"Patty must be pulling her hair out!"

"I imagine!"

Dolan thought about Hannah and her family when he got off the phone. He wondered if the sheriff's office would inform the family that Josie's killer was on the run. Of course, it most likely wouldn't matter to them, but they should know.

Ever since he was down in Shawneetauka, he'd been thinking about Hannah. He couldn't help himself. She was beautiful and kind and seemed to have a heart of gold. But it was stupid and impossible. He was a fool for even getting the notion. But still, he had a powerful urge to see Hannah. He'd stop by Shawneetauka on his way back to Arizona. He'd try to see her, at least. He wouldn't go past without trying.

CHAPTER TWENTY-FIVE

Their community, or *gmay* as they call their church district, had two funerals for young people during October. A common thread connected both funerals. Hannah could barely look at him. Unlike Josie's box, which was sealed and never opened for obvious reasons, Noah's face was visible to all. Even though he was in a plain pine box at the Miller's home and could no longer hurt another girl, Hannah was afraid to look at him as she walked by with her family. She was also ashamed. It was the murmurings and whispers. The faces and expressions. The way everybody eyed her with a mixture of sympathy yet also suspicion. Of course, everyone knew she was with him. It was a typical buggy ride—the courting ritual. But the timing of the tragedy, only a few weeks apart from Josie's death, made the common thread so apparent. It was all too interconnected to ignore. She felt like hiding, but there was nowhere to hide.

In the days following the funeral, she was only at ease with Danielle and her father. By the first week of November, after an argument with her mother, she went over and stayed at Danielle's. It wasn't really an argument. Hannah was thinking over everything that happened around the time Josie left. All the drama surrounding her sister and Noah Miller. So she asked her parents about that day the bishop spoke regarding Josie. She wanted to know what was said. She never knew, never asked anyone, and at the time, assumed it was none of her business. But her perspective changed, and she wanted answers. She was no longer going to live with her head in the sand. But her mother was intransigent and said it was a private matter between herself, her father, and the bishop. Her father impassively sided with his wife.

Hannah was hurt. Her mother didn't understand at all. Hannah tried to be a good person who minded her place and loved her family, community, and God. She worked hard and seldom questioned things. Her biggest shortcoming was that she wasn't yet baptized and hadn't yet gone through the baptismal courses, so community members could have questioned her faith or her willingness to "join church," and maybe some did, and perhaps even her mother did. Hannah was a little behind the curve, a late bloomer perhaps, and what worried her was that, had she been baptized and joined the church, she would have been expected, and pressured, to find a partner to marry. She didn't want to be prodded and pushed, then merely settle. That's not what she wanted. She wanted a fairy-tale romance. It had to be a true love affair, like in those sweet and simple paperbacks she read on lunch breaks. It may have been silly, but that's what she hoped for. So aside from her procrastination regarding baptism, for which she could be faulted, she felt maltreated by her mother. And even worse, she started to feel that her mother didn't love her—maybe even disliked her. Just as Josie said before, and at the time, Hannah couldn't understand it. Now she understood it perfectly well. She felt the same.

↔

Her eldest brother Jacob was the first to come by Danielle's house to check on her. Hannah and Jacob hadn't seen each other often. He'd been working many hours at the RV factory while also building a modest home on land owned by the parents of his special friend, Amanda. They planned to marry soon, and he spent most waking hours either at his job or on their property, working to build their future.

Hannah found Jacob standing on the porch, tugging his suspenders. He smiled at his sister and said: "So . . . what's going on?"

She showed a half-frown, half-smile and shrugged.

"You know, I'm not very *gut* at talking. You do most of that in our family," he said.

"*Jah*, I suppose I do," she said.

"I know it's all been rough for you lately," he said. "But it'll get better."

"What's been rough is living with *Mamm*!"

He chuckled and started pulling at his suspenders again.

"Can it be that bad?"

"I don't know," she started. "It's like I'm being ignored and silenced."

"What about?"

"I don't know. Nothing. And everything."

"You sound like Josie now," he said and frowned.

"True," she replied. She was becoming more like her sister. She knew that. Hannah had never been rebellious or disobedient, or cynical in her entire life. But something changed within. Something changed the night the bishop's son tried to assault her. Something changed when Dixon, the horse, drove him into the dirt and killed him. Something changed because he was dead, and she felt no remorse.

"I'm worried for you, you know. And *Dat* asked me here too. So he's also worried."

"No reason to worry," she said.

"So will you come home with me?" he asked.

"I think I'll stay here with Danielle and her *dat* for a while."

"Look. If you want to be away from *Mamm,* why not visit one of our cousins? Kayla or

Sarah would love for you to spend time with them. I could take you tonight," Jacob said.

"No, it's fine. Everything is alright here," she said. He meant staying overnight at the cousins was one thing, but staying with *Englischers* another.

"*Jah*, well, I guess I tried," he said.

"You did *gut*," she replied and smiled.

He nodded and said, "I'll see you again soon!"

"*Denki!* You did make me feel better. Just stopping by."

He jumped from the steps, hopped on the buckboard wagon, and rolled away. Hannah waved goodbye and sat down on the front of the porch. The buckboard went down the road, and Rosie's shoes made a clippety-clop sound on the pavement. She closed her eyes and tried to pray, wanting to ask forgiveness for feeling the way she did. It was wrong that she had unpleasant and disagreeable feelings toward her mother. But she couldn't help herself. She also had no remorse as far as Noah Miller's death. She felt nothing. Cold. She should have felt some guilt—not nothing. It may have gone beyond that. She may have been thankful that he was dead. But, of course, she had been traumatized and distressed. Fear caused this reflex of feelings. So she tried to pray, but it was no good—too soon. If she asked forgiveness for these angry and disagreeable thoughts—towards her mother and dead Noah—she would only go on having them over and over. So it was pointless to pray and ask forgiveness now. She would only have to do it again the next day and perhaps the next. So, instead, she merely thanked the Lord for His understanding and loving, even if she was slightly wayward and presently undeserving of His great kindness.

Danielle popped her head out the door, and Hannah turned and stood up from the porch. "Aren't you cold out here? It looks like it could start to snow!"

"*Jah*, I'm getting a little cold!"

"I wanted to show you where all the towels are and other stuff you may need to use,"

Danielle said and held the door open for her. Hannah followed her to the room at the end of the hall.

The guest bedroom had a bathroom attached. It wasn't very spacious, but it had a toilet, shower, and a small vanity with a mirror. Hannah was pleased. Her own bathroom! Embroidery hoops of various flowers and designs covered the walls of the bedroom and bathroom: a white daisy, a yellow sunflower, a variety of wildflowers, and numerous other creations, including kittens, puppies, and a giant rooster. Hannah stopped and inspected the embroidery work.

"My mother and grandmother made those. I never wanted to learn, but I suppose I should have. Not that I'm Suzy Homemaker or anything!"

"I could show you how to do stitchwork if you ever wanted to try!" Hannah said.

"Well, maybe . . . someday!" Danielle said less than enthusiastically.

"You know, I've never spent the night at an *Englisch* home," she said. "I do appreciate you letting me stay a day or so."

"You can stay as long as you need," she replied. "It's just Daddy and me here, and I could use a little sister around!"

Danielle opened the vanity drawers and the linen closet door to show Hannah the contents.

"Towels are here and washcloths. A few bars of soap in here. Shampoo and conditioner. A new tube of toothpaste is here. Even a new toothbrush!"

Hannah inspected the shower compartment.

"It's easy to use. Turn this handle, and it's on. Turn it all the way on, and it'll be hot enough to burn, so you'll only want to turn it halfway!"

"Nice! I like hot!"

"I don't suppose you'll need my curling iron or anything?" Danielle asked playfully. "But I'd love to put make-up on you and do your hair someday. You'd look like a gorgeous fashion model!"

"I think I'll pass on that, thank you," Hannah said as she pulled down on the strings of her white prayer *kapp*.

"Well, you wanna make hot cocoa? I bet Daddy would like a mug."

"Sure!"

They entered the kitchen, and Danielle grabbed a pan for the stove. Hannah got the milk from the fridge. They had a microwave, but she liked making it the old-fashioned way.

"Look!" Danielle shouted, pointing to the kitchen window. "I guess I was right!"

Big snowflakes were drifting down slowly, illuminated by the bright mercury lamp next to the house.

"Yep. Perfect time for hot cocoa!" Hannah said.

They dropped a dozen miniature marshmallows in their nearly-full mugs, sat at the table, and started talking. Hannah wanted to tell Danielle what happened the night Noah Miller died. She considered it for a moment as she looked into her mug. Finally, she told her.

"My god!" Danielle said, "I knew he was a bad one! But this?"

She immediately got up and hugged Hannah, still sitting in her chair. Hannah got teary-eyed and let her know that she had not told anyone else what he did. She also admitted she intentionally spooked the horse. She only meant for the horse to scuttle. Guilt came, perhaps for the first time since it happened—a good thing.

"I wish you had let me know sooner. You didn't need to keep this all to yourself. Carrying that burden! And you did what you had to!"

"Another thing—I think Noah Miller did this and much worse to Josie."

"God! I suppose it's possible."

"I've been having these feelings . . . you're going to think I'm crazy . . . but ever since that night, I've been feeling like I'm turning into my sister. I'm thinking like her. Saying things as she would say— feeling strange. It's like we have a bond. Like she's trying to speak with me—through me. And she understands too."

"I don't think you're crazy at all. Sisters can have connections that no one else could imagine."

Hannah tried to smile and drank cocoa from her mug.

"Unfortunately, I had a similar experience in high school. I don't want to think about it. I won't go into detail. It was bad, though. It affected me for a long time."

"I'm sorry!" Hannah said.

"It's fine. I'm over it now. But I'm here for you. I'll listen. So don't be afraid to tell me anything."

"I'm already feeling a lot better. Thanks! Maybe it was your perfect hot cocoa!" Hannah said, smiling.

"Yes, it's one of my great talents . . . mixing powdered Nesquik into milk! But, of course, it goes along with my wonderful TV dinner heating expertise or my microwave popcorn-popping abilities!"

"I want to try your microwave popcorn!" Hannah replied. "It sounds dangerous, though!"

"Daddy, you want more hot cocoa?" Danielle asked in a loud voice. He was watching *60 Minutes* on the television.

"No, no. I'm good, dear. Thanks, though! Andy Rooney is almost on if you want to watch!" he replied.

"He loves that curmudgeonly old fool! —I do too!" Danielle said to Hannah. "I should go watch the TV with Daddy for a minute. Then we'll make popcorn!"

"*Jah!*"

Hannah followed her into the living room, and they sat with her father. While Andy Rooney was on television for his three-minute segment, Hannah thought about her English boy, as Danielle called him. She hadn't thought of Dolan since the night of the horrific buggy ride. She'd been daydreaming about him excessively until that point; then, her innocent silly-girl fantasies were interrupted by the reality of violence and death. What had he been doing that past week up in Michigan? Had he thought about her at all? She hoped he had.

Loneliness suddenly crept over her. *Would she ever see Dolan again?* She feared the answer.

CHAPTER TWENTY-SIX

Monday at the Red Barn was uneventful. Hannah was usually a little down and depressed on slow days at the restaurant. Like they cleaned and prepped and stocked for no reason at all. As if they were preparing for a big production but never drew the curtains asunder. Nothing ever happened. It was also disappointing financially, as the tips were few and far between for two waitresses taking turns on tables. Mindy also acted nervous on slow days; she still had to pay the bills. She frequently opened the cash drawer to add up the few receipts, only to look disappointed.

Hannah volunteered to clock out early, and she sat at the break table in the back. She picked up the latest paperback left by Gloria, one of the night waitresses, and thumbed through it. She wasn't in the mood to read. Usually, in the past, had she volunteered to clock out early, she would have headed out to run errands in town, or maybe she'd start walking home if the weather had been nice. But since she was going to Danielle's, she'd wait.

The paperback cover had an attractive young woman in a white wedding dress, holding a bouquet, glowing with anticipation. Gloria only left clean and nice romance novels for the others to read. Mindy had teased her, saying she must've kept the steamy ones all to herself. Hannah slid a finger across the cover and started to daydream. In the past, when she imagined her special day, she pictured the plum-colored wedding dress that she and her mother would create and sew. Of course, it would have a lovely white apron cut from the same delicate material as her prayer kapp, and her attendants would also dress in plum purple. The cut and fit needed to be comfortable, as she'd also wear that dress on regular church Sundays thereafter. The delicate apron would be special, though. After the wedding, she'd carefully pack and store the apron in a keepsake box. Then, on a far-away, future day, upon her death, the family would clothe her body with a lovely dress along with that special apron to be buried in, following the district's funeral practices.

But now, would she ever be married in the Amish way? A month ago, that question would never have crossed her mind. She was confused and conflicted. On the one hand, she felt free. Free like a feather floating around a gentle breeze, weightless and surreal. Anything possible; opportunities limitless. But, on the other hand, she was fearful of the unknown. The world was wide open. But she was still so afraid.

Hannah picked up the book and thumbed through it. She read a sentence more but then stopped again. It was no good. She couldn't distract herself with words. She placed the book back on the windowsill.

Danielle walked up to the table, already wearing her brown suede jacket. "Mindy will wait on any customers until the evening girls get here. So we can take off!"

"I thought she may do that! —It sure is slow!"

"It's because of the crazy weather. My last customer said her brother called from Minnesota and said they've had three feet of snow since Halloween!"

"Wow, that's plenty!"

They slid out the back entrance, got into the Oldsmobile, and drove off. Later, when they were passing her farm, Hannah thought she should return home. Perhaps if she was proving a point to her family, she had done so. But unfortunately, she didn't have the courage to do more than prove a point; she couldn't stay away from her family. It had been a useless exercise in futility. She was disappointed; she'd have to give up her rebellion and head home. But Danielle wasn't a mind reader, so she continued driving down the road. Besides, Danielle loved that Hannah was staying with her. She told her so. She'd been lonely as of late, more so than usual, and having her little sister around—as she called Hannah—a nice change. Ever since her mother died when she was thirteen, only Danielle and her father lived in that house. And now, according to his doctor during the last appointment, his *amyotrophic lateral sclerosis*, or Lou Gehrig's disease, had progressed as expected. Perhaps it would be another year until he couldn't speak, eat, or breathe—a frightening and lonely prospect for Danielle. Her father took the news in stride. Being ever the optimist, he pointed out to his daughter that a small percentage of those affected by this disease have lived well beyond ten years from diagnosis. Danielle, ever the realist, knew that ninety percent, the majority, die in two to four years. Hannah felt for her friend.

"Do you want to show me how you make your chicken noodle casserole for dinner? We've got time to bake from scratch tonight! It's early," Danielle said.

"Sure! Your *dat* will like it!"

"I'm sure it will be great. Tomorrow I'll bring home Mindy's fried chicken and mashed potatoes. That's Daddy's favorite. Maybe after tonight, your Amish casserole will be his favorite!"

"No, Mindy's chicken is everyone's favorite!" Hannah replied.

After dinner, which was a culinary success, there was a gentle knock on the front door. This time Hannah's brother Caleb came to check on her. Hannah went outside to the porch.

"Hallo, wie bisht du?" Caleb asked.

"I'm fine."

"Gut."

"It was your turn? —To come to check on me?" Hannah asked with an intentional grin.

"Jah, but I would have come anyway. Even if *Dat* didn't ask!" he said, mainly speaking English again.

"So, how are things?" she asked.

"Not bad. But everyone is missing you," he said. "Even your cow Lena is missing you!"

"You're being funny!"

"No, she's only put out half her normal milk! And she's months away from her dry period. So she needs you to come and stroke her on the head and whisper to her!" he said, keeping a serious face.

"Okay, let me get my things," she said abruptly, pretending to be concerned.

She was planning on going back home after dinner anyway. So at least she could let her brother think he influenced her decision, even in half jest. Caleb stood on the porch with a satisfied look and waited for her to return.

After thanking Danielle and her father for the accommodations and promising to pay them back somehow or another, to which they refused, she ended up on the buckboard wagon with Caleb, and they went down the road toward their place. There was no rain or snow—only a peaceful, pleasant evening. When they rolled past the pond, across from the Bontrager's property, Hannah didn't want to look over there, at *that spot*, so she eyed her brother handling the reins. He was a lovely young man, and a fortunate girl would marry him someday. Her two older brothers were too perfect. They were both kind and gentle and good-looking and hard-working. In addition, they had caring hearts and understanding minds. Her brothers significantly influenced how Hannah assessed and compared the other young men courting her. So, of course, the other young men fell short.

When she returned to the farm and went back into the house, her little sisters hugged her on each side. Her younger brother was standing near the sink, drinking a glass of punch. Aaron wore his black wool cap. Not the traditional brimmed straw hat. Brimmed hats were corny, he'd say, and black wool caps were cool. Hannah smiled at him and gestured for him to come to her, and he did. So she had all three young children around her, and she was glad.

Later that evening, she was alone with her parents. They sat at the kitchen table—the place for serious discussions. The gas light above the table was set low, and the room was dim. Her father sat at the end of the table. He had his hands clasped together and fumbled with his thumbs. Hannah and her mother sat next to him and across from each other. Her mother looked dour but only slightly more so than usual. Hannah wondered what they would discuss.

"Your mother and I have decided we will tell you about that meeting with the bishop, about your sister, if you are still of a mind to hear us."

Hannah was surprised and didn't expect this.

"*Jah* . . . please."

He looked up from the table and nodded to his wife. He didn't want to be the one to speak on such a delicate subject. So her mother took over.

"That morning, Bishop Miller said something disconcerting. That certain gossip about Noah and Josie made it around to his ears. He confronted Noah about this, and Noah did not deny what was being said: that he and Josie had been together as man and wife. So the bishop immediately suggested, and we agreed, that they would be married. So it was settled."

Hannah was struck dumb.

"So that morning before church, you told Josie that she had to marry Noah?"

"That is what we did."

Hannah pressed her hands to her face in disbelief.

"We made the right choice. There was no other way."

"So this must have been Noah's plan," Hannah said, aloud but musing. "He knew the bishop would make them marry if he found out about such a thing."

"I don't understand what you are saying."

"So you were aware of this and still allowed him to come around, sit with me, and court me?" Hannah said, now with anger in her tone. "Perhaps you'd offer your other daughter to the bishop's son to make up for the first!"

"Don't be foolish. It was not like that!"

"You demanded that she marry him . . . you drove her away! Don't you see?"

"It was the only thing to do."

"If you only knew!" Hannah said. "I wonder if it would have made any difference?"

"What are you saying?" her father asked.

"No . . . I don't think it would have made any difference to you," she pondered aloud.

"You would've still made her marry. Even if you knew."

"What are you saying?" her father asked again.

She stood up from the table and shook her head. She draped her arms across herself, held herself, and shook her head again in disbelief.

"What do you mean?" he asked. "What is it?"

"He tried to *rape* me!" she said, tears trickling down. A word Hannah had never uttered, nor had it ever been spoken in that house—a word too violent to exist in the vocabulary of such a peaceful community. "He tried to . . ."

She collapsed back down to her seat at the table. She covered her face. Her father slid from his chair and knelt next to his daughter. He placed his hand on her head. He looked stunned. He prayed for a moment. Then he quietly said, "I'm sorry."

"He tried . . ." she started to speak again, whispering, as her father knelt close beside her. "He tried . . . but the horse . . . he fell . . . do you understand? Maybe it was worse for Josie. Don't you see?"

Her father stayed close to her and put his arm around her shoulders as tears fell from her face.

"I understand," he whispered. "I'm sorry."

Luckily her mother kept silent. Whether carefully worded or apologetic or sympathetic, anything she could have said would have merely sounded empty and hollow. Her father stayed by her side for a long while, clearly not wanting to leave his little girl. Her mother kept still and silent for a moment, then she slowly went over to the sink, picked up a towel, and began wiping the countertops. Satisfied with the state of cleanliness, she folded the towel carefully and neatly, then placed it again next to the sink. Finally, she retreated quietly to her quilting room while Hannah and her father remained.

Hannah hardly slept that night. It would be the last time she ever slept under that roof. She made up her mind while climbing the stairs to the bedrooms. She'd see about staying a short while with Danielle and then, after a bit of saving, go out and travel and experience the world beyond. Maybe volunteer with a church group helping disadvantaged orphans in some faraway land or help feed the homeless masses. She'd heard such things from her Mennonite friends, which piqued her curiosity. Or maybe go out on her own and try to live like an *Englischer*. That was her right. She could return to the community and take her vow in a year or two. It wouldn't be impossible.

Lying awake on her bed, she quietly decided to become courageous and bold. The fear that brought her back home that day was unacceptable. She prayed for the courage needed to venture out. She tasted the slightest bit of freedom and wanted more. It was also about individuality. She was a singular being who had the right to choose for herself. Not just follow the motions of the community's convention. She even had the right to fall in love. To fall in love with persons who previously would have been unthinkable and off-limits. As Danielle said, she had the right to follow her heart and go wherever it may take her.

She was finally falling asleep, and as she did, she pictured Josie Jane in a summer field of green. Josie was wearing her blue dress. She took off her prayer *kapp* and let her long, blonde hair down. She twirled around in the tall grasses, and a light breeze blew—smiling, carefree, and happy. In this memory, Josie was about thirteen, and even then, so unique and free-spirited. She rose above and beyond all others around her. As if she had special access to secrets of the world that no one else did. She was special and free and blessed, and others in the community grew to resent her for it. Perhaps Josie herself became a little bitter and disillusioned because of the subtle backlash from the others. But Hannah fell asleep with only the memory of that sweet thirteen-year-old girl in the field of green, who was still free of bitterness and disillusionment; she fell asleep with that pleasant memory of her sister in her heart and was content and satisfied.

CHAPTER TWENTY-SEVEN

"So the people who volunteer get meals and living quarters?" Hannah asked her friend Lavina, who worked at the Mennonite visitor center in Shawneetauka. On her lunch break, she went to the center and found Lavina at the desk.

"Most of these mission and volunteer positions provide meals, shelter, and provisions," Lavina confirmed. She was going down an entire list of Mennonite opportunities that Hannah could apply for. Most were out of the country, in other parts of the far-away world, like Africa, South America, or Asia. Hannah was thinking about volunteering for mission work, but perhaps she could start at a place in North America. She never left the Indiana-Ohio area in her entire life, so she'd take baby steps as far as becoming bold and courageous.

"These camps in Oregon and Colorado . . . are they year-round or only summertime?" she asked Lavina, pointing down at the pamphlets.

"The youth portion is during summer, and it's actual camping and fun stuff for the kids. But they are staffed year-round because they also do women's retreats and quilting courses, and there's a nature center at the Colorado camp too, so the animals need to be taken care of all year."

"I'm experienced at quilting and working with animals, so this position in Colorado sounds perfect!" Hannah said excitedly.

"I worked at the Colorado camp! You'd love it. So fun! It's near a town called Cortez, over by Four Corners. There are lots of parks and national monuments around. The San Juan Mountains are nearby. The Ute Indian Reservation. Mesa Verde. It's beautiful. I was there when I was your age," Lavina said.

"It sounds so nice! What did you do? Was it the same position?"

"I believe so. With these types of volunteer opportunities, you'll find that you go to do one thing, then nine times out of ten, you'll be doing other jobs. They will pay you a stipend if you decide to help with cooking. It's good to get extra spending money. It all adds up."

Hannah leaned against the counter and flipped through the glossy pamphlets with their color photos. She was so excited. Volunteering was her chance to get out into the world but still do good Christian work with the Mennonites. A poster hung from the wall with quotes by the founder, Menno Simons. She was inspired as she read what he said.

Lavina stood up. "Here is the form to fill out for this position." She handed her the clipboard with a pen.

"*Jah, denki!*"

"Don't worry whether or not they will say yes. After I fax the form, I will be personally calling over to the Cortez Camp & Lodge," Lavina assured her.

When Hannah left the center and crossed Van Buren Street to head back to the Red Barn, she felt lighthearted and good-spirited. Things were going so well; her friend Lavina was confident she could help her attain the position, so doors appeared to be opening right before her. To be in Colorado soon—she was giddy.

As she got across the road, three Amish women assembled near the restaurant's side entrance. They were waiting for her. It was her cousins Kayla, Sarah, and her aunt. Her Aunt Rebecca, her mother's older sister, stood behind them with a dark hooded cape draped over herself so that only her glasses, nose, and chin were visible. Her aunt, like her mother, didn't speak freely. She wasn't a big believer in idle chit-chat. But Kayla and Sarah were much like Hannah, could speak freely and, perhaps, too often.

"We were picking up thread and patchwork supplies and thought to see you," Kayla said.

"*Jah*, we hoped to catch you when you weren't busy," Sarah added, nodding and motioning her head toward the restaurant. "How are you?"

"*Denki*, I'm fine. Just fine." Hannah said. They were not just out for quilting supplies.

She knew what this was. As she walked toward them, she could tell that they had a strange seriousness to their faces. She could tell right away that this was more of an intervention than a friendly hello.

"We have been discussing it and would like you to stay with us for a while. At our homes." Kayla said.

"For as long as you need," Sarah chimed in.

"It would be *gut* times, like when we were kids," Kayla added.

Her aunt bundled herself ever more tightly and slowly nodded in agreement.

Sarah grabbed Hannah's hand, cradled it between hers, and pleaded with her: "We don't want to lose you! Everyone is worried. Please stay with us!"

They knew she'd been staying at an *Englischer's* home for several days. She'd been with Danielle and her father again. She also didn't attend church with the family that previous Sunday. It was the only time she'd missed church except when she was nine years old and came down with measles.

"Come stay with us!" Kayla pleaded as her sister did but with greater urgency.

The wind picked up; it became colder and colder. Finally, her bundled-up aunt added: "Please, child!"

"I've talked with a Mennonite friend about doing volunteer work, and I'm excited about the opportunities."

"Here in LaGrange County?" Sarah asked.

"No. These opportunities are far away."

"But we will lose you!" Kayla said. "You will be gone."

"We are your family, girl!" her aunt insisted. "You belong here. Not out there!"

"We want what is best for you, Hannah!" Sarah said.

"I want to feed the hungry. I want to clothe the naked. I want to comfort the sorrowful," Hannah responded to them with passion. Five minutes before, she read those words for the first time. She read them from the poster on the visitor center wall. It said more and more suitably and eloquently, but Hannah couldn't remember the rest. She also felt slightly disingenuous for repeating those words, considering her first position would be doing none of those things at the camp in Colorado. But she meant it all regardless.

"At the expense of your family and community here?" her aunt questioned. "And at the risk of losing your soul?"

Her cousins shuddered as their pious mother said this. They each grabbed one of Hannah's hands again. Kayla's eyes welled with tears, and she begged her to stay.

"Please don't go!"

Hannah also became tearful. Their reaction wasn't an act. They were dead serious. She could tell they were distraught and sincere. They truly believed if she left and went out into the world, it would be all over for her.

"I'm sorry," Hannah replied. "I'm sorry."

She'd already made up her mind to leave the community. It was a slow-developing decision that started more as a far-away, impossible thought, to suddenly—her destiny. The Mennonite opportunity sealed her fate.

"I've decided," Hannah said emotionally, "to leave."

She dropped her hands and hugged both of her cousins. Her aunt, who sounded so much like her mother, said: "But look what happened to Josie Jane!"

Hannah had been waiting for such a retort. She expected her Aunt Rebecca to say such a thing. However, it didn't bother her or make her angry. Instead, she smiled lightly but sincerely, took a few steps toward her aunt, and planted a Holy Kiss onto her lips, as she previously witnessed the deacon's wife do the same to the newly baptized females of their district. A kiss of peace but also a farewell kiss. Her aunt seemed thunderstruck by the gesture and said nothing more.

The next day Lavina came into the restaurant. She was holding a manila file folder and stood near the cash register. She smiled as Hannah approached her.

"All the information you need," she said, handing her the file. "You can start any time in the next couple of weeks . . . Whenever you get there."

"*Denki!* Wonderful!" Hannah said with great emotion. "They responded so fast!"

"Yes, this fax came from Margaret, the camp secretary, this morning. I spoke with her last night."

Mindy and Danielle came up to Hannah, and she turned to them.

"I'm going to Colorado!" she said, smiling.

Both Mindy and Danielle had reasons to want Hannah to stay. But regardless, they seemed genuinely happy for her.

"Sweet!" Danielle said. "Now we have to figure out how to get you there! A bus, I imagine."

"I wish you luck!" Mindy said. "And whenever you are back around Shawnee, you'll always have a job here!"

"You're the best!" Hannah said to Mindy.

Hannah and Danielle had to return to the customers, so they broke up the little meeting near the cash register and resumed their business. Lavina grabbed a coffee-to-go and headed out to cross the street. Hannah went from table to table for the rest of the afternoon as if floating on clouds. She was so excited and happy about her new opportunity. She even volunteered to fill Danielle's section's salt and pepper shakers. The ketchup bottles too. Danielle did not argue.

↔

When Hannah told her parents, brothers, and sisters about the opportunity in Colorado, she emphasized that it was a Mennonite camp and retreat. She'd already been staying with Danielle for several days but thought it would be best to make a special effort to let everyone know her plans as soon as possible. The fact it was a Mennonite operation undoubtedly reassured them. It wasn't as if she was going full bore into the English world only to float away into their corruption and distractions. No, she'd be doing wholesome work with people of similar faith. Also, she made sure they understood that she intended to come back to Shawneetauka someday, at least to visit them or even stay. But that was far into the future, and now she was talking about today.

Unsurprisingly her news was known, as her intentions were already conveyed to them by her cousins and Aunt Rebecca. They stopped by the previous day after encountering Hannah outside the restaurant. Still, the family seemed glad she'd come by to explain her plans. Even her mother seemed grateful that she did, and unexpectedly she insisted Hannah stay for dinner, which she agreed to. Even Jacob made it home early, so the entire family was present. However, Jacob did make her feel slightly guilty when he reminded his sister that she'd be missing his wedding in December.

"I will pray for you and Amanda on your day!" she said.

"We will be grateful to you," he replied.

All in all, the visit with her family went splendidly—with no animosity or tears. On the contrary, they all appeared to be glad-hearted. Her mother even packed up her two extra blue dresses. She also bundled the quilt from her bed and had it ready to take with her if she chose. Hannah never considered what she'd wear when she left. She was unsure about wearing English clothing. But this gesture made her realize she didn't have to change. She'd continue wearing her prayer *kapp* and most likely continue wearing her plain clothes unless she was required to wear something different, depending on her job duties or physical activities.

She left her family feeling joyful and relieved. She was departing on good terms, not running away or escaping. She did not burn bridges or scorch any earth as she headed out that door. On the contrary—the bond with her family was as strong as ever. As she pushed forward into her new endeavors, she was doing so with only positive and self-affirming motivations behind her. She expanded her world by being bold; any fear and apprehension she formerly harbored vanished. Her prayers were being heard.

↔

Danielle showed Hannah a road atlas that night and suggested she take a bus to Gallup, New Mexico. A Greyhound bus would go through Albuquerque and continue along I-40 to Gallup. Next, they needed to determine if a taxi or bus service ran from Gallup to the Four Corners area.

"You should call the camp tomorrow and see if they have any suggestions," Danielle recommended. "We can check in with Greyhound to figure out the exact routes."

"You are being too kind to me with all your help!" Hannah said.

"Well, I don't want my little sister to leave, but since you are, I want to get you there properly!"

"*Denki!* You are a true friend!"

"It's going to be bad enough for me to break in a new waitress on the day shift! I don't want to be worrying about you in the meantime!"

Hannah grinned and shook her head.

The next day Hannah and Danielle worked out the proper travel itinerary for the Greyhound bus service to Gallup. She needed to take a shuttle van from Gallup to Cortez, with a stop in Shiprock, a town on the Navajo Indian Reservation, still in New Mexico. The thought of stopping in a Navajo town was exciting to Hannah. The initial bus wouldn't leave Middlebury until 5 pm; there was no longer a morning pick-up. So she could work with Danielle the day she left and get a ride to the bus terminal after they finished. However, all the calling and planning were for naught and unnecessary. It was a fortuitous and unforeseen circumstance that made it all unnecessary.

The day Hannah was expected to leave, while at the Red Barn helping Danielle train a new waitress, her English boy stopped to say hello. He was all packed up and on his way to Arizona. Dolan sat in the booth near the window and spoke with Hannah. Upon seeing him, Danielle bit into the back of her hand with an animalistic disposition and turned to

Mindy with her hand still in her mouth. Mindy laughed and said: "I told you he was a dish!"

Dolan wasn't there long before Hannah told him about her planned travels to Cortez, Colorado. Since he was driving right through Gallup, he mentioned to her that his passenger seat was empty, and he preferred it not to be. She happily accepted the proposal and told him she'd gladly occupy the vacant seat without hesitation or deliberation. It was all too perfect; she said yes without thinking.

When Danielle was introduced to Dolan, she was on her best behavior. Even when she learned about the change in plans, that he and Hannah would be driving cross country together, she barely made a peep. Not until she walked back into the kitchen, where Mindy was pulling out the order of fried chicken to hand to Hannah, did she erupt: "THIS IS A FLIPPING FAIRYTALE! —When will *my* Prince Charming walk through that door?"

CHAPTER TWENTY-EIGHT

Hannah promised to call Danielle as soon as she arrived and at least once a week thereafter as she left through the rear exit. Dolan finished moving a few things from the back seat of the Jeep and into the small U-haul trailer attached. As she stood by, he placed Hannah's bags in the newly created space in the Jeep. Dolan previously pulled around to the rear of the building and parked next to Danielle's Oldsmobile, where Hannah's things were. As he opened the passenger door for Hannah, a tall and gaunt man with a long beard stood on the sidewalk and stared back toward them. The man looked like Abraham Lincoln's twin, only with a longer beard and an Amish hat. Old Abe had a mildly menacing gaze as if waiting for them to respond in kind. Hannah turned to Dolan. "That's Bishop Miller," she said. "I think he may want to speak with me."

"I'll go to that gas station to top off the tank," he said, pointing to the Phillips 66 station. "And I'll leave you to the bishop. Unless you don't want to speak with him."

"No, I should. It would be the right thing to do."

Dolan pulled away in the Jeep with the trailer, and Hannah walked to the bishop. He pumped the fuel and looked across Van Buren Street to see Hannah and the bishop in conversation. He couldn't believe they'd be traveling across the country together. He suddenly felt like a million bucks.

↔

When Hannah approached the bishop, she could see the look in his eyes. He knew she was leaving. She assumed he would plead with her to stay. But he didn't.

"Your dear Aunt Rebecca informed me of your pending departure. She's a fine woman; I believe she is deeply concerned and worried for your immortal soul. I told her not to worry. We will never know the mysteries our Father has planned, nor should we be arrogant enough to think we could understand what He has chosen or shall devise for us. *It is what it is.*

And worry is the most useless of all emotions. Jesus said no one gains a minute of life by being anxious or worried. *Gotte* will always provide as long as you first seek entrance into His kingdom. So do not worry about your niece's soul, I told your aunt, not even your own. As long as you first seek out The Almighty, you need not worry."

Hannah didn't know what to say in reply. She fumbled with her thoughts and said: "I'm blessed to have an aunt so concerned for me."

"This is true," he said and paused. "But girl, there is only one thing I came to see you about today, just one thing I want you to know: I used to have a son, and now I do not."

Hannah eyed him cautiously as his demeanor and tone quickly changed; her stomach sank.

"First, your sister dragged him down into the filth and muck with her pretty little face. He could not help himself. You and your sister both; your ridiculously beautiful faces. Like sirens calling from across the seas to drown a man to death. Your allure and beauty are too great, and he had no chance. You do not even know it—the power you possess. You just smile and can sink a thousand ships. But he was my boy. He may not have been perfect, but he was my only son. And now he's gone."

Hannah backed up slightly in fear. And as she did, the bishop reached out with his extended right arm and held her shoulder. She winced, and he placed his other hand on her shoulder and pulled himself closer to her. He looked into her eyes and said: "Do not be afraid, girl! Look at me! I am not my son. I would never hurt you!"

She was shaking and full of fright. She fell to her knees, and the bishop gripped both hands tightly on her shoulders. The bishop knew what his son had done. Her mother must've told him.

"Look at my face, girl! I want you to remember it. I want you to remember my face and my son's. Do not ever forget it your entire life. No matter where you may be! I want you to remember my pain!"

Hannah exploded in tears.

Dolan finished fueling. Across the road, something was happening that he didn't understand. The bishop stood above Hannah with his hands around her neck; she'd fallen to her knees. *Just like her sister.* Adrenaline surged through his veins. His heart pounded. He sprinted across Van Buren—darting, twisting, and weaving through the traffic like a madman. The bishop released Hannah and turned as Dolan tackled him at full speed. The two men rolled along the pavement, over the curb, and tumbled into the hedgerow. He pressed his forearm against the bishop's neck and raised his right arm intending to break his face with one punch. But he didn't. He turned to Hannah. Was she okay? The bishop pleaded with him: "Leave me . . . I would never hurt her!"

Dolan jumped up and went to Hannah. Aside from tears, she did seem fine.

"You okay?" he asked

"Fine. Just afraid. And upset."

The bishop sat on the curb and started to weep. He was a sad figure of a man. He covered his face and bawled. Dolan helped Hannah lift herself from the pavement and slowly went to the bishop. She sat on the curb next to him and said: "I'm sorry about your son. Truthfully, I wasn't before; but now I am. I'm sorry for you as well. I will remember your pain. I always will. Please believe me. I'm so sorry . . ." She reached out for his hand.

He nodded and held her hand gently as Dolan stood by.

"I'm truly sorry about your son. It was a terrible thing . . ." she said and was cut short by developing tears. "Please forgive me."

He reached his other hand to Hannah, nodded, and smiled slightly. She was forgiven. Forgiven even if he had no idea the extent to which he forgave her.

"But you must also forgive me," the bishop requested. "And my son. Please forgive him!"

"I have. I already have."

Two Amish women—who had stopped their buggy on the street when Dolan disrupted traffic—approached. Hannah knew them, of course, and as she regained composure, asked if they would see to the bishop. Get him back home. Without questioning anything, the two women helped the bishop to his feet and walked side by side with him to their buggy.

By the time they hit the Indiana Toll Road, Hannah had explained to Dolan all that had happened between her sister, Noah Miller, and herself. Dolan absorbed what she said and what she'd gone through, especially the past few weeks. He said, "I'm sorry about all this; what you had to experience. And the way you asked for forgiveness—and gave forgiveness. You are a truly good person. You *do* have a heart of gold."

"*Denki* . . . I mean, thanks," she said. "But I can be selfish, prideful, cowardly, and moody. I'm not perfect."

"If you say so," he said, smiling. "But I was thinking back to when I first met you. I thought you were a good person with a good heart."

"So you thought about me then?"

"Yes."

"I thought about you too. One night I cried myself to sleep thinking I would never see you again," Hannah admitted. "So you think I have a heart of gold?"

"I'll be straight with you. I've known a few beautiful young women. Some women are beautiful on the inside, and some are beautiful on the outside. They generally don't overlap. But, truthfully, those most beautiful can be the ugliest on the inside."

"You think I am beautiful on the inside?"

"I do."

"And the outside?"

"You are gorgeous."

"Thank you," she replied quietly, almost ashamed of it. "The bishop said I could sink a thousand ships with a smile. So I suppose that's a compliment."

Dolan nodded and grinned.

Hannah stared out the passenger window as they sped along I-80.

"You'll be doing the police training when you get to Arizona?" she asked.

"Yep. The police academy. I'll be starting a week after I get back."

"You were a hero today! The way you came out of nowhere and knocked him down. Impressive!"

"I shouldn't have. What I thought I saw happening to you and what was happening were two different things. So maybe I do need training."

"I was petrified, though. I thought the bishop would hurt me."

Dolan couldn't mention that all he was thinking and seeing at the time, in those few seconds, was Luke Staley strangling her sister on the side of the highway.

"I protect people," he said. "If I could do one thing, that'd be it. Or try at least."

"I know," she said. "I feel safe with you. Even driving on this highway—I thought I would be worried and afraid, but I'm not!"

"So . . ." he started while he changed lanes to pass a slow-moving semi-trailer, "you cried yourself to sleep thinking about me?"

"I knew I shouldn't have said that!" she said, embarrassed. "I was feeling weird and lonely. It wasn't long after what happened with Noah Miller. I was staying the night at Danielle's house. It was also the first time I spent the night away from my family. I started thinking about you and how maybe I would never see you again."

"I wasn't going to let that happen," he replied. "But truthfully, I was also worried I wouldn't see you. So as I walked into the restaurant, I thought that if you weren't working, I wasn't sure what I'd do. Maybe stop by your farm. I'm not certain."

Dolan pulled off the highway into a rest area. They could stretch their legs and use the facilities if needed. He parked in front of a picnic table. It was a nice warm day for the middle of November.

"We could have a bite of the fried chicken Mindy packed for us," Hannah said.

"Good idea!"

She went to the facilities, and Dolan sat at the table and waited for her. A little girl and her mother waved to Hannah and said hello as they passed each other. Since Hannah still wore her long, plain blue dress with her white prayer *kapp*, she probably looked like a character from *Little House on the Prairie* to the girl. She was most likely curious anyway. Her mother whispered into her ear.

Hannah got back, and she and Dolan sat side by side on the bench, with their backs pressed against the table.

"Wing or a drumstick?" he asked as he pulled open Mindy's box.

She grabbed a leg, took a few bites, and pointed toward him with it. "You are going to need a napkin!"

His lips and fingers were already messy from eating a wing. He looked at his greasy fingertips.

"I think I have a bunch in the glove compartment," he said, getting up.

"I'll get them," she said, popping up instead.

She opened the glove box and pulled the napkins out; when she did, a photo fell onto the floorboard. She picked it up, looked at it, then put it back. She carried the napkins over.

"The girl with you in the photo . . . with reddish-blonde hair. Is that your girlfriend?"

"Oh, that's Bree."

She took bites from her chicken leg and glanced at him when he didn't seem to answer the question. "Bree?"

"Yes, my girlfriend."

"She's beautiful!" Hannah said. The look on her face changed slightly. Her lips twisted.

"Yes, she was. But, unfortunately, she died back in February."

"No . . . I'm sorry."

"Yeah, pretty sad. Childhood sweethearts and all. But we hadn't been together in a long while. We'd broken up way back when. It was an accident up in Michigan. I was in Saudi Arabia when it happened."

"The war?" she asked quietly.

"Yes, the Gulf War," he said. "Bree was a fashion model."

"Like Cindy Crawford?"

"Not quite, but yeah."

"I only know of Cindy Crawford because she is on dozens of magazine covers at the grocery store," she said. "Sadly, we both lost people this year."

"Yeah," he said, reflecting. "It's been a tough year. But I think we've each found somebody too. A new friend? What do you think?"

Hannah looked up, and her eyes got big. "Maybe even a *special* friend?"

"I have feelings for you. You may know this," he said softly.

She smiled. Dimples showed on her face, and her cheeks went rosy. She twisted and twirled the string from her prayer *kapp* around her index finger.

Dolan finished up another chicken wing and playfully smiled at her. Hannah reached over with a napkin and dabbed his lips. She leaned in and stole a quick kiss. That took him by surprise. "Definitely a *special* friend," he added.

CHAPTER TWENTY-NINE

Once they were back on the highway, Hannah skimmed through Dolan's CDs in the center console. He had told her she might like *Simon and Garfunkel's Greatest Hits,* which was pretty mellow. The song "America" was perfect for traveling down the road.

"What's this baby?" she asked, holding up Nirvana *Nevermind.* "He's swimming for the dollar!"

"I just got that CD. It's excellent stuff! They were doing cool things in Seattle when I was overseas. They're calling it grunge-rock. That one, too—Pearl Jam."

The music played, and they continued driving past various towns, landmarks, rivers, and fields. Hannah enjoyed Simon and Garfunkel's melodious tunes and lyrics. Even later, with Nirvana playing, Hannah continued smiling.

When they stopped for gas near Champaign, Illinois, they were already listening to Pearl

Jam's *Ten*. She'd like *John Denver's Greatest Hits* so that one was on cue for the rest of the trip through Illinois.

Later, Hannah got excited as they approached the wide Mississippi River and the Gateway Arch beyond. The complete scene—the water, the cityscape, the silvery arch—was picture-perfect. They were almost to St. Louis.

"The gateway to the West," Dolan said.

"I still can't believe it. I should pinch myself to make sure I'm awake! We're really going out West!"

Dolan pulled off the highway after crossing the bridge over the massive river. They stopped and visited the national park that contained the arch. They walked along the promenade. A few leaves still clung to the hardwood trees; the manicured lawns were green. There were other people out along the path, taking in the sights, mostly couples. It was close to dusk, the orange sun glowed on the horizon behind the city, and the enormous silvery arch had a copper-like hue. The others were holding hands and walking closely. It seemed to be date night for everyone at the park, a romantic evening stroll at sunset. She looked over to Dolan and grabbed his hand. He smiled and pulled her closer. They paused along the rail as the big river boats and barges floated up and down the Mississippi. He draped his arm around her shoulder. Being with her was so right; he couldn't believe it.

Several large white pelicans flew past the big boats along the water, heading south. He checked Hannah to see her reaction. But she didn't seem to be looking. All at once, she appeared downcast. She was biting her lower lip nervously. He didn't understand.

"What's wrong?" he asked, looking at her concernedly.

"I'm worried this is all too perfect . . . like an impossible dream. Us being together, I mean. You'll think I'm being silly and childish, but I guess I'm just afraid again. Maybe I'm afraid of getting my heart broken."

He couldn't help but chuckle. Hannah appeared confused.

"And here I'm wondering where we should stop for dinner!" he laughed. "I'm kidding . . . But seriously, I think I may be feeling the same as you. I think I know what you're feeling. Vulnerable, I suppose."

He held Hannah closely. She was smiling after he said that. She turned and placed her arms up over his shoulders.

Dolan nodded and said: "It does seem impossible that we should even be standing here together. But we *are* here. And all that happened to bring us together. The terrible things. Even the good things. This has to mean something, right?"

Hannah smiled. She pulled herself up and kissed him.

"All I know is I don't want to be anywhere else in the world other than right here with you," he said warmly. "And I don't know what's going to happen from here on out . . . in ten days or ten years from now . . . but I do hope, and truly believe, this is the beginning of something special."

Hannah wrapped her arms around him and pressed her face to his chest. They held each other tight.

They stayed a bit longer, looking out across the river. It started to get dark, and the city's lights showed. A young female park ranger strolled along and advised them the place was closing for the night. So they left the riverside and headed for the Jeep. After returning to the parking area, Hannah looked up at him and said: "You better visit me in Colorado every chance you get!"

"Visit? Once I get you to Cortez, I may never leave you!"

"*Jah?* —Promise?"

Dolan smiled. She knew he had to start at the academy the following week. But what about the week or so they did have? He opened the passenger door and helped her up into the Jeep. When they drove off, he asked: "Would you like to see Arizona?"

"Arizona?"

"We both have a week or so . . ."

"We would drive straight to Arizona?"

"Yeah, we could stay at my aunt's estate in Sedona. She has a big place. Lots of extra rooms. It'd be great!"

"Yes! That sounds fun!—Exciting!"

"Next week, I'll run you up to Cortez, to your Mennonites!"

She laughed.

"What?" Dolan asked. "Did I mispronounce it?"

"No," she giggled. "Danielle was calling you my *Englisch* boy. So when you said *your Mennonites*, I thought it was funny!"

"Hey—I think I'm gonna like being your English boy!"

Hannah fell asleep in the passenger seat, and Dolan kept driving. He pulled off twice for gas; he told her she could keep sleeping as she woke up each time. So she slept. It was very late, almost morning, when Dolan stopped. He was fighting to stay awake, so he pulled into a rest area outside Shamrock, Texas. They'd just made it through Oklahoma. He reclined his driver's seat and fell asleep instantly.

He woke up with the sun hitting him in the face, rubbed his eyes, and looked over at Hannah. She was brushing her hair. He never saw her hair, aside from the little that showed below her prayer *kapp*. She was also wearing jeans and a t-shirt top. Normal clothes. He felt like he woke up in an alternate universe. But he didn't say anything. Instead, he watched her brush her light-blonde hair.

"I need to brush my hair every morning," she said to him as if apologizing. "I freshened up a little in the bathroom here."

He kept staring at Hannah. The morning sun was bright on her face and hair; she was glowing with radiance, like in one of those ridiculous shampoo commercials on television.

"You *really* are beautiful."

She smiled, continuing with her hair. "Danielle gave me these clothes. I wasn't going to take them, but after I tried them on at her house and saw myself in the mirror, I didn't mind."

"It's strange to see you this way," Dolan admitted. "But strange in a good way!"

She laughed. When she finished, she pinned her hair in a bun and put on her white prayer *kapp*. Dolan reached for his ditty bag from behind his seat.

"Time for me to brush my teeth and clean up a bit." He slapped on his baseball cap and headed for the restrooms.

Hannah wandered around the grounds and picnic areas. She said hello to an older woman walking her small black dog, then went to the lookout. They had a telescope mounted for viewing. You could see for miles in all directions. The ground was mainly flat, with the occasional small butte or hill, with patches of range grasses and cedar bushes. Unfortunately, she discovered that looking across the wide-open space made her feel dizzy. She had had enough of that.

She strolled back to the main building and examined the Texas-themed plaques and other monuments they had on display, like a stone carved in the shape of Texas and a granite slab with a star cut out in the center. It was cute that even the barbeque grills were Texas-shaped. Along the edge of the main building, where the grass was tall and natural, a warning sign stated: *Beware of Rattlesnakes. Stay off the grass!*

"Any rattlesnakes?" Dolan asked.

Dolan had come up from behind her. He was clean-shaven, and his hair was neat and pomaded. He was back to his *GQ* look. She was startled when his voice came from behind, still spooked from reading the sign.

"I'm looking for them!" she said. "But I think I'll stay off the grass just in case."

They held hands and walked back to the Jeep.

"It's about ten more hours until we hit Sedona," he told her. "Unless we go sightseeing and get sidetracked."

"Getting sidetracked sounds fun!"

"My goal is to get sidetracked all this week until next!"

As they were pulling away from the rest area, Hannah asked: "Will you do something for me?"

"Anything." He responded quickly.

"I want you to treat me like you would any other girl . . . like any *Englisch* girl. I want to know that *this* is genuine. I don't want you to be afraid to say or do anything around me. I want to know you are yourself."

"Hannah, I'm a pretty simple guy. I never try to be something I'm not. I'm pretty darn honest. I can't lie. There's no scheming or calculating in my head. With me, it's a matter of what you see is what you get."

"But still . . . If you want to swear and cuss around me, drink alcohol, or whisper things in my ear that would even make an *Englisch* girl blush—I'm ready for all that."

He laughed and said, "Now you have me wishing I was Don Juan! I'll need to think of a few hot and spicy words to whisper!"

Hannah reached over and dragged her index finger along his smooth face in a playful way. Their weeklong adventure together was only beginning. Hannah was ready for this. Perhaps dreams do come true, and prayers do get answered. She looked out the passenger window as the wide-open scenery went past.

Dolan pressed the button on the CD player and, using a strained country-boy voice, started singing along with John Denver, making up half the words as he went along. His singing was comical enough to make Hannah laugh out loud.

"I'm happy!" he shouted. "I can't help it. You, me, and John Denver all together—cruising along the Texas Panhandle. It doesn't get any better than this!"

He started singing again, torturing the song.

"Look at that, Mr. McBride! Could you eat all that?"

She was pointing to one of the "72-ounce steak challenge" billboards. *Get the big steak FREE if you can eat it in under an hour—If not, it's $32.95!*

"Well, Miss Yoder, it's almost lunchtime, so I believe so! I bet I could eat two!"

"Get ready, Amarillo . . . here we come!" Hannah shouted and clapped her hands, smiling.

Dolan laughed and let out a big rebel yell: "Yeeeeeah-haw!"

↔

They arrived in Arizona late that night. Hannah and Dolan spent a fun Saturday with Red and his aunt. Hannah called her brother Caleb and also her friend Danielle. They were both thankful she phoned and happy and excited for her. Danielle said she wanted *details* the next time she called! Hannah laughed.

Early Sunday, she and Dolan hiked around Cathedral Rock. They ended up along Oak Creek at his favorite spot, nestled in the mystical canyon, surrounded by cottonwood and sycamore trees. Hannah was amazed and in awe by it all. She said she had no idea places like Sedona existed on this Earth.

"This is as close to God as I've ever been," Dolan said, of his special place, hidden near the creek below Cathedral Rock. "And it's Sunday, so I guess this *is* my church."

"*Jah*, this is peaceful and enchanting. How I picture the Garden of Eden."

Sun rays flickered through the remaining leaves of the trees as a gentle breeze swirled.

"Speaking of church . . . If you want to go to an actual church today, there's an incredible chapel on the other side of the road, built onto the top of a red-rock butte. Being Sunday, they may have services too. It's the coolest little church I've ever seen. I think it's called the Chapel of the Holy Cross."

"I'd like that."

They sat on a flat sandstone ledge and listened to the relaxing sounds along the creekside. Hannah leaned back onto Dolan, and he wrapped his arms around her. They were a perfect couple. She never knew love, and he never knew love like this. They fell hard and fast. Hannah was trying not to think about the coming week when she'd have to say goodbye. She was already feeling the aches and the longing. She wasn't having second thoughts about the opportunity with the Mennonites; she was still excited about going. But it would be hard to leave Dolan; maybe the hardest thing she'd ever do.

CHAPTER THIRTY

Marge heard on the radio that the fugitive Luke Staley had been captured near Paulden. When the breaking news came through, she was listening to the oldies on the country station. It was the first good news she had heard in a while.

Marge followed the case closely ever since word first came that a deputy sheriff discovered a young woman's body near I-40, between Seligman and Ash Fork. It was peculiar, but she had a terrible feeling it could be the girl Josie, who had stayed the night with them a few days before. George was on a long-haul trip with his rig, and Marge was home alone when she first heard they found a body. Even before the sketches went out in the newspapers and television, she feared it could be Josie. That night, George called her from a truck stop in Laredo, Texas. He called her any night he couldn't make it home. She told him the news story and how it could be Josie. Marge was upset by it. But George said it couldn't be Josie because she would've been traveling east on I-40. Seligman was west of Flagstaff. Almost seventy miles west. So it couldn't have been Josie. This reassured her. But a couple of days later, the sketch appeared on the local TV news, and when she saw that sketch, her heart sank; she cried that entire endless, sleepless night.

George was home in Cordes Junction with Marge when they announced the capture of Staley. He was in the living room looking through his trucker magazines. Marge let out a cheer when she heard the news.

"They got the bastard!" she yelled out to George.

He came into the kitchen and put his arm around his wife.

The Tuesday Jane case was known throughout the county and well beyond. As Patty Malloy said, the murder of a pretty blonde girl is a story that gets the media humming. Marge never did call the sheriff's tipline. Between the heartache and guilt, she could never bring herself to call. Besides, Marge and George didn't know much that the police hadn't released, such that her name was Josie, and she was traveling to Indiana. Josie never said much about herself when she stayed with them. Marge didn't ask either. They were just happy to have her around. The day Marge almost had the courage to call the tipline about Josie, her identity was released anyway. That morning she remembered Josie was going to Shawneetauka. That would've helped, but it became a moot point after the news was released.

Interest in the case grew substantially once Luke Staley escaped. The manhunt had lots of press, but the original story of the murder of a Hualapai Native American, and a pretty Ex-Amish girl, had already piqued the public's curiosity. Soon, tribal members and other good-hearted individuals set up memorial shrines at the fuel station for Fred Mohon and the site along I-40 for Josie. In addition, the Hualapai people held a sacred ceremony in the middle of the gravel parking lot at the Seligman

Tex-Gas. There were hundreds of flowers at both sites and a few votive candles left. For weeks travelers stopped at Tex-Gas and along I-40 to leave notes, flowers, or whatever gift they may have had.

The prior week, George drove his Peterbilt past Josie's makeshift memorial on I-40. He didn't stop, but after he and Marge heard about the capture of Staley, he got an idea. He would take Marge on a road trip around Northern Arizona. They could stop in touristy places like Sedona and the South Rim of the Grand Canyon. But most importantly, he wanted to bring his wife to Josie's shrine along I-40. Marge had been bugging him for years to go on a sightseeing trip, but considering he traveled on the highway for a living, it was the last thing he wanted to do. But he owed this to Marge. So George said to pack for an overnight stay. He'd get them a room up near the Grand Canyon.

Marge was excited. She packed a suitcase and even found her extra-large floppy-brimmed sun hat to wear. She hadn't worn it in a long while.

They loaded the Chevy and headed for the open road. George never told her about stopping at the wayside shrine. They could stop by after they finished their touring. It would mean a lot to her.

↔

When Dolan pulled off I-40, another vehicle was already parked on the wide shoulder. He came around and opened the passenger door for Hannah, and helped her down. She was holding a single red rose. They stepped over the rusty chain strung across the opening to the old highway yard. After Hannah stepped over it, she stopped and smiled. A small cross was erected, painted white, and behind it was a pile of stuffed animals, flowers, and notes. A man and a woman were kneeling to place flowers. Hannah held Dolan's hand, and they stayed near the chain, trying not to disturb them. The couple placed the flowers, and the woman wailed. She cried loudly. Her husband comforted her. Hannah suddenly got tears in her eyes and pulled close to Dolan. She couldn't believe a stranger could get that emotional over her sister's death. But maybe they weren't strangers. Perhaps they knew her sister. With that thought, she slowly approached the couple.

"I'm sorry to disturb you," she said to them. "Did you know Josie?"

The man turned to see Hannah. He smiled lightly and said: "Yes, we did. My wife and I."

His wife looked at Hannah and smiled, her face red with tears.

"I'm Josie's sister. My name is Hannah Yoder."

"Your sister stayed with us for a day," the woman said through tears. "Only a short while, but it was such a blessing."

"I'm George Jones, and this is my wife, Marge," George said, walking toward Dolan and Hannah.

Marge lifted herself and went over to Hannah, and hugged her.

"I'm so sad about your sister," Marge said. "It breaks my heart."

Marge and George explained to Hannah how her sister ended up in Cordes at their home.

They told her about the bus fare and how they discovered she had gone off without taking it.

"You look so much like Josie," Marge said to Hannah.

"And Tammy," George added quietly.

"Tammy?" Hannah asked.

"Our daughter," Marge said breathlessly. "We lost her too. Your sister reminded us of her. So much."

Marge told the story of Tammy and how she ran away all those years ago. How she followed up regularly with the police until finally, one day, she stopped. She could tell the detectives dreaded seeing her walk into the office. They couldn't give her any news, good or otherwise, and it pained them as much as her. She still thought about their daughter daily but admitted that she'd lost hope that Tammy would return. With Josie, it was nearly the same. The pain and suffering and guilt. Like it all happened again.

After hearing her story, Hannah hugged Marge again. She felt an immediate bond with her and George. They were kindred spirits who all suffered a loss.

"Marge, why don't we let her visit," he said, pointing to the pretty red rose Hannah was holding.

"Oh, I'm sorry, dear," Marge said. "But I'm going to go to the pickup truck and write down my phone number and address for you. We could keep in touch."

"That would be nice!" Hannah said. "I'm not sure what my mailing address or phone number will be because I'm heading to Colorado, but I'll write or call you when I'm settled in."

Dolan and Hannah went to the shrine, and Marge and George went to the truck.

↔

Marge opened the passenger door and said, "Isn't that something, George?"

"What?"

"That her sister, Hannah, is here. They just happened to visit too! The Lord has His ways—"

"Possible," George said. "I just wish Him and His ways were around a hell of a lot more often!"

He sat in the driver's seat and eyed the wooden rosary beads and crucifix hanging from the rearview mirror. Marge wrote down her information and walked back to Hannah. George watched his now-happy wife approach the girl's sister. Marge was happy because she saw a little bit of their Tammy in Hannah. As with Josie, a small part of Tammy came back into their lives, so her presence helped lift a tiny bit of their grief. To lose a child, and carry that loss through life, is the heaviest of all burdens. So anything to lighten that load is a godsend. He suffered all those years the same as Marge had. But luckily, they had each other. That's how they kept going. Marge had her faith, and she had George. George didn't have much faith, but he had Marge.

↔

A few days later, Hannah was in an emotional state at the Mennonite camp in Cortez. She was face to face with Dolan, saying goodbye.

She was wearing one of her plain blue dresses and had tears in her eyes. Dolan cradled her face in his hands and kissed her.

"I should've made you promise," Hannah whispered, smiling lightly.

"You know I don't want to leave," he replied.

"I'm being silly," she said. "Underneath these tears, I'm the happiest I've ever been in my life."

"Me too."

"I suspect you'll be glad to be rid of me for a while, though!"

"Not a chance," he said. "Not for a minute."

"Good luck with your police academy," she said. "I'll write to you every day!"

"Every day?"

"Well, maybe every few days."

"I'll use the phone and call you," he said. "Letter writing isn't my strong suit!"

"I also wanted to thank you, Mr. McBride."

"What are you thanking me for, Miss Yoder?"

"For making me happy."

Dolan smiled and pressed close to her. He whispered, "I must be the luckiest son of a gun on this planet . . . I don't deserve you!"

Her tears started coming again.

"What did I say?" he asked.

"Just go!" she said forcefully, yet playfully, through sniffles. "All this crying is making my head hurt!"

Dolan held her face in his hands again, wiped the tears off her cheeks with his thumbs, and kissed her one last time. Finally, he jumped into the Jeep and drove off, waving his arm from the open window as he left. She watched him roll away until he disappeared around the first bend of the road, where the red Jeep vanished behind a stand of grayish-green cedar.

"I'll be missing you, Mr. McBride," Hannah whispered. She waited until she could no longer see the Jeep through the trees and slowly ambled toward the main entrance of the Mennonite lodge, where she'd begin her new work, which she believed would be enjoyable and satisfying. In the distance, the San Juan Mountains were glowing a beautiful reddish-orange, opposite the setting sun. She paused before entering the building to glance back over her shoulder.

☒

EPILOGUE

Detective Patty Malloy was with the sheriff at HQ when their contact from the Oklahoma City FBI called regarding the suspected serial killer, Rodney Russell Lee. The part-time truck driver confessed to numerous abductions and homicides spanning six states and twenty years. Three of those were in Arizona. One kidnapping and killing originated in Yavapai County. The FBI wanted the county's files on any missing girls from 1975.

Rodney Russell Lee was a busy man in '75. The first killing he admitted to was a pair. He befriended the young couple while visiting the Lake Mead Recreation Area. They all stayed in an old miner's shack for a few days. One night they got heavily intoxicated, and Lee killed the young man with a rusty pickaxe. Lee wanted the man's wife for his own. A day later, when he quickly tired of the young woman, he killed again. He put the bodies into their little green Ford Maverick and rolled them into the deep reservoir. Nobody had ever discovered the car or its contents in all those years.

A few months later, he picked up a girl outside Cordes Junction, Arizona. He kept the cute blonde captive for a few weeks in the storm cellar of his elderly mother's home in Oklahoma. He said he accidentally asphyxiated the girl one evening when she made too much noise. He was only trying to keep her quiet. Later he buried her body in a field of derelict oil and gas rigs located east of Lawton in the Ardmore Basin. Those remains were discovered in 1983 by a crew of oil workers doing field workovers. Unfortunately, authorities never matched the remains with open cases beyond Oklahoma.

As soon as she heard the confession regarding the girl from Cordes, Patty knew what file they needed to pull. For several years, Marge Jones followed up with the sheriff's office about her daughter's disappearance. They were never able to give her any answers back then. Now, unfortunately, they could. That was the worst part of her job. Patty dreaded talking to a victim's family. The bad news was hard to dispense.

That afternoon, she was scheduled to visit the Bar-T Ranch with Johnny Mohon and the owner Jimmy Tilley. Mohon invited Patty to see the caverns the day they captured Staley. He advised her this would be one of the final opportunities to see that underground world. Jimmy Tilley decided he'd no longer work with the state park service to open the caverns to the public. The state was already working with a rancher in Southern Arizona to purchase an extensive cavern system near Benson, and Tilley thought they were dragging their feet on his deal. So he told John Mohon that he'd allow a few guests to visit over the next couple of days, but then he was closing it all up. His new idea was to donate the property to the Hualapai Tribe upon his death. This change of plans made Johnny quite happy. But Patty wouldn't get up to the Bar-T Ranch that afternoon. Instead, she'd go to Cordes Junction to dispense news that was a long time coming. Patty hadn't thought about sending anyone else to inform the family. Even though she hadn't worked directly on that case back then—she was a rookie on patrols—Patty remembered Marge. She couldn't forget her pain. She remembered the last time she saw her at the office, how she could tell Marge had lost all hope, how her face turned emotionless and cold. Marge went out the door, and Patty never saw her in the office again.

Patty thought of Marge over the years, like others that never got justice or answers. She remembered all of them—all the faces. She worked to make sure that rarely happened. It was part of her motivation. So Patty would go above and beyond for this task. Marge deserved it—that and much more.

As she knocked on the front door of their home in Cordes, Patty took a few deep breaths to settle her nerves and tried to think of the right words to string together, but they didn't exist. The door opened.

"Hello, I'm Detective Patty Malloy of the Yavapai County Sheriff's Office. You are Mrs. Marge Jones?"

"Yes. Yes, I am."

"Could I come in to speak with you? I have news. I'm sorry to tell you this, but I'm afraid—"

"George!" Marge yelled into the house, overwhelmed with emotion. She tried to steady herself with the edge of the door. "I think . . . I think they've finally come to tell us about our Tammy!"

↔

Rodney Russell Lee died in 1992 while awaiting trial for the abduction, rape, and killing of two sisters, Julie Atkinson, sixteen, and younger sister Veronica Atkinson, fourteen, of Sayre, Oklahoma. With his death, there would be no legal justice for these sisters or the nineteen other victims, including Tammy Jones.

Due to the scope, nature, and number of crimes, the FBI had been working with Lee and federal prosecutors on a plea deal; they would take capital punishment off the table if he confessed all of his crimes. These were federal cases because most of his victims had been kidnapped and transported across state lines. However, the Oklahoma attorney general later chose to prosecute Lee for the Atkinson murders, so the state could still pursue the death penalty; therefore, a trial would proceed.

Lee had been boisterous and cheerful as the trial date approached. As if he got a warm, fuzzy feeling anticipating the photographs and other evidence that prosecutors would introduce at trial. He'd relish the media attention. Lee told one of his jailers that Julie and Veronica Atkinson were *two of his tastiest treats*. The guards had to endure Lee's sickening antics and perpetual bravado for weeks. Then one day, it was over.

The day before the trial was scheduled to begin, Rodney Russell Lee died in his sleep. He died of natural causes: acute myocardial infarction. Lee wouldn't get his circus spectacle of a trial or his perverted *remembrance of things past*. He was just dead. And so perhaps there was a modicum of justice in the world: justice dished out by heart attack. Those that knew him best—his guards and jailers—did not agree. They said he got off easy. His death came quickly, with no bloody torture or agony or misery. He did not have to wait, sweating for days and hours in anticipation of the midnight strike of the clock. The electric chair would remain lonely and empty; the burning-lethal chemical concoction never mixed for special injection; the hangman's knot never tied and strung. So to the guards, his death was all a bit anticlimactic. It was not good justice.

↔

Marge and George received their daughter's ashes not long after his confession. They held a ceremony of life service with close family and friends in Arizona. Father Domingo Flores made an appearance and said words during the vigil. Later, their daughter's urn rested above the fireplace mantle in their home. But that was only a temporary placement. Marge and her husband took that urn on a trip to San Diego and visited the stunning sandy beaches and blue waters—where Tammy was set free in the wind, and Marge and George said a final goodbye to their beautiful daughter.

They arrived at the same spot they had visited while on vacation when Tammy was nine years old. She loved that beach. She collected pretty seashells and flew her rainbow-colored kite along the shore next to the high bluffs. They remembered that trip as if it were yesterday.

Walking along the sand, Marge pressed the urn to her chest, holding it lovingly and carefully as she once cradled her child. She smiled with simple satisfaction. George felt it too. *He smiled, knowing they would all be together again.*

Marge spread her ashes far and wide; George held his wife close. They watched the evening sun dip from the rose-vanilla sky into the great blue expanse. She whispered, "I love you, sweetheart."

The white-foamy waves rolled harmoniously from the sea. They walked hand in hand along the shoreline in peaceful, reflective silence. The sand was soft on their bare feet. A cool breeze moved inland; large seabirds glided gracefully along the thermals high above the tall sandy bluffs. Serenity prevailed.

Made in the USA
Monee, IL
25 January 2023

26246764R00288